Estrel

Keri A. Kitson

First Printed - 2012
Reprinted in Trinidad and Tobago - March 2016
Revised Edition March 2019

Published by Keri A. Kitson – New York, USA & Trinidad and
Tobago, West Indies

Estrel, rev. ed. Paperback - **ISBN 978-976-95857-2-0**
Estrel, rev. ed. Ebook – **ISBN 978-976-95857-3-7**

Dedication

This book is dedicated to both my
my grandfathers: Wilmot Oswald Kirby (1919-2011) and
Oswald Wolseley Kitson (1928-2005) who taught me the value
of determination.

Table of Contents

Foreword by Keri

We are each born into this world at a particular time for a specific purpose.

It matters not the length of the life - span.

Sometimes our purpose can be as simple as bringing joy to others for a time.

Other times, it may be as profound as impacting change in this world.

Yet at all times,

our responsibility while fulfilling our own purpose

is to help others along their respective journeys.

Do not doubt that you matter in this life.

Sometimes, it takes us a little longer to find our purpose than others.

However, know at the end of it all,

That you do matter!

So hold onto your dreams.

Follow your heart.

Keep close to your Maker.

And always believe that you can!

By *Keri A. Kitson*

Acknowledgement

Many many thanks for all those individuals (known and unknown) who supported me over the years in this venture. To Cynthia who edited my work, and put up with my endless emails and nagging. Any errors in this book are attributable to me. To Junya, who patiently listened to my ideas, and created a cover design to suit me perfectly. To my family, neighbours and friends who supported me (even when they thought I was crazy).

Special thanks to my Aunty Cathy, who came through when it was really needed, without even realizing why. Always remember that you are never too old to pursue your own dreams, and that you are precious in your own right. And last, but by no means least, to my grandmother Irene Merle Akal Kitson, my mother Jacqueline Kirby-Kitson, and my father John Kitson.

CHAPTER ONE

Dueling Arena – The Final Duel

Talia didn't remember walking into the dueling arena. Her only awareness was of a seething anger that made her feel cold. Her sister, Delia, had often commented that Talia had a tendency to go frigid when she was mad. However, this was the first time she had ever been this angry, and soon her anger would have a focus. Her smile was grim as she spotted her opponent. He was older than her, perhaps in his early thirties and wore one of those half-masks that prevented injuries to the upper face. She could sense his exhilaration and anticipation, as if he had sized her up and thought to himself that the outcome was decided in his favour. To him, she probably looked like a mere slip of a girl who he could easily best.

She turned away from him so that he wouldn't see her eyes. In doing so, she noticed that the final arena had been changed. The two duelists stood at opposite ends of a bridge that was raised a few feet over dark swirling waters. The bridge was narrow and made of a lightweight material that didn't appear to be capable of holding their weights. In the dead center of the bridge was a jewel suspended in a bubble of air. Much like the semi-finals, this was another hostile environment, and the object was to see who obtained the jewel first. Unlike the other duels, there were no rules for this one: anything was permitted. She was glad for that concession, because she was not interested in winning as much as making him rue the day that he had crossed paths with her.

As the referee signaled a start to the duel, Talia's eyes connected with her opponent for a brief moment. It was the complacency that she read in his eyes that triggered her anger. Even the referee was caught off-guard by the ferociousness of her attack as she unleashed her full fury. Her opponent's over-confidence vanished as he rapidly revised his original assessment of her. Within the first few moments of the duel, it dawned on him that this mere slip of a girl might actually be an adversary worthy of his full attention.

*

Somewhere close by - The Observation Section

Delia felt a shiver run down her spine as she felt Talia's rage. The coldness that descended upon her twin to replace the feelings of rage was worse. She tried to calm her through their twin bond, but Talia deliberately shut her out. This was the first time her twin had ever completely blocked her. A sense of foreboding filled her as the referee signaled the start of the duel. She could see that Talia's opponent had no clue what her sister was about to unleash. If he had, he wouldn't have looked so complacent. She almost felt like warning him, but Talia was her sister and she trusted her. Whatever it was he did to make her sister mad, he was now about to face Talia on the warpath. She just hoped that her sister didn't do something she might regret later.

*

Nine Hours Earlier – Fair Grounds

"Who are we going to see?" sang Delia.

"The best!" responded Talia.

"Who are we going to see?" sang Delia in a higher pitch.

"The best of the best!" replied Talia.

"Where shall we see them?" queried Delia.

"At the fair…at the fair!" answered Talia.

"Hurray for the tournament…!" sang both girls.

Delia and Talia had been in the habit of inventing ditties since they were toddlers. So, this little ditty was no exception. It was sung in a high-pitched sing-song guaranteed to irritate their father had he been around. Dutra de Novo, a well-known Merchant Mage from the province of Siente within the Merari dome, was none too pleased that his beloved daughters were to be in attendance without a chaperon. As a father, he took pride that in an era where most parents neglected to ingrain certain values in their magelets, he had endeavoured to ensure that his daughters had been raised to be ladies. Whether or not they chose to act as such was another matter for discussion. Yet Dutra was a great believer that in the fullness of time, his daughters would appreciate his efforts.

As it stood now, after all of their arguments concerning their ability to run his booth at the fair, his daughters felt it better to err on the side of caution where their father was concerned. They could hardly resort to their childhood pastime in front of him. So they waited patiently for his departure before they began arranging, then belting out the lyrics of their new tune. By the time they arrived at their destination, various improvisations of their little ditty had been sung to the general amusement of passers-by.

They were greeted by a hubbub of activity upon their arrival at the fairgrounds. They had to side step numerous persons laden with parcels and other paraphernalia, rushing around in a great hurry. Although their father's booth had been set up the day before by his two helpers, he had still insisted that they arrive at the booth by 7 o'clock. He insisted that the displays be arranged in a manner designed to catch the eyes of passers-by. Dutra de Novo was an excellent merchant and knew how to market his merchandise. So even though he was none too pleased that they were running his booth, he fully intended to ensure that they worked hard to sell all of his merchandise.

He had also warned them ad nauseam about the dangers that could befall simple country mages such as themselves. In fact, his parting words had been to urge them not to stray off and to stay together. According to him, 'foreigners' and 'royalty' were in attendance, and though most of them were generally good sorts of mages, there were always a few bad apples, and he urged them to be careful. Their father had been at his most impressive when he issued these warnings to his daughters. His eyebrows had risen into two arcs that resembled the two crescent moons that could be seen in the sky above Merari on clear nights. Yet, they had not dared to tell their father that he resembled a grumpy gnome. Instead, they had done their best to stifle their amusement.

Despite it all, nothing could dampen their excitement. Their exuberance fairly hummed, almost like a live wire palpitating with pure energy. They were still tickled pink in anticipation at being able to attend what had been touted as 'the tournament of the year'.

"Thank goodness that Merari was chosen as the venue," said Delia.

"Yes, it was fortunate that Merari was picked over Luz, Babel, Varga and Saba domes in the lottery. Though, I do believe that we need to be more thankful that father is on the Committee for the Merchant Guild. Otherwise, he would have decided to run his booth himself when Ted and Darcy fell ill."

Delia nodded in agreement.

They had chuckled in their identical manner as they recalled how a mysterious quirk of fate had landed them there. Soon after Ted and Darcy had finished constructing Dutra's booth the previous evening, they had both complained of feeling unwell. Dutra had immediately taken them to Merari's Healing Centre. An examination by the healing mages had revealed that his assistants had developed a particular strain of the flu that had been virulent through the Merari dome over the past few weeks. The healers had reassured him that Ted and Darcy would recover within a few days, provided that they rested and took the prescribed medication. Unfortunately, they were not going to be able to work for the next few days.

It was a testimony to their father's aplomb that he went into action immediately. He had started canvassing his usual helpers to see if any of them were available at such short notice. Everyone he asked had other commitments. Delia and Talia fondly recalled how they had seized the opportunity to attend the fair. After shamelessly eavesdropping on a conversation between their father and another committee member, they had cornered their father and volunteered their services.

His first response had been an empathetic 'no'. The merchant in him had warred against his instincts as a parent. His daughters knew their father well, so they had employed arguments that catered to his merchant side. His parental side was of the opinion that they were too young to attend and they had been raised to be ladies. They had countered his argument by pointing out that they would celebrate their twenty-first birthday on the fair day. Thus in the eyes of the general mage populace, they would no longer be considered magelets. Notwithstanding that, they were quite capable of being both ladies and salespersons without violating any arbitrary standard of decorum. It was at this point that Delia and Talia had played their trump card. They had reminded their father of how their mother had proved herself to be quite a capable assistant to him on many occasions, both before and after their marriage.

This knowledge had been gleaned from their mother's penchant for telling them bedtime stories when they were younger. One of these stories had been about her arrival to the Merari dome, and finding her first job as a salesperson working for the same company as their father. Alyssa de Shulto had always laughingly described how she had proven herself to be indispensable to the firm, and this had attracted her employer's attention. Their father had been a rising star in those days, and had been travelling throughout the other domes when his employer had requested that he work with her. They had distrusted each other at first. Then, a quirk of fate had caused them to be stranded together one day, and somehow their hearts had thawed and they had fallen in love. The rest, as their mother had liked to say with her winsome smile, was history.

It had been a risk to bring their mother's memory into any argument with their father, because he had never gotten over her passing. They had felt a bit low to even mention it, yet they had, because no one could possibly deny that their mother had been a 'real' lady. Her ability to make even the most mundane of tasks or events appear special by her mere presence was remembered fondly. She had an inner grace that made one notice and respect her in all circumstances. Their mother had been a delightful mixture, and she was the best example they could possibly use to counter their father's argument.

Unfortunately, though acknowledging the validity of their argument concerning their mother, Dutra had stubbornly clung to his opinion. Thankfully, he was forced into acceptance once he discovered that no other help was available for that day. Of course, his forced consent had been accompanied by dire warnings that Delia and Talia had dutifully listened to but mentally shrugged off. They hid their gleeful anticipation as best they could, for they knew that once all the merchandise was sold, they would be able to attend the 'live' tournament.

Typically, the yearly fair at Merari was comprised mainly of mages from the Merari dome showcasing their various wares, trinkets and delicacies. The inclusion of 'the tournament' in this year's fair made it extraordinarily special. In an effort to teach the general populace more about their history (but more likely, in Dutra's opinion, it was to collect data on a pool of potential future leaders), the Mage Council had decreed that the tournament be reintroduced. According to the folklore that surrounded the legendary exploits of old, the tournament had been held on a regular basis after the great battle between Mother Gaia and the Demigods, to determine those worthy of leading their people. The Demigods may have created and ruled the mage race, but Mother Gaia had created and defeated the Demigods, and after the epic battle, the Demigods had quite literally disappeared from the face of their world, leaving the mages to rule themselves.

The tournaments had originally been formulated as a way of determining the best mage to lead them. The winner of the final tournament was then crowned their ruler. This ruler would be known as the Mage King, and would retain this position until he or she died. From amongst the bested participants of the tournament, the Mage King would choose his or her advisors. Upon the Mage King's death, another tournament would be held, until a new Mage King was chosen. As time passed and peace reigned in the world, the criteria for being selected as Mage King changed, and the position of Mage King became an elected one.

Today's tournament would be fought between the most powerful mages of the younger generation. The qualifying ages ranged from twenty-one to forty. It was the first time in a long time that mages from the different domes and strata within their society had consented to showcase their talents. Everyone, from the royalty amongst the mages to those of dubious heritage, would be allowed to duel, once they qualified. Both girls could still recall their mother's voice as she drilled into their heads that the one thing guaranteed to level the class structure within their society's hierarchy was talent. According to their mother, all mages with great talents were respected, regardless of their background. In fact, the stronger a mage's talent, the higher that particular mage could rise within the class structure of their society. They knew from snippets of conversations between their father and fellow Committee members that contestants and spectators alike from the Luz, Babel, Varga and Saba domes had been flocking into Merari in the weeks leading up to the tournament. It seemed that everyone was taking this tournament quite seriously.

"Talia look!" exclaimed Delia, as she directed her sister's to the breathtaking iridescent colours that danced enchantingly along the dome walls surrounding the fairgrounds.

"Just smell the freshness of the air. It makes me feel like taking as many deep breaths as possible. Look at all these mages…Do you think that we might come across any 'royalty'? Oh my, look at the outfits… Do you think we look good enough?" Delia asked.

Talia merely smiled at her twin in amusement. Delia was always happy over the small things in life, yet could be a paradox in other respects.

"Yes, it is quite magnificent… Yes, it is possible that we might come across 'royalty'. We look fine…Now focus! If we don't start arranging these trinkets, the Mage Council will start the official commencement of the fair before we're even finished. We have to draw the bulk of the purchasers in quickly. Do you want to end up with a terrible seat in the observation section?" Talia's brisk tone brooked no argument.

"You're right…from the looks of this crowd that's milling around it is possible to sell our merchandise quickly."

"Do you really think that the organizers would start the tournament promptly at midday?" Delia asked thoughtfully.

"You bet…look how organized they were for the preliminaries."

"True…they eliminated the majority of candidates in the space of a few days in the initial competency test. Remember what Darcy and Ted said? The preliminary test administered was standard in all domes, and so too the preset benchmark, hence the high failure rate."

"Well on the flip side of it, no one can claim any sort of bias. According to the rules, one representative from each dome was on the testing panel. There is no re-testing of a candidate. With only twenty-five allotted entrants for each dome, they had to be strict."

"Plus, only twenty of the allotted spots would be filled prior to fair day in the preliminaries, while the other five would remain open for each dome in case of late entrants. Even father thought that the organizers were being rather generous to the maverick mages by keeping these spots open up to half an hour before the tournament commenced."

"I dare say I disagree with Father. I'm sure the organizers realized that for one reason or the other, some mages could not attend the preliminary trials. Take us, for example. We celebrate our twenty-first birthday today. Since twenty-one is the minimum age for participation, I'm positive that there are others who may have come of age after the preliminaries. Or alternatively, they had other equally good reasons for being late entrants." It was the slight undertone in Talia's statement that triggered Delia's 'trouble' antenna.

Perhaps, it was the calmly reasoned explanation which hinted at Talia's intention to do more than just observe. Nevertheless, her tone had alerted Delia that Talia's epiphany had been made earlier than this moment. From past experiences, Talia's epiphanies were usually precursors to some hare-brained adventure. So Talia had gotten quite adept at not letting on before she was ready to act. It was at that moment that Delia's brain connected the dots. Talia had been the one to bring up the argument about their mother. She had pushed and pushed until their father had caved.

"Tal…let's pretend that you're not planning on trying out, shall we? Aside from the apoplexy that our father will undoubtedly have; what about your new talent? You still have kinks to work out before you can be truly sure that you mastered the new one. Dueling 'sounds' exciting, and even I admit that being pitted against other duelists, as you each try to knock out your opponents until a clear winner emerges, has an allure to it. Not to mention the grand prize and the wonderful accolade of being declared the most powerful mage throughout the domes. But seriously, Talia, what if you get hurt? None of us know how safe the magical safeguards in the dueling arena really are.

Not to mention what Mother always told us… the truly great mages keep the publicity surrounding their powers on a very low key. And we both know that she was rather powerful. So do you risk the exposure just for a title which would only be limited to those who opted to participate?"

Delia still didn't like the gleam in Talia's eyes, nor the fact that she had not even tried to counter her argument.

"Tal…are you listening?" Delia asked.

At this point Delia just sighed. Her sister would find a way to try out, and she would be sitting in the observation bleachers by herself. She was not going to be dragged into this adventure. She wanted to be a spectator. She had no doubt that Talia would qualify once she tried out. She had seen her sister in action whilst their mother had been alive. Talia fairly glowed when she was pitted against difficulties and had to rely solely on her magical abilities.

Their mother had trained them in various mannerisms, styles of address and defensive tactics that would serve them well wherever they went. No one knew from whence their mother came, since her life before arriving in Merari was one topic she never discussed. Yet, the manner in which she conducted herself spoke volumes. She had either belonged to the higher strata in society or associated with them long enough for their mannerisms to become ingrained.

It was this mode of conduct, along with a few other useful tidbits, that she had passed onto her daughters. She had drilled defensive tactics into her daughters until they became second nature. If they had known that the skills she had taught them were known to only a select handful of mages in the five domes, they would have been more appreciative of her training. Nonetheless, they still had supreme confidence in her training.

"Tal…were you listening?" Delia asked.

Since no response was forthcoming, Delia just threw up her hands and groaned. She knew her sibling. Talia was going to find a way to enter. They were identical, right down to the moles located at the nape of their necks. In fact, only their mother had been able to tell them apart. However, looks were all they had in common, as their personalities and powers were poles apart.

"Come on …there's our father's booth…Let's see what we can do to get you there in time." As she spoke those words, Delia felt a faint tingling along her senses. It had the feel of a power greater than any belonging to a mere mage. Delia recognized the Deity's hand, and sighed as she bowed to the inevitable. Talia did not know it, but she was about to embark on a path of destiny. She just hoped that they were both prepared for the change that would inevitably come.

*

<u>Sometime Later at Dutra's booth</u>

The official commencement at eight o' clock had been brief. By half-past eight that morning, sales had been brisk, as mages wandered into their booth to purchase their trinkets. Their clientele had been mostly female. All of them had wanted to purchase trinkets either for themselves or as gifts for some relative. The few males who had stopped by their stall were young, and interested more in flirting than in the trinkets. Delia was delighted to discover that she had a knack for turning their flirtations into actual purchases. She had appealed to their chivalrous side when persuading them to purchase items from their stall. Her ploy worked rather nicely, and none left without a few purchases and a fervent wish that she and her sister would sit next to them at the tournament.

As luck would have it, by ten o'clock all their trinkets had been sold. The last trinket had been sold to a mage in his mid-fifties. He had wandered in out of curiosity. Most of the items had already been sold, so Talia had to direct him to the last trinket. He had gotten a rather peculiar expression on his face when he saw the last trinket, nestled discreetly on a cushion in an out-of-the way spot. Everyone else who had come in had bypassed it in favour of trinkets with more obvious beauty.

Personally, Delia had liked this trinket the best. She thought that it had an understated yet somewhat otherworldly elegance that only those with discerning eyes would appreciate. To Delia, it was much like a person, easy to overlook in favour of flashy or loud individuals, but a true diamond in the rough. The mage had been so taken with it that instinctively she knew that he was meant to have it. He had purchased it immediately then left.

"Whew…we did it…that was the very last one."

"I'll close the booth.…you go deliver the proceeds from the sales to Father. I'm going to assume that's the last I'll be seeing you in person for the rest of the day…so good luck and be careful," Delia said with a smile, as she gently started pushed her twin out the door with the proceeds.

Talia had stood at the door for a second and laughed.

"Why do I even bother to hide stuff from you? You know me so well…I'm not doing it for the title or accolades. I just need to find out whether I'm good enough."

On that note, Talia had squared her shoulders and looked Delia straight in the eye.

"To be more accurate, I need to find out if I'm as good as Mother believed I could be."

That was good enough for Delia.

"I'm sure you are…Mother believed in you and so do I."

"You know you can always come with me for try-outs!"

"Nope…I have a feeling that this is something you need to do on your own…"

"Besides, I would like to secure a good seat to cheer you on," Delia replied with a smile.

Talia felt touched. It was moments such as this that made Talia appreciate her sister for the thoughtful soul that she was. In a few simple words, Delia had reassured her that it was all right. Talia had her doubts about qualifying. However, if her sister was going to be in the observation stands waiting to cheer her on, she would make very sure that Delia was not disappointed.

"Thank-you" Talia said softly as she gave her sister a quick hug and bounded out the door like a bolt of lightning.

"Good-luck, and may Mother Gaia bless you," whispered Delia as she watched her sister weave quickly through the crowd.

She then turned to tackle the mundane task of closing the booth. As she did, she started humming the short ditty that she and Talia had created that morning. Perhaps her creative juices were still flowing, for she found herself adding an additional stanza. If anyone had stopped in they would have overheard strains of the new verse.

"We going to the tournament,

And we shall see the best,

But the best better beware,

Cause Talia will be there!"

As she slid the last bolt into place, Delia felt quite pleased with herself. Talia would approve of her last stanza.

It was approximately eleven o' clock, and the tournament was scheduled to start promptly at midday. If she hurried, she should be able to secure a seat with a good view of the dueling section. She just needed to figure out the location of the observation section.

Her sense of direction was horrid, so she closed her eyes and picked a direction. It was while wandering in the direction she had chosen that luck guided her. She had inadvertently bumped into an older mage while trying to get her bearings. Fortunately, he hadn't taken offence at her clumsiness, and was kind enough to steady her. His clothes were nondescript and his mannerisms a bit odd. Yet, something about him tugged at her maternal instincts.

He had an aura of loneliness that most would simply mistake for aloofness. However, her talent for empathy was able to distinguish this subtle nuance. What surprised her was the compelling urge she had felt to soothe away some of the incredible loneliness she felt surrounding him. This urge had been a strange one, given that he was the first person other than her sister, whom she felt so compelled to soothe.

So, in what she later considered to be a completely uncharacteristically bold move, she had asked if he would like to accompany her to the observation section. She had felt askance as soon as the words left her lips. What was she doing? She had just invited a perfect stranger to accompany her to the observation section. Not only was he a stranger, but he was older, and quite possibly had other plans.

Along with such thoughts, her father's warnings flashed though her mind until she was half contemplating how to retract her invitation as gracefully as possible. She felt her cheeks flush in embarrassment as he turned to look at her fully. The look that he gave her was measured. It was a look that felt as if he could see into her very soul. It was not an assessment that should belong to one of his years. It was one that felt centuries older than his appearance implied.

Yet, whatever he saw in her had pleased him. He gave her a half smile. Then, he gallantly bowed to her as if she was one of the mage royalty, and extended his arm in a courtly manner. It was more of a paternal gesture, but she did not mind it one bit. His aura of loneliness subsided slowly as she took his arm. He knew the way to the observation section and gallantly escorted her there while regaling her with amusing anecdotes of tournaments of old, according to folklore. His knack for storytelling made Delia almost believe that he had actually been at the ancient tournaments. In return, she surprised herself by sharing the little ditty that she had invented with Talia. He had complimented their inventiveness, and even smiled at her last stanza. She enjoyed herself so thoroughly that it was only later that she realized that they never asked each other's names.

*

Fair Grounds-Near the dueling section

Talia had found her father on the other side of the fairground arguing with a fellow Committee member about the placement of the Merchant Guild banner. She had interrupted them, handed him the proceeds from the sales, then hastened as quickly as possible to the dueling area. She was on a mission, and she didn't want to be distracted. She hadn't been sure whether her father would be more displeased to find out that she had tried out or that she had placed. Either way, he was going to have an apoplexy. Even he didn't know the real extent of her powers. Her gifts were powerful, and she had only recently begun to master them when an additional one had popped up. She had tried mastering the new one by using the techniques taught to her by mother. It was now more or less manageable.

She had a deep longing in the recesses of her heart to know whether her power levels were sufficient to meet the benchmark. Delia's gift of empathy, though considered in some circles to be one of the softer powers, was powerful, but not adaptable to such a game as this one. It could not be measured against any benchmark like Talia's. However, unlike Talia, Delia never yearned to know how powerful she actually was. She had always calmly accepted her natural gift as it was. Talia had yet to reach that stage of acceptance. At times she felt like a silly dolt for longing to know, when compared with Delia's calm acceptance. It was during those times that she sometimes wished she was more like Delia.

She had been so caught up in her musings on the way to the dueling area that she failed to sidestep a well-dressed male mage. He had inadvertently backed into her rather hard, causing them both to tumble to the ground. Luckily, Talia had quick reflexes, and had been on her feet within seconds. As she looked around, she noted that a group of three male mages had stopped to assist them. A quick appraisal on her part placed them in the higher stratum of society. They were all a few years older than her. Whether they all belonged to Merari or to the other cities she didn't know. They were all remarkably handsome specimens.

"Oh, I dear say I'm sorry about that. I'm awfully clumsy sometimes."

This came from the mage who had backed into her and was still flat on the ground. He looked so forlorn that she couldn't help but smile. He had such a lost puppy dog expression on his face that it was guaranteed to make him a favourite with the ladies. Yet, it was so genuine that one couldn't help but smile at him. Talia had never realized that when she smiled and felt happy that she glowed. It was that glow that made her look extraordinarily beautiful at times. If she had known, she might have thought twice about smiling.

As it was, when he saw her smile, the mage on the ground felt as if he had just experienced a pure surge of power. In fact, the entire group had similar reactions in differing degrees. Fortunately, Talia remained blissfully unaware of the internal havoc she was creating in their systems. She had never considered her beauty, and living with an identical twin had a tendency to make appearances unimportant. So she was a bit surprised when all of the mages insisted on her joining them as they tried out as late entrants. They wouldn't take no for an answer, and then finally admitted quite sheepishly that they were lost.

On learning they were headed to the preliminaries, she mentally blessed her Creator for sending her companions. She led them to the area then let each one go ahead of her, as she worked up the courage to follow her mind. It had come as a surprise that they all qualified, even the one who had made her fall. They had joked excitedly with each other as she congratulated them. She was surprised when the same one who had given her such a puppy-dog expression turned to her and encouraged her to try out. He even took her by the hand and led her to the sign-up sheet for the qualifying tests. He told the organizers that she was a part of their group, and wondered if she could try out. The organizers had one spot left and had been about to close the qualifiers. However one puppy-dog expression from him, as well as a glance at his name on the sheet, had them all agreeing to allow her to try out for the last spot.

As she stepped into the enclosed area in which the qualifying test took place, she drew in a deep breath. The tests involved all the elements and basically tested her ability to defend and in some instances neutralize potential threats. It was somewhat similar to the games she played with her mother as a child. As she drew upon her power she glowed, and by the end of the trials she felt invigorated. She exited the qualifying area knowing that she hadn't used even a fraction of her full power.

When she came out of the enclosed area the organizers were huddled in a group poring over the dueling schedule. Once they confirmed that she was indeed twenty-one, they assigned her the last spot. They also made her sign a waiver in the unlikely event that anything happened to her, so that they would not be held liable. It was pretty much the standard liability waiver that she saw in her father's contracts when he was selling his merchandise. The others crowded around to congratulate her, and joked that it was fate that had made them bump into her. The one who had led her to the organizers merely smiled a quiet soft smile that made her glad that she had listened. She had turned to thank him when it occurred to her that she didn't even know his name.

She grimaced, knowing how horrified her father would be at her manners. So she sank into a deep curtsy to the group as a whole, and then introduced herself in the formal manner her mother had taught her when addressing the highest of mage nobles.

"I am Talia Ramona Jeremieu de Shulto, of the Merari dome, descended from Dutra de Novo, Merchant Mage of the province of Siente. Born to Alyssa de Shulto who has since passed on to Mother

Gaia, and sister to Delia Abigail Jeremieu de Shulto."

Everyone remained silent for a moment. They were astonished at her formal introduction, since only those mages belonging to court royalty would know their identities. It surprised them that she had guessed that they came from some of the most distinguished lineages within their society and had addressed them as such. Their respect for her had risen considerably after she had qualified, for they realized that there was substance behind her appearance.

Then she had addressed them in the correct manner as befitted their rank, even though they had deliberately tried to downplay their status. It was at this point that they realized that she was no mere country girl from Merari. So they treated her with the respect due to one of similar rank, and introduced themselves in the same manner. That was how she learnt that the mage who knocked her down was called Thom Raule Rahmut de Arrea of the Varga dome, who, as it turned out, was the grandson of the last Mage–king of their society.

*

Later that Afternoon: Observation Section

The duelists were announced by their surnames, thus leaving the audience clueless as to the duelist's gender until he or she entered the dueling arena. The arena had been enclosed, but the audience could view them clearly through an oversized focal mirror that zoomed in on the dueling arena. So when Talia walked into the arena for her first duel, Delia felt a simultaneous mixture of pride and foreboding.

Pride that her sister had qualified and that the extent of her true power would soon reveal itself to Talia. However, these feelings were mixed with a sense of foreboding at what their father might do once he found out.

Thus far, Talia was one of the few female mages participating, and the announcers were calling her by the lesser known surname of their mother. As was the custom in their society, the males took their father's surnames while the females took their mother's surnames. So brother and sister would have different surnames even though they belonged to the same house. It was a tradition meant to preserve both family lines. In their case, they never knew their mother had another name until she told them on her death bed. The scroll she left them to be opened on their twenty-first birthday at the precise time of their birth was supposed to answer the questions they had surrounding their maternal family. Unfortunately, they had been born at dusk, so they still had a few more hours to go before the scroll would unseal itself and allow them to view its contents.

In the meanwhile, the afternoon had proven to be an immensely satisfying one. Delia had cheered on as Talia made short work of the opponents she faced. Her sister had become a crowd favourite as she had dispatched her competitors in a quick efficient manner. Delia had recognized her use of some of the tactics their mother had taught them. The use of these tactics minimized the actual use of Talia's powers, thereby allowing her to conserve her energy. Even as the duels progressed and Talia faced more difficult and experienced opponents who were older, to Delia, it had appeared as if Talia's power level flourished rather than became depleted by its constant usage. Her duels were becoming longer and she had switched her approach to more subtle attacks, since the pure energy blasts were guaranteed to drain.

Delia had chatted animatedly with her companion after each of Talia's duels, and had shared some of the scrapes that her sister had gotten into when younger. Her companion smiled at the obvious pride that could be heard in her voice. They had managed to obtain seats together, and he had amused her with anecdotes until the duels had begun. Then he had commented on the performance of each duelist until his companion's sister had walked into the arena. If he had not been seated right next to his companion he would have sworn that it had been her walking into the dueling arena. The resemblance had been uncannily identical. After observing her sister in action, he had been suitably impressed. He could see that she had the skill to make it to the finals. Yet, she had not displayed that drive to win that typically set apart the champions of such games.

Nevertheless, her skill alone had already set her apart for notice by the echelons of their society that were in attendance. He suspected that the Kao would recruit her, for she had a certain elusive quality that suited that group. However, for the time being, he was contented to sit and listen to the excited chatter of his companion. She reminded him of her mother at that age. Alyssa Shulto de Tierney had always amused him and had earned his friendship. Alyssa had been unpretentious in a court full of pretension, and had disappeared from it quite abruptly. He recognized her in this little one, but did not reveal his knowledge to his companion. It seemed that fate had decreed that he would once again be intertwined with the Tierney lineage.

*

The Dueling Arena and its enclosure

As the evening wore on, the duelists had dwindled to four, three males and Talia. Due to the point system that had been implemented to assess the wins, the two mages with the lowest points would be pitted against the ones who had attained higher scores. The winner of each respective duel would move on to the final duel of the day. Talia was pleased to find out that Thom had made it to the finals. Luckily she had not dueled anyone from the group she had met at the fair, for the others had lost to different opponents. Even she had been surprised that she had made it this far. Not only was she the only female mage left, she was also the youngest.

The organizers had decided that she would duel against the mage with the lowest points scored, while Thom would duel against the mage with the highest score. The duelists had been split into four groups originally and kept in separate areas so that there could be no fraternization between groups as they awaited their next duel. Each group was provided with sustenance, medical aid and an update by the attendants assigned to them by the organizers. She and Thom had ended up in the same group, while the others had been assigned to different groups.

Even as the duelists had dwindled, the organizers had still

maintained the groupings. So she was still able to talk to Thom and render any aid he might need after their respective duels. Although there were standard safeguards designed to prevent serious bodily injury, mages had still come out of the duels with minor injuries and lowered power levels. Once a mage tapped into his power reserves and became depleted, he was susceptible to bodily injury, since the safeguards were meant to be additional protection to a mage's natural defenses. However, in order to power those defenses, the mages had to have a sufficient level of power remaining. The duels had been a drain on the mages' natural power.

Thom's power level had waned considerably, and he had been drawing on his energy reserves. Her power hadn't seemed to flag one bit but felt as if it was finally being given full reign. Like a feline that had been cooped up too long, it had unfurled and blossomed the more she used it. When they had both been called to their respective duels, she had impulsively hugged him, inadvertently transferring some of her power to him through skin-to-skin contact, thereby bolstering his energy reserves. It had taken them both by surprise, since energy transfers were typically done consciously and with the permission of the other. Not many mages could transfer some of their own power to others, and it was rare for it to occur between strangers.

Such spontaneous power transfers were known to occur either between members of the same lineage or with close loved ones. It had happened once before successfully when Delia had been sick. Yet, for some strange reason, her power felt akin to his, so much so that it had instinctively sought to raise his depleted reserves. She hadn't had the time to discuss this with him, and had decided to wait until after the duel. She had been curious as to why her power reacted to him in such a strange manner. He had been equally surprised, and had given her arm a quick squeeze to signal that they would speak later.

As she entered the arena she was surprised to see that the organizers had re-arranged the space into three raised daises. A referee indicated that she was to face her opponent from the bottom dais. Both duelists were to try to reach the top dais while defending themselves from attacks by the other as well as from hidden traps in the arena. Talia was a bit surprised at the change. It was no longer duelist against duelist, but had been expanded to two duelists battling in a potentially hostile environment. She barely had time to digest the information before the referee gave the signal to commence the duel.

Immediately, her opponent, in an attempt to take her out of the game early, shot a bolt of pure energy at her. Though she deflected it, she realized that he was definitely playing to win, and would have no compunction injuring her in the process, if he could get away with it. That thought made her realize that with the change of arena for the duels, there was a strong possibility that the safeguards might not operate as they were supposed to. However, that was as much time as she had to think, as bolts of light and fire streaked towards her from somewhere in the arena. The dais she was on had also begun to sink into the ground with amazing speed. As she dodged, deflected and tried to reach the second dais, she was able to shoot her own brand of power at her opponent. He seemed to be having problems getting to the second dais, since he was being bombarded with spurts of fog and gusting winds.

Somehow she managed to land on the second dais, and immediately started going for the third. But the dais started spinning and going up and down in rapid spurts of movement. So she dropped to the ground in order to get her bearings and realized that the movements were timed. She had a brief five- second interval to move on between the changes in movement if she was to progress beyond the dais. When the next interval came she went for it. So did her opponent. However, for once her tomboy days came in handy as she propelled herself to the third dais while taking a shot at her opponent. He had left himself open as he tried to maintain a levitation spell to take him to the last dais. It was his mistake, for her flash of power hit him squarely in the middle of his tunic, and he fell straight to the ground. She learned the answer to her earlier question about the safeguards as a cushion of air gentled his fall. He would still be black and blue the next day, but for now he was not seriously injured. However, she was now on the third dais and her opponent had been knocked to the ground, making her the clear victor of this round.

She had been so excited to find out how Thom had fared. She wanted to discuss the changes in the arena as well, and had bolted from the dueling arena as soon as the dais she was standing on sank to the ground. She checked on her opponent first, then walked as quickly as she could without appearing unladylike. As she got to her grouping area she saw the assigned attendant frantically gathering Thom's outer clothing that he had taken off before starting to duel. A sick sense of fear nestled in the pit of her stomach. She was almost afraid to ask what had happened.

When the attendant saw her she motioned her to accompany her. She walked her straight to the space they had designated as the medical bay, and that was where she found Thom. He had been badly injured when his opponent's energy blast had caught him on the broadside, and the safety mechanisms had failed for some unknown reason. They were still amazed that he had survived. The energy bolt without the safety mechanisms to filter it should have rendered him comatose, but luckily his natural defenses had saved him from the full brunt of it.

As it was he was unconscious, and they were arranging to move him to the best healing center in Merari. Thom looked so pale and lifeless on the small cot. From the whispers of the attendants and organizers, they were all worried. The opponent who had injured him came from an equally titled family, and was rumoured to be the top candidate for the position of Mage-King, which had become vacant when Thom's grandfather had passed on. If Thom was to pass on after the duel with this particular candidate, there would be huge repercussions in the court, and those ripples would be felt by everyone. So they had been trying to keep this as quiet as possible.

Talia took it all in while staring down at him. Unfortunately, as she was about to hold his hand, she was hustled off to the final duel. A sense of helplessness and rage had descended upon her and for the first time in her life she wanted to hurt someone, and hurt that person badly at that.

*

The Final Duel:

The Observation Section

Delia's companion had been amused by this little mage. She had excitedly pointed out her sister when she had entered the dueling arena. She had then cheered her on throughout all the duels. Then suddenly, she went very still. A few minutes before her sister had just entered the arena for the final duel, she had unconsciously gripped one of his hands in a death-like vise. He was surprised, because nothing appeared different. Whatever had disturbed her was more than anxiety for her sister to win. It was almost as if she was afraid. He gave her hand a little squeeze of reassurance, and made no comment on her death grip on his hand. Then he settled back comfortably into his seat and watched as the referee signaled the start of the final duel. Whatever it was that this little one was worried about would soon reveal itself.

*

Final Duel: Inside the Dueling Arena

Talia had been holding back prior to this bout. However, the image of Thom lying on the cot unconscious and barely alive was enough to make her forget everything. She forgot her mother's cardinal rule and allowed her power full rein. Her first shot almost vaporized her opponent. Luck had been on his side, as he had managed to throw himself unceremoniously to the ground as her bolt whizzed by. After that, he had rebounded remarkably quickly as he blocked, parried and deflected her, as best he could. He played to win, and shot blasts at her that would have hurt her badly had they connected. Luckily she made herself a difficult target, thereby rendering accurate shots nearly impossible. She then returned in kind until the rapidity and intensity of the flying bolts of power made even the referee concerned for his own safety. Within two minutes, the power level emanating from within the dueling arena was more intense than it had been for all of the previous duels.

As the solid surface on either side of the bridge began melting away, the duelists were forced onto the bridge. It was a tad sturdier than it had looked at first; but when her foot went through the material, she realized that she couldn't stay in one spot too long. Her opponent realized the same as well, and opted to levitate instead. Talia didn't bother to waste time with disbursing her power, but instead took a gamble. She trusted that the bridge would hold her weight, and decided to sprint to the center. In tandem with her sprints she sent enormous waves of energy crashing against her opponent. During her mad dash to the center, huge fist-sized blocks of hail came out of nowhere and started falling onto the bridge. The weight of these hailstones created haphazard tears in the fabric of the bridge and in some places tore it completely, causing her to jump.

She was caught by a power blast from her opponent as she was jumping across one of the larger tears. It sent her tumbling towards the swirling waters beneath the bridge, but luckily she remembered a spell of Delia's. Delia had insisted that she wear a flower in her hair that morning, and had ruthlessly pinned it in. Now, with most earth magics one had to have a piece of the element to work with. It was not possible to call into existence, something of nature from nothing. So she yanked the flower from her hair and called a flower rope into existence and bade it to fasten itself unto the bridge supports. As she dangled halfway between the water and the bridge, she started swinging back and forth until she had achieved enough momentum to swing unto the bridge with a little boost from her power. She was aiming for the dead center. It didn't matter to her if she was hurled into the water afterwards. As long as she got to the jewel first and knocked her opponent out, she would be fine with any subsequent injuries.

So she kept swinging. Once she had attained sufficient momentum to reach the center she boosted herself upwards. As she cleared the top of the bridge she could see her opponent within an arm's length of the jewel. The unexpectedness of her appearance made him pause for that crucial second, which was enough for her to summon all the power she had left within her and blast him. The close proximity of the blast sent her flying backwards as well, but not before she grabbed the jewel from right underneath his nose. She saw his eyes register complete and utter shock as he went tumbling into the swirling waters below.

The last image he had before he lost consciousness was the absolute coldness of Talia's eyes as she blasted him. Surprisingly,

what came to him before his mind slipped into a state of oblivion
was not that he had been bested by this slip of a girl, but rather that
she had beautiful eyes.

* * *

Chapter Two

'REVELATIONS'

<u>Sometime afterwards</u>

Talia hadn't stayed for the accolades and congratulations, but had slipped away as soon as she had changed into some borrowed clean clothes. As fate would have it, she hadn't fallen into the water after the blast had propelled her backwards, but she had landed in dirt just beyond the dueling arena. The blast had been so powerful that it had caused a rift in the arena, and she had fallen through. Luckily the referee had found her immediately; and since she was still clutching the jewel, had declared her the winner.

She had taken one glance at the flock of people bearing down on her and begged the referee's indulgence to let her go change before she dealt with anyone in such a dirty state. He had been surprised at her request. Having seen her in action, he had not realized that she was capable of being concerned about anything as mundane as being dirty. Nevertheless, he had gallantly directed her to a discreet side entrance located nearby and promised to hold them off while she changed.

She had grabbed the first available clothes that fit, then freshened herself. Slipping out the opposite entrance with the jewel in hand proved easy. She then discreetly made her way to where Thom had been placed before she left for the duel. She was in luck, as the attendants were now loading him into the enclosed conveyance that had arrived from the healing center. As soon as they turned their backs she slipped into the back with him and rested the jewel on his chest. She took the hand nearest her and prayed to Mother Gaia.

Their mother had instilled in her daughters a deep and abiding respect for Mother Gaia, and in complete sincerity she asked that Thom be healed. She didn't know how long she held his hand; but while holding it, she felt her pores rise and her own power flare as another power flowed over and around them. This power had a gentle quality to it, almost comforting, really. It was like a mother caressing her loved one who was hurt and trying to take away the pain. This power bathed them in a golden light, and it wiped away all remnants of Talia's rage. She felt it as it infused Thom, gently healing each cell in his body.

As the power faded, Talia was left in a state of awe. She had just experienced Mother Gaia's loving touch, and knew from then on, she had been given a wondrous gift. Few mages could claim to have been touched by the deity in such a way, and her mother had taught her that when Mother Gaia bestowed such a gift, one needed to give thanks. As she looked at Thom, his cheeks were rosier and his skin no longer had that ghastly pale hue. His fingers were also beginning to curl around hers. As he opened his eyes he saw her and smiled. Smiling back, she kissed his hand; and taking the jewel from off his chest, closed his fingers around it. She realized that he was not fully awake as yet even though his eyes were opened, but she was hoping that he would remember her last words to him as she left him.

When the attendants opened the back of the vehicle where they had placed their unconscious and badly injured patient, they were met with a surprise. They discovered him seated in an upright position, clutching a jewel in his hand and with a bewildered expression on his face. They were amazed at the transformation. He positively glowed with wellness. If they had not loaded him into the carriage earlier they would have disbelieved that it was the same mage. His first words to them surprised them even further. He greeted them with an ancient saying used by the older generation of mages and true believers. As the attendant later told his superior, he looked them straight in the eye and with the greatest sincerity and humility told them: "To Mother Gaia, our Creator, I give thanks and praise."

*

<u>An Hour Later</u>

<u>The Country Manor of Dutra de Nova</u>

When Talia returned home, Delia was waiting by the entrance to the foyer. She looked as if she had been there for a while, and her countenance was one of concern. Talia felt guilty for that concern. She knew that it was the first time she had ever completely blocked out Delia. She had not wanted the ugliness of her emotions to spill over to her sister. So she had protected her the only way she knew how. She had never known that she had such a dark side, and realized that she must have been like an avenging warrior during the final duel. Yet, her anger and rage was gone. The experience with Mother Gaia had soothed away all the ugliness and the rawness of her emotions. She felt renewed and at peace. She wanted to share that wonderful experience with Delia to make up for blocking her out earlier.

However, once Delia hugged her, she knew that something wonderful had happened to her sister. Delia felt the lightness in her twin. It was as if Talia's rage had been wiped clean and a more serene Talia was before her. She also felt a vestige of the otherworldly presence on Talia that had raised her pores earlier that day. She didn't know what had transpired between her sister and the deity. However, she was profoundly grateful for the change that had occurred between the dueling arena and now. Her sister was better, and that was all that mattered to her.

So she congratulated Talia on winning, and then hustled her towards the library where they could view the contents of the scroll their mother had left them for their twenty-first birthday, once it unsealed itself. She had taken the liberty of retrieving it from their mother's hiding place when she got back from the fair. So by the time they got to the library and flopped onto the divan, the last rays of daylight had started fading into dusk. It was at this time that the scroll began to unfurl.

Their mother certainly knew why she had be-spelled the scroll to open on their twenty-first birthday. A heritage that surpassed even their most vivid imaginations was unveiled. Not only was their mother a direct descendant of one of the old royal lines of their society; she was one of three children born to the mage they had previously known only as the last Mage King. She was originally born in the Varga dome, and in fact was a Tierney, the maternal line to that of the Arrea branch. Their mother spoke of her twin sister,

Sunni, whom she said Talia resembled in temperament. This previously unheard of aunt was also a member of the Kao. For Talia that raised Sunni's credentials several notches and made her long to meet her. The Kao didn't extend its membership to anyone lightly. All persons belonging to the Kao earned their place regardless of their social standing or connections.

Their mother knew her daughters well. She went on to elaborate in the scroll that if either one of them wished to seek out Sunni, she was to be found in the Holy Citadel of Rhys. She apologized to her daughters for cutting them off from her family, but she wanted them to lead normal lives. She had wanted them to know the value of simple joys and true friendships. They would not have had such, if she had revealed their heritage sooner. She had never told their father, because he had told her once that her past didn't matter to him. So the decision had been hers alone, and she had protected her daughters. As their mother's voice emanated from the scroll, Delia and Talia felt her presence surrounding and enveloping them. They knew without a shadow of a doubt that their mother had firmly believed that her decision was the right one.

Being the practical person in death as she had been in life, their mother had hidden two items that would assist them in reaching their destination. Few persons knew the actual location of the Holy Citadel of Rhys, so the items she left them was priceless as they could enable her children to come and go anywhere in the world in a matter of moments. The location of the items had been enclosed in a riddle within the scroll. Their mother's last words were of love and of how proud she was of her daughters. She told them to seek their own path in this life, and to be thankful that they were able to choose their own destiny. With that the scroll vaporized, and they were left with a smaller sheet with the riddle which had been embedded within the scroll.

The riddle was surprisingly easy to solve, since they knew their mother's idiosyncrasies. They found the matching amulet and ring hidden within the center of her most prized rosebush in the garden. It had been secreted in an invisible element-proof pouch that would have been impossible to find if they didn't know where to look. They always wondered why their mother had asked them to take care of her roses while on her death-bed. The reason they had complied was because they felt closer to her in the gardens she had loved so much. So fulfilling her last request had been easy.

Talia gave the amulet to Delia and took the ring for herself. There had been a charm spelled by their mother in the pouch with the items, and it gave detailed instructions for their use. The charm stressed at length the importance of not revealing the true nature of their inheritance to anyone. It had also made the simple request that the items be passed onto the first pair of twins born to either one of them on their twenty-first birthday. The items were surprisingly simple to use. All they had to do was summon to mind the person or place they wish to go to and their respective inheritance would take them to within a few feet of the place or person. They had to be very specific in their request, otherwise they could end up in mid- air or worse.

Typically, when one needed to be transported to other domes or inter-dome, one used the mirror system that operated as the main transportation system in the domes. The only places that did not have the mirror system onsite were the healing centers and the mysterious Holy Citadel of Rhys. For some reason the magic of the mirrors caused interference with the healing magic at the centers. With respect to the Holy Citadel of Rhys, few persons actually knew its location, and the magic that surrounded that place was hardly likely to allow the mirror system to work. It was unheard of to be transported using such items. The gifts from their mother were indeed priceless treasures and answered the mystery of her frequent appearances and disappearances in various places when she had been alive.

For Talia it was a godsend. She had an overwhelming desire to seek Sunni. She knew that there would be a furor over her winning the tournament, and she wanted something more. Her experience with Mother Gaia had awakened a yearning within her to make her life count. She didn't want to waste it going through the accolades and public attention. She had an intuitive feeling that she would find her purpose with the Kao, and that her aunt Sunni, would be able to point her in the right direction. So to her, the ring was a blessing.

From beyond her passing, her mother had given her life some direction. Something was calling her, and she needed to follow that call. She had so many questions about her power, about their mother's family and about Mother Gaia. Delia looked at her quizzically when Talia mentioned Mother Gaia. Talia was the last person she expected to hear who wanted to know more about Mother Gaia.

It was at this point that Talia shared her encounter with Mother Gaia. Even her twin agreed that the Kao would be the best source of information with regard to this incident. When the Divine deigned to show up in one's life and grant a boon, quite often the Divine had something special in store for that person. Their mother had taught them what she knew of Mother Gaia. If Sunni still belonged to the Kao, then she would be able to teach her the true path, because the Kao were the most devout followers of Mother Gaia.

So, if their mother's instructions were correct, if they summoned to mind the person or place they wished to go, the items would transport them. There was an image in Delia's amulet that showed two young women identical in appearance wearing elaborate formal robes. They had both known instinctively which one was their mother by the look in her eye. So Talia would have to summon to mind Sunni's face based on the image they had of her, then ask the ring to take her to her aunt. Of course, she had experimented with Delia first. Then she experimented on their favourite pet that they had left inside curled up on the kitchen mat. The third experiment was to an old blind teacher who had retired years before and resided some distance away in the Luz dome.

Once all the experiments were successful, she transported herself back to her starting point. She debated with Delia whether to wait and tell their father good-bye, but decided against it. They both knew that Dutra de Novo was going to be upset with respect to her entering (and winning) the tournament. She loved her father, but knew he probably wouldn't understand her overwhelming yearning to seek her aunt. Also, she suspected that if she returned to the city at this time she would find it difficult to maintain a low profile. So she packed all items she considered essential, then bade her sister farewell.

Their parting was bittersweet, as Delia refused to accompany her to meet their aunt. Delia felt deep within her soul that this was Talia's journey. Someone needed to be home to tell Dutra what had transpired. Her own destiny differed from her sister's, and she needed to flow into it much more gradually. She had questions about their mother's family, and wanted time to mull them over. So with a gentle smile, Delia bade her life-long companion farewell. For once Talia hugged her sister of her own volition. Then she drew in a deep breath and disappeared in the twinkling of an eye as she sought her own destiny.

*

A few Hours Later - At the Manor

When Dutra finally arrived home that night, he was informed by Delia of Talia's departure. There had been a series of delays that had prevented him from viewing the tournament and thereafter from leaving earlier. First, there had been a problem that he had to sort out in conjunction with the Merchant Guild. When that problem had been solved, a pesky administrative one had cropped up. He had just breathed a sigh of relief and was headed home when one of his wealthy clientele, whom he dealt with on a regular basis, had sought him out. He had offered him congratulations on his daughter's triumph at the tournament, and enquired whether she would be interested in becoming a spokesperson for his place of business.

Of course, Dutra had hastened to correct the mistake. None of his daughters was powerful enough to win that event (which he had missed because of the Merchant Guild meeting). In fact, he even joked about Delia's inability to create a medium level charm or Talia's inability to master simple merchant magic. Yet, his client had insisted that one of his daughters had won, and she had been a fearsome sight to behold in the final duel.

He had remembered Dutra's children quite well from an enjoyable evening he had spent at their home about three years before when Alyssa de Shulto had been alive. On the spur of the moment, he had stopped off at their manor on his way back to the city in order to pick up an order instead of having it delivered as usual to his business place. It had been an unscheduled stop and Dutra had been in the city. Alyssa de Shulto had welcomed him to their home. He had met Dutra's daughters, and they had entertained him while his wife had retrieved the item for him.

His departure had been delayed by an unexpected storm, and Alyssa had invited him to stay for supper. He had been astonished how like their mother the twins were. Alyssa de Shulto had reminded him of someone, but to this day he still didn't know who it was. Nevertheless, he always remembered what a wonderful time he had had that evening with them. It was one of the reasons he kept doing business with Dutra. So he had been pleasantly surprised when he saw one of his daughters dueling in the tournament.

After he heard his client's tale, a seed of doubt had been planted in Dutra's mind. He had begun to wonder if his children had really hidden their abilities. He had known instinctively that their mother had been quite powerful, but for some reason she had been contented and happy to be his wife. She never flaunted her talent, and even he couldn't tell what her actual power level was, even though they had been married eighteen years. It was just an aura that had surrounded her that he recognized from dealing with powerful mages. It was not what they did, so much as how they acted that distinguished those with a great deal of power from those who wished desperately to be known as such. He was a shrewd judge of character when it came to his business, but not apparently when it came to his children if his client's tale was true.

So he made his way to the dueling grounds in order to sort out the matter. Images of one of his daughters were encapsulated in bubbles everywhere. Most showed her plucking a jewel right out from under a rather surprised-looking mage as she was blown backwards. Replays on the bubbles showed her almost falling off what looked like a bridge over some dark swirling water, then swinging from what seemed to be a rope of flowers, and finally grabbing a jewel suspended in the center and blasting the other mage with an extremely powerful energy blast that propelled her back and him off the bridge into the water. Somehow they had managed to capture the faces of both contestants right before the blast had sent them flying backwards. His daughter had worn a cold, ruthless look on her face, while the other duelist had one of pure astonishment. If he had not seen the bubble replays Dutra would never have believed it. He had never seen such a look on either of his daughters' faces.

After the organizers discovered that he was the father of their absent winner, they cornered him and made him accept her prize and title on her behalf. Everyone was offering him congratulations, and he still felt dazed. Folks were approaching him from all sides asking if they could meet with her to discuss various offers. By the time he was able to get away and return home it was quite late. Surprisingly, he wasn't upset when Delia informed him of Talia's departure. It had been a day of surprises, yet it had also been one of revelation. All the time he had been warning his daughters about the dangers of the fair, he never once considered that his daughters were more than capable of taking care of themselves.

Perhaps it was the strain of the day, but his mind kept picturing Talia's face as she blasted the other finalist. He started chuckling at first, but then he roared with laughter until tears trickled down his face as he recalled the astonishment on the other mage's face as his slip of a daughter blasted him away. Wherever his daughter was headed, he knew now that she would be fine. He kept grinning as he went to the kitchen for a late repast. Whosoever had the ill-fortune to cross her would eventually find themselves with more than they had bargained for.

Delia smiled as she heard her father chuckling in the kitchen. She knew exactly what he was thinking. So she smiled to herself and hummed the ditty from that morning.

"Who are we going to see?"

"The best!"

"Who are we going to see?

"The best of the best!"

"Where shall we see them? "

"At the fair…at the fair!

"We going to the tournament"

"And we shall see the best"

"But the best better beware"

"Cause Talia going to be there!"

When her father looked in on her a little later, Delia was fast asleep with a smile on her face. Dutra shook his head as he wondered what this daughter was capable of. After seeing what Talia had done to her final opponent, he wasn't going to make the same mistake twice and underestimate Delia. As he closed the door to his girls' bedroom he snorted and whispered to his late wife as was often his habit when alone.

"Really Alyssa, they are your daughters."

With that he took himself off to bed, but not before he could have sworn that he heard his late wife's voice whispering back.

"I know, dearest, I know…"

* * *

CHAPTER THREE

' NEW BEGINNINGS '

PART ONE

<u>Three Months Later - Varga Dome</u>
<u>The Palace</u>

"Breathe, Delia...Just breathe."

With that thought, Delia unconsciously squared her shoulders then let her hand nestle gently in the crook of Thom's. With an elegant inclination of her head she indicated that they should proceed to the Major-domo. Her stomach clenched in knots as they slowly approached the dignified Major-domo. She knew that once they gave him their invitation, and he announced them, all eyes in that glittering throng below would be upon them.

"Did I tell you how gorgeous you look right now?"

"Yes, but I wouldn't mind if you say it again."

"I guarantee that you will be a smashing success amongst the male population here tonight…Of course, the female portion will probably want to zap you back to Merari."

"Thom, don't exaggerate so much!"

"What, just because I'm your cousin doesn't make it any less true. If I wasn't your cousin, I would probably be amongst the moonstruck males. Honestly coz, I feel hurt that you don't feel sorry for me!"

Delia gave an elegant little snort at that comment from Thom.

"Pray tell, why should I feel sorry for you?"

"I'm the one who would be stuck all night keeping the rakes and other disreputable characters away from you. After all, you're beautiful, the grand-daughter of the last Mage King, fabulously wealthy courtesy of our dearly departed Great-Uncle Broderick, and on top of all that, you are the twin sister of the infamous and elusive champion of the tournament who bested at least half of those gathered at this ball."

"Well, when you put it like that, I can see why you will have such a tough job escorting me tonight."

"Good, I'm glad you're seeing it from my perspective."

Delia had to laugh at her cousin's wistful expression as he eyed the exit door.

"Come on Thom, all of this is your doing. You're the one who dragged me to Varga to live. You're the one who made me take the etiquette and court protocol lessons. And who was the one that bullied me into attending this premier haute couture debutante ball of mage royalty?"

"Well, I did…. but in my defense I did it for your own good. I wanted to make your transition to your rightful place in society as smooth as possible. This was the only way I could think of to effectively silence all the nasty rumours one of our 'dear' relatives has been spreading about you after she got cut from Great-Uncle Broderick's Will."

Delia knew that Thom had been livid when he found out that a certain relative had been blackening her reputation even before she stepped foot in Varga. So upon her arrival in Varga, she had been immediately whisked to her new home and then inundated with lessons. Thom had been resolute in his intention that Delia make a mockery of the malicious rumours. Delia knew that her cousin was trustworthy, so she complied with his request. For nearly three months she had endured an intensive and thorough grooming course with only Thom, her three instructors and the staff for company. Of course, there had been the one time she had snuck out, but generally she had abided by the confinement. As fortune would have it, because her mother had taught her the fundamentals, the lessons had been easier than expected. In fact, they had merely enhanced and polished her innate grace and charm.

So here they were. The debutante ball was to be her test. It was the pinnacle of all her preparations. This was the annual ball whereby all the young mages of the most distinguished families would be presented. They were deemed the 'mage royalty' of their world. Yet this circle was still a small exclusive one, whose ranks would close against any potential usurpers they deemed unworthy regardless of family connections.

"Delia Abigail Jeremieu Shulto de Tierney accompanied by Thom Raule Rahmut de Arrea" rang the deep velvet tones of the Major-domo as he announced their names.

Thom gave her fingers a quick squeeze as complete and utter silence descended upon the entire ballroom. As one, all conversation below ceased, and all eyes turned in their direction. Ironically, it was at that moment that the bells of an ancient clock in the foyer started to chime. As she gracefully glided down the ivory staircase in her emerald robes, one thought kept running through her mind, 'Just breathe.'

*

<u>In the Ballroom Below</u>

He couldn't believe his eyes when he first saw her at the top of the staircase. She looked incredibly stunning. He could not believe that the same girl who had humiliated him in the tournament was actually being presented at this premier ball. His first thought was that they had begun to let the rift-raft into their ranks. He almost smiled in anticipatory glee at the embarrassment, that she would endure by the older tabbies who were renowned for their brisk set-downs of upstarts.

It was a pity, because she looked wonderful. She wore an emerald creation which clung to her curves and made her look utterly feminine. She had a pixyish appearance combined with an air of elusiveness that gave one an irresistible desire to discover more. He remembered how beautiful her eyes were, and smiled as he recalled what a ruthless look she had before she snatched the prize away. He had respected her greatly in that moment. If she managed to win over the mage echelons, she would infuse this staid circle with some life.

As he watched, he saw her approach the Major-domo escorted by Thom Rahmut de Arrea. Her selection of escorts was impeccable. The Arrea lineage was the most distinguished of their exclusive society. He wondered how she had managed to wrangle the grandson of the last Mage-King into escorting her here. The Arreas didn't associate with anyone they deemed unworthy. Therefore her appearance with Thom Arrea showed their approval, and that had effectively sealed her acceptance into this close-knit society, more so than being formally presented. No one would dare risk cutting her openly with the Arreas' backing. It was a stroke of ingenuity.

He was further surprised when the Major-domo announced her name. The Major-domo had not only called her 'Delia', but 'Tierney' as well. When he had regained consciousness after the tournament, he had made extensive enquiries as to the identity of his opponent. The report stated that she had a twin sister named 'Delia'. However, none of them ever mentioned that she was a 'Tierney'. That explained the Arrea connection. The Arreas was the male counterpart of the Tierney line, which made them cousins.

Now that he knew his opponent's true identity, he felt immensely better about his loss. For months his colleagues had ribbed him endlessly about being beaten by a no-name mage of dubious origins. However, his loss now had a different context to it. He had lost to the grand-daughter of the last Mage-King, who was well-renowned as one of the most powerful mages of their time. Judging from the blast that had rendered him unconscious, at least one of his grand-daughters had inherited his power. He wondered if this one had as well. He fully intended to discover more about this sister. She just might prove to be a likely candidate in his quest for a suitable wife.

He had need of a wife, for the Council had recently informed him that he had been chosen to be the next Mage-King. It would not be officially announced for a few months. However, they had urged him to seek a counterpart quickly, before it was made official. Ironically, it was his loss at the tournament that had swung the vote in his favour. Afterwards, one member had told him privately, it was the manner in which he had handled his defeat and subsequent ribbing that had won him their final approval. The Council was of the opinion that one saw a person's true colours when the tide was against them more so than when it was in their favour.

So he had deigned to attend tonight's proceedings with the goal of perusing the current batch of eligible debutantes for a potential mate. He knew that when the news was made official, he would be hunted by those wishing to become Mage-Consort. Perhaps he was old-fashioned, but he preferred to do the hunting. After all, marriage was a life-long commitment, and he wanted to at least like the person. Plus it had a delicious irony to it; not only was this sister an excellent choice as the grand-daughter of the last Mage-King, but he would live each and every day for the rest of his life with the same pair of fine eyes that had wiped away his complacency at the tournament. Chuckling to himself, he headed towards the maharani, hoping that he would be able to wrangle an introduction.

*

<u>Three Months Earlier-Varga Dome</u>

Thom shifted uncomfortably in his seat in the front parlour of his lately departed Great-Uncle Broderick. He had genuinely liked his great-uncle, whom most of his other family members had avoided like the plague because of his sharp wit and acerbic sense of humour.

Quite often the other members, including his grandfather who had been his younger brother, had come under heavy criticism from his great-uncle when he thought they were doing something wrong. For someone who rarely moved around in society, Great- Uncle Broderick had been surprisingly well-informed. When one was summoned to his home, it was usually because he had found out about their transgression. Yet, no one dared disobey his summons, because he was the acknowledged patriarch of the family.

To Thom, he had been a wonderful man who kept their family from becoming a cesspool of self-indulgent rakes or, at the other end of the spectrum, self-righteous prigs. He had maintained balance and order for as long as Thom could remember. Surprisingly, Thom had gotten along well with him, and would visit as often as his schedule permitted. During those visits, their discussions would range over a variety of topics. His last visit had been right before his entry into the tournament. He had been in Merari when he had received word of his uncle's passing.

As Viceroy Chen entered the room, everyone became silent. Viceroy Chen had wasted no time as he got down to business. Privately Thom could see why his Great-Uncle and the Viceroy had been such good friends. With all eyes trained on him, he attached the scroll containing Great-Uncle Broderick's last Will to a stand in the center of the large desk situated at the front of the room. The scroll had slowly unfurled upon being activated by him and confirmed the date and time of its making. Thom had been surprised, as the scroll's date revealed that it had been made a few days after the tournament.

As the holographic image of his Great-Uncle appeared, Thom felt a pang of sorrow.

"I , Broderick Gerrol Rahmut de Arrea, being of sound mental, physical and magical capacity do hereby confirm this to be my last Will and Testament. I hereby bequeath all my possessions, with the exception of a few legacies, to be shared equally amongst the following individuals:

Thom Raule Rahmut de Arrea, my great-nephew, who has displayed admirable qualities his entire life, and who has been a wonderful source of companionship during my last few years. Thank you for being the child I never had.

Delia Abigail Jeremieu Shulto de Tierney, my great-niece, who was a joy as a child and continues to be a treasure as a young lady. She taught me the value of cookies, milk and children's stories on a rainy day.

Talia Abigail Jeremieu Shulto de Tierney, my great-niece who has brought honour to our lineage by her display of talent and skill. She was a hellion as a child, and has turned into someone I am proud to call family as a young woman.

To the rest of my family, I leave absolutely nothing except the profound wish that you would handle your affairs with more discretion and sense and refrain from embarrassing our family line.

To my faithful employees I have directed Viceroy Chen to distribute certain legacies. I thank you for your loyalty throughout these many years.

With that, his Great-Uncle's voice faded. Thom got to his feet quickly and walked out before the tears he felt threatening to run down his face embarrassed him. He had not expected it. As he closed the door he heard the pandemonium break loose behind him. All the family members who had been cut out in this new will were stridently contesting its validity. They had not dared to contest Thom's inheritance. It was generally accepted that he had been the favourite. They were more miffed that two previously unknown relatives had been inserted in their stead. No one, with the exception of Thom and the Viceroy, knew who these family members were.

Thom left the Viceroy Chen to handle the explanations, as he was well suited to the task. He brooked no nonsense, and could be relied upon to deal with all the drama that was unfolding. His Great-Uncle had chosen well. As Thom wandered through the elegant townhouse, he found himself in the study. It had been his Great-Uncle's favourite room. He was surprised to see that two new images had been added to the photographs on his desk.

One was the image of Talia snatching the jewel from right underneath her opponent's nose. It was a smaller hand-sized one. Their Great-Uncle had installed a larger version in the entrance foyer. Thom's father had been surprised that their Great-Uncle had chosen to display such a vulgar picture of an unknown hoyden in such a prominent place. Since Thom and his father had never gotten along, Thom had wisely opted to keep his mouth shut at his father's remark. The other picture must have been taken a few days later, for it showed Thom and Delia laughing as he swung her around. He had been surprised at that one, since he had been unaware that he was being photographed. His Great-Uncle had definitely been keeping an eye on them.

He was reminiscing on his first meeting with his cousin a month before. He had been in search of Talia, and had stumbled across Delia. He had shown up at their country manor under the guise of returning the jewel that Talia had somehow managed to leave with him while he was unconscious. He knew that he had heard her voice when he was semi-conscious; but when he had come to, she had disappeared. Once the healers had reassured themselves that he was well, he had been discharged. His friends had delayed him from seeking Talia that evening, but by the next morning, armed with her address, he had gone searching for her.

He had seen Delia at the edge of an old well- worn path to the woods just beyond the manor, and mistaken her for Talia. Happy to see her, he had engulfed her in a huge bear hug, then lifted her in the air and swung her around before she could even say a word. As Delia later told him, she had been taken by surprise at his strange antics. It was only when she recovered her senses that she had sternly ordered him to put her down. She had explained that she was Talia's sister, and her sister had in fact left to live with their aunt. He didn't believe her at first, and thought that Talia was playing a prank on him. However, Delia's sincerity eventually convinced him, and he had turned red at first before sheepishly apologizing for his behaviour. She had forgiven him and invited him to the manor upon learning his identity.

She had set about making a meal for him, after his stomach had given away the fact that he had missed breakfast. He had followed her to the kitchen, and even assisted her in preparing it. Whilst in the kitchen, they had talked about Talia and how he had met her. Then they had started talking about a variety of topics. It was with a start that both of them had realized that they had spent the entire morning talking in the kitchen. Time had flown by so quickly that Delia had lost track of everything. For his part, he had felt so comfortable talking to her, that Delia had seemed more like a dear old friend instead of a new acquaintance. They had a light lunch soon afterwards, and she had offered to show him the woods where she had been about to go for her daily walk when they first met.

It was while walking with him that she told him about their mother. Unlike Talia, she wanted to know more about their mother's family before even venturing to make contact. So, given that Thom was from the Varga dome and moved within the higher stratum of society, she had asked him what he knew about her mother's family. Thom had been a bit taken aback that she had asked him about that particular family, since that was actually his father's branch. When she explained why, he started beaming from ear to ear and engulfed her in an enormous embrace. Then he had swung her around until she laughingly told him that it was becoming a habit. He had even started twirling her around in a country dance before she put her foot down and asked him to explain his mad antics.

Of course, he had apologized profusely for his behaviour, but she could see he wasn't a bit sorry. Delia had been rather perturbed, and started poking him for making a joke of her. When he saw that she was upset, it had sobered him a bit. So, he had started giving her a rather long and boring history of that family. To be more precise, he had actually gone back ten generations before he got to the one that mattered the most to her. It turned out that they were first cousins. His father had twin sisters, one of whom had died a few years earlier. Her mother had been an infrequent visitor at his home when he was younger. Then his grandfather and her mother had fallen out over something, and the family had been divided. Her twin had sided with her sister, and his father had sided with his grandfather.

No one aside from their grandfather, Great-Uncle Broderick, Aunt Sunni, and his father knew what the falling out was about. However, soon after her mother had ceased to visit his father or grandfather. To the best of his knowledge, Alyssa had never stepped foot inside the palace again. His Great-Uncle Broderick had been the most upset, because Alyssa had been a favourite of his. So no one had been surprised when shortly thereafter, he had stopped speaking to his brother.

Delia had been a bit overwhelmed by the fact that she and Thom were cousins. It was amazing that someone directly related to her would just waltz through her front door soon after she discovered her mother's secret. It seemed akin to fate that the person would be an actual cousin she was beginning to like a lot. Stuff like that just didn't happen to her. She was so doubtful that Thom realized she needed proof. So, he told her of how Talia had shared power with him during the showcase when his own power levels had been low.

He realized now that given his kinship with Talia, their powers had recognized each other on an elemental level. So he had proposed a test. If he could transfer some of his power to her, then the likelihood of their being related was high. He doubted it was possible for power transfers to occur between him and two different unrelated mages. Although he was merely hypothesizing, the theory made sense, so she had agreed to the experiment.

They had found a grassy knoll and sat down. Delia had been nervous but Thom had been like an eager puppy with a new toy. He had instructed her to just relax and breathe. Delia was compliant as she did as she was told. It was only when she was so completely relaxed that he had taken her hand gently. His touch was warm and reassuring, so any latent hesitation she had disappeared. The power transfer was surprisingly pleasant. There was warmth and a soft golden glow that accompanied it. He felt his own power meld with hers in such an intimate way that he knew without a doubt that they were related.

It had been somewhat similar to the time it had occurred inadvertently with Talia. With Delia, he had sensed the difference. Her power was much like his own, powerful but gentle at the same time. Delia had attempted to transfer his power back to him. However, much like him, it refused to leave her. It seemed that the power he had transferred to her was quite taken with her and didn't want to return to its rightful owner. A bit embarrassed, she had asked Thom if he could take it back. Smiling gently, he denied her request. He told her to consider it a gift and to let it be.

After that, Delia had grilled Thom about everything concerning their family. She had insisted on his staying over. Her father was due home later that evening, and she wanted them to meet. Thom and Dutra had instantly hit it off. Thom was like the son Dutra never had. He and Dutra de Novo had spent hours discussing a range of topics. Once Dutra discovered that Thom was family, he had insisted upon Thom staying with them for a few days. In return for staying there, Thom had insisted on assisting her father in all sorts of plans for the Merchant Guild.

Thom had quite enjoyed his stay. He had let down his guard and just been himself. Every morning he would traipse through the woods at ridiculously early hours. Delia had once asked him why, and instead of just shrugging it off sheepishly, he had admitted that he just liked being alone with the world and opening his senses to a new day. He loved to hear the birds start off their mornings chirping. He had especially liked the yellow bird with its brown, white and black crown that had its own particular morning sound. He confided to her once that it served as a reminder that no matter what mages may do, the world was still a beautiful place. He even admitted that after his injury and miraculous healing he appreciated the little things more.

Delia said nothing, but merely smiled. He knew that she had suspected that growing up as the grandson of the Mage King and having a powerful mother who was renowned throughout the mage academic community was probably daunting. From his youth, everyone had constant expectations of him. He had no siblings, and before he met Delia and Talia, no close cousins. So now that he had discovered that he had cousins, both of whom had treated him just like any other mage, he was happy. Delia accepted Thom as family, and that was all that mattered to her. She soon became like the sister that he never had. She had spent hours telling him of her childhood with Talia, and he had felt a deep affinity with them.

Unfortunately, his stay had been cut short by a terse missive sent via courier by Viceroy Chen, who had urgently requested his presence. Given the tone of the message, Thom didn't think it was wise to disobey. Thom didn't know who had been sadder at his departure. They had all been like forlorn puppies when Thom shared the contents of the missive with them. Delia had helped him to pack, while her father had made travel arrangements for him to Varga. When it was time to say good-bye, Dutra had insisted on seeing him off. Delia didn't think she could without falling apart and crying, so she said her farewells the night before, and stayed out of the manor until he had left. He had left a note for her with the jewel that Talia had won. His note had consisted of one line: *'See you soon'* and he had signed it *'Cousin Thom.'*

Upon his arrived in Varga, Viceroy Chen had been there to receive him. It was from him that Thom had learned of his Great-Uncle's passing. Thom had attended the funeral and delivered the eulogy. Now it was time to go back into the room with all his relatives and confirm the truth. When he walked back into the room, he found his relatives more subdued, but one was still bitterly angry. They had discovered that the will was airtight and would stand up in any mage court. Once he had their attention, he quietly confirmed that Talia and Delia were indeed the daughters of his aunt Alyssa. He briefly outlined how he had found his cousins. At first no one would believe that the 'hoyden' that had won the tournament from under the nose of the favoured mage king candidate was related to them. When Alyssa had broken off contact, she had not contacted anyone in that room. So no one even knew she had had two daughters.

The Viceroy had known what he would be facing, and had produced evidence to support Thom's assertions. One was a document from Sunni, Alyssa's twin sister, confirming that her sister did indeed have twin daughters. One of whom was the 'hoyden' who had won the tournament, and whom she was now training as a novice Kao member. Most had been aghast that two members of the younger generation of their branch had been living in some forsaken dome without the benefits of having access to the finest schools and privileges that was their birthright by virtue of their being the only grand-daughters of the last Mage King. It was an affront to them that Alyssa hadn't chosen to share this information with them. Privately, Thom thought it was a whole bunch of nonsense, but he kept his mouth shut.

After everyone had left, the Viceroy had told Thom that his Great -Uncle had kept in contact with Alyssa after she and her father had fallen out. He had known of his great-nieces, and had in fact visited them when they were younger. Alyssa had always arranged these visits whenever her husband was away on business. She had always been one of his favourites, and he thought his brother a fool for being so stubborn. He had kept an eye on them without their knowledge since Alyssa's passing. In fact, their father traded quite regularly with his contact there. His contact had always kept him abreast of the girls' lives.

When he found out that Thom had been injured in the tournament, he had immediately ordered his contact to locate him and arrange to bring him home. When his contact had reported that Thom had gone to stay with his cousins and that Talia had departed for parts unknown, his great-uncle had realized immediately that Thom had discovered the connection. So, he had his contact keep an eye on them as usual (and judging from the recent picture on his Great-Uncle's desk it had been a close eye) and had tried to locate Talia. He had gotten lucky, as his contact with the Kao in the Holy Citadel of Rhys had informed him of Talia's impromptu arrival. Personally, Thom had been in awe at the formidable network of contacts his uncle had developed over the years.

His Great-Uncle had taken the initiative and written to Talia. Since he and Sunni remained on good terms, she had facilitated this communication. According to the Viceroy, his Great-Uncle had grilled her about her sister and their life. Talia had politely told him to mind his own business. Yet, they both seemed to have taken a shine to each other. That was when he had ordered an enlarged image of Talia snatching the jewel from right underneath the nose of her opponent in the final second of the tournament to be displayed prominently in the foyer of his home. Talia had not attended his funeral, but had sent her condolences to Thom.

Over the next few days Thom and the Viceroy had dealt with everything quickly, since his Great- Uncle had made the necessary arrangements for the transfer of his estate. The only stipulation his Great- Uncle had given in a private letter he had left to each of his beneficiaries was that Delia be brought to Varga to live for a year. He didn't bother to make such a request of Talia, because he knew she had found her purpose with the Kao. However, he had wanted Delia to be exposed to opportunities she would never experience if she was left to live in Merari. If she didn't like it, she was free to leave after the year was completed. His house in Varga had been left for her use. He had urged Thom to make her transition as smooth as possible and to keep away the feckless fortune hunters from her. He had ended his letter to Thom with gruff words of love that had left Thom weeping for the grand old mage he had called friend.

*

Merari Dome – A week after Thom's departure

Delia and her father had moped around after Thom's departure. He had become so much a part of their family that with him and Talia gone, the manor had felt empty. He had filled their lives with laughter, and his presence right after Talia's departure had eased the void she had left. Delia still hadn't heard from Talia since her departure, but she hadn't felt any danger surrounding her twin. She didn't know if her sister had become more adept at blocking her, or if she was simply well. However, she had trusted her instincts, and believed deep down that her sister was fine. Talia would contact her when she was ready, and Delia needed to continue her life.

About a week after Thom's departure, he returned. Much like the first day they had met, she had been walking along the path in the woods and had seen him. It was so déjà-vu that at first she thought she was daydreaming. It was only when he engulfed her in a bear hug and swung her around like a rag doll that she accepted he was not a figment of her imagination. Of course, she was so pleased that he was there that she had dragged him to the manor to see her father. Thom had filled them in on everything that had transpired since he left. He had also given her the letter their Great-Uncle had left for her. His own letter had been creased and she was sure re-read countless of times.

Delia was still reeling at the fact that a stranger had left her a fortune and she was to leave all that she knew and move to Varga for a year. It seemed that every time Thom came into her life it changed. She still couldn't recall meeting her Great-Uncle. It was only after reading her own letter that she recalled him. When he had visited her mother had introduced him as an old friend, and he had let her play tea with him. She had been tickled pink when he had produced actual milk and delicious cookies in her teacup and tea plate. Talia had turned up her nose at that display of magic, and had been about to prance off when he berated her for having bad table manners. He had then proceeded to woo them with a fascinating story that had them thoroughly engrossed. From that time on, whenever he visited, they would automatically drag him to the library, where he would tell them other fascinating stories while their mother served them with tea and cookies.

She had almost forgotten those memories. He had stopped coming after their mother had died; but he had sent a huge bouquet of Alyssa's favourite flowers to her funeral and a book of classics for them. After that they hadn't heard from him. So when Thom told her that their Great-Uncle had been keeping tabs on her, she was amazed. She felt like she had been hit with a ton of bricks and was still reeling. Yet Thom and her father took it quite in stride and put their heads together to see how quickly they could get her to Varga. Everything was ready in Varga for her. It was up to her father whether he wanted to accompany her for the year, or entrust her to Thom's care.

At the end it was decided that Dutra and Delia would accompany Thom back to Varga. Her father would stay with them until she got settled and explore potential opportunities in the region. He would return home soon after, and visit as necessary. Dutra trusted Thom to keep an eye on her. Both men were in one accord when it came to that. So, a few days later, Delia had found herself packed up and on her way to Varga.

*

VARGA -Two days before the Ball

Delia could hear the bells chiming from the clock in the foyer below, signaling to her that her instructor would soon be here. She was in no mood to be instructed on proper etiquette of the mage court. In fact, it was her least favourite lessons. Privately, she thought it was a bother which she might have been inclined to skip if Thom wouldn't start on her case about the upcoming debutante ceremony where all the young mages of so-called 'mage royalty' would be presented.

She was learning things that were taught to the others from birth in a few short weeks. Surprisingly, it turned out to be easier than expected, since it seemed that her mother had been teaching them the fundamentals since birth. Although her magical abilities were more empathetic in nature, in the court setting they would be an asset. However, she needed to learn how to keep a tighter rein over them, as one of her instructors had warned her. In fact, he had insisted that if she ever felt like her protective shield was low and she was beginning to feel overwhelmed by the various emotions she picked up, she was to find a quiet place away from everyone and recharge her batteries for a while. He had placed great emphasis on this point.

Now, it was two days before the event and she was tired. She wanted to leave the house, but Thom had told her no. So, in an uncharacteristically rebellious mood she had disobeyed him and stepped outside the house for the first time in nearly three months. She had borrowed one of the staff's uniforms which had a hood. The hood had shielded her features from view. So early that morning when everyone was still abed, she had crept out. It was to be a quick exploration of the immediate vicinity. As she crept through the back gate that led to a minor road, she felt a sense of exhilaration. She was on her own in a strange place, and it felt wonderful.

As she walked through the streets there was still a slight fog in the air, yet she gazed in wonder at her surroundings. Everything seemed so much bigger in Varga than it was in Merari. The buildings were taller, the streets were wider, even the artistically crafted miniature open spaces in the midst of these imposing buildings were amazing landscaped creations. At one point she wandered into an open space and stared in awe at a reflecting pool that changed to show various picturesque scenes. She would have gone on staring at the pool but for the sounds of life she heard stirring around her.

She saw vendors getting ready to hawk their goods for the day. Off-site staff busily trying to get to their respective workplaces before their employers awoke. A few security mages passed along, keeping a watchful eye on the day's proceedings. She saw the streets come alive as the soft glow that signaled daybreak gently blanketed the dome. As she watched the dome come alive, she forgot she was standing in a pathway. It was only when someone bumped into her and had to steady her that she was jolted back to her immediate surroundings.

As she turned to thank the person, she was pleasantly surprised. It was her old friend from the tournament who had spent the afternoon entertaining her. It was such a coincidence to see him there at this hour in this particular dome. She felt a prickling in her senses that it was an omen that she should not ignore. She used to tease Talia concerning her ridiculous notion that when a butterfly crossed one's path, one's life was about to change. Now, she wasn't so sure that Talia's notion was as absurd as she first thought it. She was actually tempted to let him go without revealing her identity. However, the choice was taken out of her hands as he recognized her and acknowledged their acquaintance. He couldn't see her face, yet he knew it was her. He even teased her about her outfit in a rather sapient tone of voice. She responded in kind, and their easy bantering would have continued if she hadn't been mindful of the time.

He insisted on escorting her back to her home, so she filled him in on how she came to be in Varga and what was happening in her life. She confided her fear to him that she would make a total cake of herself at the debutante ball. He glibly told her that such an occurrence would be welcomed, if only to liven up the party. He had not attended that particular event for more than a decade, as he found it a ghastly bore. However, he promised that he would endeavour to be there, if only to witness her make a spectacular faux pas that would make such a boring crush worthwhile. She felt like clouting him after that remark, but restrained herself quite admirably. As he bid her adieu by her new home, she felt more confident that she could pull this off. Thanks to him, she was ready to face the world of 'mage royalty' and set them on ear if the need arose.

The Night of the Ball

Thom let out a low whistle of masculine approval as Delia glided gracefully into his line of sight. For the first time since they had met, he felt it a pity that they were cousins. Now, he was going to be stuck all night being bombarded by requests for introductions to her. He knew for a fact that he was in for a rough time of it, being her guardian. He was almost tempted to tell her to go right back upstairs and change into something less alluring.

It was then he glanced into her eyes and saw the uncertain expression in them. She stood at the bottom of their staircase, outwardly poised but with the air of one ready to flee. He felt like an ogre for even contemplating the notion of asking her to change. So, he mentally resigned himself to having a rough night ahead. Bowing elegantly he addressed her:

"Delia Abigail Jeremieu Shulto de Tierney, of the Merari dome, descended from Dutra de Novo, Merchant Mage of the Province of Siente. Born to Alyssa Shulto de Tierney, daughter of our esteemed Mage-King Arrea, and sister of Talia Ramona Jeremieu Shulto de Tierney… I would be honoured if you wore this small token of my esteem."

Delia smiled at Thom's thoughtfulness, and allowed him to fasten a corsage unto her wrist.

"I am deeply honored, and I thank you for your gift."

The small smile that tugged at her lips, made him glad that he had decided to purchase this small gift for her. It had been an impulsive purchase, but when he had seen it in the window of a store, he had known instinctively that it would suit her. His instincts were urging him, to wipe away the lack of confidence he saw reflected in her eyes. So, ever so gently, he squeezed her arm in reassurance.

By the time they arrived at the ball, most of the other debutantes had been announced. As expected, once the Major-domo announced their names, as one the entire ballroom below went completely silent. He felt proud as Delia elegantly tilted her head then glided down the crystal stairwell almost in sync with the chiming of an ancient clock. As they reached the bottom, the maharani, who was the presiding lady of the court for that year, greeted them. As Delia and the maharani chatted a bit, both he and Delia discovered that she had presided as maharani the same year that Delia's mother and aunt had been presented. The maharani had archly informed her that she had also been a close confidante of her maternal grandmother.

In fact, their families had been close when her maternal grandmother was alive, and she had liked and admired Alyssa and her sister. She was saddened to hear of Alyssa's passing. The maharani had pressed Delia into promising that she would visit her as soon as she could. That was not an invitation that was given lightly, so even he was taken aback. As another debutante was being announced, Delia gave her word and moved out of the receiving line to make way for the other debutante.

When Thom cleared the receiving line with her, one of the most distinguished mages of their set greeted her. Thom was stunned that she knew this particular mage. With a twinkle in his eye, he introduced himself to Thom as Ravi. Thom recovered his wits after a few moments, then politely but firmly enquired as to how the two had become acquainted. As Ravi filled him in about their chance meeting in Merari then in Varga, it was then that Thom relaxed because the expressed approval of the maharani and Ravi had cinched Delia's inclusion into their society. Others in the ballroom, seeing that both the maharani and Ravi had given her their expressed approval, dismissed any rumour which may have reached their ears, and soon flocked for introductions.

Thom and Ravi had stayed by Delia's side the entire night as she met those belonging to the mage royalty. The first question most of them asked after their respective introduction was whether it was true that she was the sister of the mage who had won the tournament. Those of her age group were in awe of her sister. It was unheard of for an unknown young mage with no previous training to best mages who had been trained by experts in their respective fields. They were eager to know if she had the same abilities. Even though she had laughingly told them no, they were still eager to know her history. It seemed as if she was a breath of fresh air to these mages who had grown up in a life of privilege.

By the end of the evening it was undoubted that she was a smashing success. Even the family members that had meant to be condescending prior to meeting her were suitably chagrined and did their duty by her after being introduced. Ravi had stuck with them the entire night, and had even accompanied them home. He had stayed for a brief chat then left. Thom had gone to bed that night feeling gloriously satisfied that he had done his duty well.

*　*　*

CHAPTER FOUR

'FAMILY CONNECTIONS'

<u>VARGA: A week after the ball</u>

My favourite nook

Dear Tabitha,

Alyssa and Sunni have been driving me to distraction. My girls are only five but today they managed to slip past Nanny Tess and Nanny Bess to glide down, of all things, the main spiraling staircase in the palace, and fly right out of doors into that dreadful Count Gladstone. According to Nanny Tess, the poor Count went sprawling with his legs sticking up in the air. And do you know what my little angels did afterwards? They were actually running back towards the same staircase to try it again before Nanny Bess headed them off.

When I found out about it and was reprimanding them, I swear their little eyes got larger and almost soulful. If I didn't have it on good account what my children had been up to, I would have doubted that my little darlings could be so naughty. I felt like an ogre afterwards, as I sternly explained that the consequences of their action would be the 'naughty corners.' Alyssa and Sunni started to cry so much when I separated them that it nearly broke my heart. Then I remembered what the little hellions had done, and I stiffened my resolve. You would have been proud of me; I managed to stick out an entire half an hour of sniffles and woeful looks by both girls. Afterwards, they both hugged me and promised me that they wouldn't slide down the main bannister anymore. It was only afterwards I realized that they neglected to promise about <u>any of the other bannisters in the palace.</u>

Cam laughed when I told him what had happened that night. He was sorry that he missed seeing his daughters glide down the main bannister. It seemed that some of the mages who did not like Count Gladstone had been snickering all day and kept mentioning seeing his daughters in close proximity within the Count's earshot. He now understood why the Count would turn pale at the very mention of Alyssa and Sunni, and had moved rather hurriedly in another direction. Cam could not control his laughter at the fact that the poor man was now terrified of his five- year- old magelets. He even had the audacity to jokingly ask if he could bring them with him next time the Council was supposed to vote on a resolution of his and the Count decided to oppose.
I swear, Tabitha, I was torn between laughing myself and throwing up my hands in exasperation. I think that it's time for me to send my little dears to my grandmother. Grandmother Dris would straighten these two out in a week. She taught me the fundamentals of being a lady before I even dreamt of marrying Cam and becoming Mage Consort. I think that it may behoove my daughters to learn some of the same lessons I had when I was younger.

So I am resolved, off they go at the end of the week to my Grandmother for some tender loving tough parenting. My girls will not grow up to be anything less than I am.

Affectionately,
Elizabeth

Delia had to smile at the letter she just re-read a third time from her maternal grandmother, Elizabeth, to her dear friend, Tabitha (the maharani at her ball), approximately forty years ago. She was currently snuggled in her late Great-Uncle's favourite recliner re-reading the batch of correspondence that the maharani had sent over the morning after her smashing success at the ball. In her note, the maharani had explained that she thought that Delia might have wanted to have a more intimate look at the remarkable woman she had been pleased to call friend for many years.

The maharani had also sent her a signed autobiography of her maternal grandmother along with the neatly tied batch of correspondence from her maternal grandmother to the maharani that had spanned nearly six decades. In her note, the maharani had indicated to her that she could keep them. The image imprinted on the book had been of her grandmother just before she had passed on. Even Delia could see the strong resemblance between her grandmother and herself. She had decided to read the correspondence between the two women before she read the autobiography.

As she read, she discovered how alike she and her grandmother were on so many levels. Like her, her grandmother loved the smells, sights and sounds of nature. Like her maternal grandmother, she loved to read. She had chosen the path of being a homemaker and had focused her energies on raising her two children and assisting her husband in his duties as Mage King. Elizabeth had married at a young age and had kept the harmony amongst her family, the 'royal' mages and by extension between the domes. It had not been an easy task, and only a select handful had ever known of the close disasters that had been averted with her assistance.

Delia had been hooked from the first letter she had read. She had glimpsed her grandmother's world through her correspondence. She knew vaguely that Thom had wandered in that morning while she was reading, but she had been so engrossed that she had barely acknowledged him. By mid-afternoon the following day she had finished reading the batch of correspondence. She had felt a strong affinity to her maternal grandmother after reading the letters she had sent to her friend. It was like seeing the life journey of a wonderful woman through her letters. She then turned to the autobiography, and couldn't put it down. She read it until she finished it entirely. Trays of food had appeared quietly when she was hungry, and had disappeared just as quietly.

She read through the night and late into the next day. It was only after finishing that she realized that she had to address some physical necessities. Yet, it had been worth it, for she felt so much more connected to her maternal grandparents after reading the autobiography. It was like a bridge had been formed in the chasm of her ignorance concerning her maternal family. She felt humbled and incredibly grateful to have descended from this woman. Afterwards she slept for sixteen hours straight.

She had just awoken to a shower of rain. Nature had released a hint of its essence in gratitude. To Delia, it seemed somewhat fitting. She loved the faint scent of this world when it rained. It was a clean earthy aroma that filled one with a sense of wellness merely by knowing that the environment surrounding one was teeming with microscopic lives. In a way, some of her abilities, like those of her maternal grandmother were tied to nature. When something was out of sync with nature, so was she. It seemed as if her abilities were connected on a fundamental level with her environment and when that environment flourished, so did she.

It was while woolgathering and re-reading her grandmother's letters that she had been surprised by an unannounced visit from the maharani. She had sent a thank-you note to the maharani and had been meaning to send a token of her appreciation, but she had not gotten the opportunity as yet. Now it seemed that the maharani had come to call in person. So after scrambling to look presentable, Delia had found the maharani in the front parlour.

From her grandmother's letters, the maharani was intelligent; and her wit, wisdom, sense of humour and good nature made her sound like a wonderful individual. Upon learning that Delia felt out of sorts with her new environment, the maharani had gently but definitely grilled her on her abilities. Delia had shared everything, since she found it surprisingly easy to open up to her. After the subtle interrogation, the maharani had considered her for a moment, then immediately announced that they were going to explore the city, because she wanted to test a theory.

Delia had been taken aback somewhat, but given what she had learned from her grandmother's correspondence, she felt as if she could trust the maharani. So she had agreed, and off they went. It had been such a fun impromptu excursion. Delia had confessed her recent escapade where she had snuck out of the house before the ball because she had been quite fed up being in the house day after day. The maharani had merely laughed and told her of some of the escapades her own children had gotten into while they were younger. She had promised to introduce her to them quite soon. She had also insisted that she call her Tabitha like her grandmother had before.

They had explored the city like two visitors who had just arrived at the dome. The maharani had insisted they travelled incognito, since she didn't want to waste time being bombarded by the other mages she knew. They visited the amazing landscape creations in the open spaces between the various buildings. The maharani took the time to explain the significance of each as well as the magical work that went into such creations. She took her to one of the most prestigious art museums in the city and they had fun discussing the various pieces on display. Their trip ended with a leisurely walk through the gardens of the palace where her grandfather had once resided as Mage King.

The maharani had told her of her grandmother's wish for nature to run free within the palace gardens. It turned out that her grandmother had not been a fan of the artificial creations, and like her, had much preferred nature. To please her grandmother, Cam

(Delia's grandfather) had the palace gardens landscaped according to her explicit instructions, and when it was completed had opened it to the general public. Upon hearing this story, Delia had felt such a profound sense of kinship with her grandparents as she continued to stroll arm in arm with the maharani. Afterwards the maharani had dropped her off and had even thanked her for putting up with an old fogey like her for the entire day. Delia had smiled at that turn of phrase. It was so quaint and lady-like, much like the maharani herself.

As soon as Delia awoke the next morning, she ate, dressed and went directly to the maharani's favorite specialty store that carried a certain tea blend that she adored. After ordering quite a lot of it, she had it delivered to the maharani's address. Her next stop was a quaint little magical trinkets stall that carried unusual pieces. She had discovered it on her early morning escapade before the ball, and had liked the feel of it. She had noticed that like her, the maharani liked jade pieces, and she spent close to two hours selecting just the right piece for the maharani. Her Great- Uncle had left her quite ample funds, and she wanted to spend some. The gratitude she felt at the thoughtful gesture of the maharani was tremendous. She had always felt as if she didn't know a part of herself, and now that part had been answered through her readings.

Delia ran into a few persons she had met at the ball on her way to the maharani's home. She wanted to personally deliver this trinket to the maharani's home. Upon her arrival, she had rung the doorbell. It was at this point that she had started to feel a bit unsure of herself. She had been running on full steam when she got up so that she had not given a thought to the propriety of dropping by unannounced. Luckily, before her nerves got the better of her, Tabitha had opened her door herself.

*

<u>Tabitha's Gardens: A short while later</u>

"Foul"

"In what dome can that possibly be considered a foul?"

"Let me see…ALL of them!"

"Would you like me to zap something up to enhance your obviously poor eyesight?"

"Thank you kindly, my dear but no…but since you did mention it, perhaps you may want to zap one up for your OWN assistance."

Delia had just accompanied the maharani (who had insisted that she be called Tabitha) to her garden when she overheard the comments. Eloise (Tabitha's eldest daughter) was going head to head with her own daughter, Ann-Marie, over what was turning into a hotly contested game. As Tabitha had explained when she had opened her own door, her entire family was in residence at this time, and they had just begun a game of 'whoosh' in the garden.

The game was between the adults of Tabitha's family and their children. The children were captained by their grandfather, the maharani's husband, Laurence, who was a professor and dean of the most prestigious university in Varga. Eloise, Tabitha's eldest daughter, had been captaining the adults, and had been vehemently defending the referee's call. The referee in question was a long-standing member of staff named Jenkins who looked quite impervious to the dirty looks being sent his way by those on the children's team as he upheld his previous decision.

Delia had found herself in Tabitha's garden by fluke as Tabitha had insisted that she stay awhile and had invited her to join her family gathering. She warned Delia that though her family was usually well-behaved, when it came to games amongst themselves, it usually degenerated into yelling matches. As a result, as Tabitha explained to her, as much as she loved her family she refused to play any sort of games with them. Her statement was soon proven true as Delia entered the garden area with her.

Her arrival with Delia had created a brief respite from the hostilities between the participants as she introduced Delia to her family. Unfortunately, before Tabitha could seize the opportunity to escape with Delia in tow, Ann –Marie managed to snag Delia for their team as they were now one person short due to what she was told in an ominously dark tone was the unmitigated and clear error of a certain short-sighted referee. Jenkins, the referee in question, merely ignored the little runt. Tabitha had made a last-ditch effort to distract Ann-Marie, but was too late, as a 'yes' had slipped out of Delia's mouth. The other children had pounced on the opportunity and taken Delia in hand before their grandmother could deflect them.

Upon ascertaining that Delia did not know how to play the game, they gave her a quick run-down of the basics, then sent her off to a position which they stressed was quite necessary even if somewhat removed from the immediate action. The adults, sensing her uncertainty concerning the game, deliberately started sending their serves to her corner. Their children shot their parents dirty looks, then proceeded to complain to the referee, who ignored them. So her team retooled their strategy. They started shifting her to different positions so that by the time the adults served, she was quickly moved to another position and one of her other teammates would replace her. Thereafter, their parents, realizing that the plan had been pre-empted, left her alone. Fortunately, Delia got better as the game progressed, and she had quite a jolly bit of fun before the match ended in a draw.

She had been invited to stay for dinner, but declined. So they had pressed her into coming over for dinner the next day. As far as Tabitha's clan was concerned, she was now an honorary member. The fact that she was Alyssa's daughter and could put up with their screeching and ungracious conduct when it came to family games made her a definite keeper in their books. In turn, Delia had been delighted at their kindness. Tabitha had merely shaken her head fondly and warned her that she had no idea what both the adult and child-sized brats had in store for her from now on.

Tabitha had seen Delia to the door, and it was there that she remembered the original reason for her visit. She gave Tabitha the trinket that she had gotten her as a token of her appreciation for the kindness that had been extended to her. As she placed the trinket in the maharani's hand she spoke from her heart. For her, it was an honour to be adopted into the clan of the woman who helped her bridge the gap to her past. Tabitha had been touched by her words and had hugged her in response. As they bade each other farewell, Tabitha had teared up a bit and made her promise to return the next night for dinner. Smiling, Delia had consented then left to return to her own household.

Delia's journey home was slow as she was a bit sore from the game of 'whoosh' with Tabitha's clan. While walking she was stopped by someone she had met at the ball. Even though she had freshened up afterwards, she had still felt a bit hot and sticky. So she tried her best to avoid a long chit-chat. She was relieved when another mage hailed them and came over to speak with the person. She was introduced and felt a rush of awareness as she realized that it was the mage that Talia had beaten at the tournament. They had met briefly at the ball, and he had seemed quite delighted to make her acquaintance, and even quipped about her sister snatching the gem from right under his nose.

Delia had been relieved to discover that he bore no outward signs of malice towards her sister. Other mages wouldn't have taken such a blow to their ego quite as well. As she bid them adieu, citing her need to see her cousin, he had surprised her by offering to escort her to her household. He felt it was the least he could do for the sister of a truly worthy opponent. Since Delia could see no way of avoiding the invitation without seeming uncouth and ungracious, she mentally griped, but smiled a gracious acceptance.

He actually surprised her. He was suave, sophisticated and quite charming. He was attractive, but not overly so. He actually went to a great deal of trouble to amuse her while he escorted her home. She realized he had a lively wit and extensive knowledge of a variety of issues concerning her own home dome of Merari. By the time she arrived at her doorstep, she had been suitably impressed. He had asked her, as any true gentleman would, if she wouldn't mind if he called upon her from now on. She had asked him 'why' before she could stop herself. He had been surprised at her directness for a moment. Then he had looked at her fully before telling her with great sincerity that he found himself wanting to further his acquaintance with the owner of such a lovely pair of eyes. His response had made her smile, so she politely acquiesced to his request. As she went through her doors she could have sworn she heard him whistling merrily as he walked away.

Afterwards, she had mused over their interlude and decided to pen a letter to Talia. She had enclosed copies of the correspondence between their grandmother and Tabitha as well as a copy of the autobiography for her sister. She had a feeling that Talia would enjoy getting to know this wonderful woman as much as she had. She even teased her in the letter about her meeting with Talia's final opponent whom she had so soundly thrashed at the tournament. When she was quite done, she gave one of the staff members the package to forward to the pick-up location for all items sent to the Citadel of Rhys. Then she found Thom and they went out to dinner.

Upon their arrival at the chic eatery, they discovered to their delight that Ravi had the same idea and had just arrived. Delia had urged him to join them. It was during dessert that Thom told her that he was going to be away for three weeks. He had recently heard about some potential business opportunities in the Luz dome. If it proved true, then it would further expand her father's business. Ravi had been surprised too, since he was going to be away as well. He had been asked that afternoon to fill in as a favour for a colleague of his, on a teaching expedition where ten students from Varga were spending a month in the Babel dome on an exchange programme. He was to accompany them and serve as a guide and protector if the need arose.

His colleague had a family emergency that made it impossible for him to leave at this time. He hadn't wanted to cancel the trip, because arrangements had been made and the students had been eagerly anticipating this trip for ages. So he had asked Ravi. He knew that Ravi had the requisite knowledge and ability. Ravi had agreed because he felt a bit restless and thought that a month elsewhere would do him good.

Thom was a bit worried to leave her on her own without either himself or Ravi there in case anything should happen. She had reassured him that it would be fine. He wasn't convinced, and was going to cancel his trip when Eloise, Tabitha's oldest daughter, interrupted their discussion. She had escaped the bedlam that was her mother's house at the moment, and had been seated at the table behind them. She was actually seated right behind Thom, and had accidentally overheard their conversation.

So she had turned around and asked if he would permit Delia to stay by her family for that three-week period. There was more than sufficient space to accommodate her, and they would love to have her. Of course, the only condition had been that she played for the adults, since the little brats were actually becoming quite horrid since they had managed for the first time ever to draw in a match against the adults.

Both Thom and Ravi were taken aback at this apparent stranger, who had just interrupted their conversation. They were also quite lost as to her condition. Delia took pity on them and introduced them to the maharani's eldest daughter, and told them of the match that she had participated in. Recognition registered in both Thom and Ravi's faces as Tabitha's name was mentioned. Given that Eloise had been away for a few years, and had just returned, neither of them had recognized her. Eloise was quite like her father in many respects, and took matters into her own hands when she saw that both Thom and Ravi were about to refuse. She swung her chair around to join their table, then countered each and every argument they could toss at her. It was a lively debate between all parties concerned, while

Delia just sat back and smiled in amusement as she watched Eloise launch a spirited campaign on her behalf.

Delia had no doubt that Eloise would win after seeing her in action at the match. She had gone toe to toe with her father and had outclassed all others in her spirited defence of her side. The only one who came close to giving her a run for her money was her own daughter, Ann-Marie, who was a miniature version of Eloise. Nevertheless, Eloise with a cause was not to be deterred. She had been trained by her father, and used her tongue like a finely-tuned instrument. Ravi had given it a decent try with his glib tongue and artful jabs here and there. But even he realized that he was no match for this spirited mage with a determined gleam in her eye. After looking to Delia for assistance and seeing none forthcoming from her quarter, they had finally conceded defeat in the face of Eloise's arguments.

Delia had no objections herself, and had rather looked forward to becoming better acquainted with that boisterous clan. However, she understood Eloise's nature and had made her promise that she would ask her mother, not tell or argue, but ask permission for her to stay with them for the three weeks. Eloise had been about to wheedle a bit on the arguing part, but Delia had held firm. So Eloise had promised, then gleefully left their group to ask her mother as quickly as possible before Thom and Ravi could recover from her verbal assault. Delia had no doubt that by the time she and Thom got home an invitation from Tabitha would be there waiting. She had thought that Tabitha's family 'adoption' of her was just mere words. She realized now that they had been quite serious. As Eloise had just aptly demonstrated as far as she was concerned Delia was family, and that was that. Everyone else, including Delia's blood relatives, just had to deal with it.

True to form, as soon as Delia, Thom and Ravi arrived at her household, an invitation was waiting. Like Eloise, Tabitha had happily extended the invitation. In fact, she had been even more delighted to have Delia join the bedlam that was her household for the next few weeks. Her invitation was an unconditional one, since her grandchildren were now arguing strenuously against Eloise's condition that Delia join the adult team. Both teams wanted her since she proved to be quite decent at the game, and aside from all that they had all liked her. Of course, the most vigorous opponent against the condition was Eloise's adolescent daughter, Ann-Marie, whom (Tabitha had confided to Delia) had cheerfully countered every argument of her mother's with her grandfather's occasional support. Tabitha had hastened to add that since she was issuing the invitation, Delia was under no obligation to even participate in the games, and was quite welcome anyway. She would love the opportunity to become better acquainted with the grandchild of her dearest friend.

After reading the invitation, Delia had waved it under Thom and Ravi's noses before archly informed them that she had told them so. Thom had grabbed at it, and after both he and Ravi thoroughly examined it, could find no further objections. Even Delia could see they were relieved at not having to leave her alone in the house. So they had discussed Thom's potential business opportunity and Ravi's upcoming chaperoning. By the time Ravi had left for the night, they were all excited at their prospective ventures. She was off to be a houseguest of one of the most respected mage households in Varga; Thom was off to sniff out and possibly cement a business opportunity for her father; and Ravi was off to visit a different dome, which would curb his restlessness a bit.

* * *

CHAPTER FIVE

' A COURTSHIP '

<u>**Tabitha's home: A week later**</u>

Delia had been a guest of Tabitha for a few days, and had been quite happy being a part of her boisterous clan. She was allowed a certain level of freedom to come and go as she pleased. Most times she was having too much fun with the maharani's family to leave. They were an intelligent, fun, and loving group, and she had fallen in love with each and every one of them. When she did leave the household, it was usually for an early morning walk in the gardens of the court.

She had been enjoying the smell of the rain in a quiet spot. She knew that it would not be long before one of Tabitha's children or grandchildren found her and got her involved in some mischievous scheme. Tabitha's daughters, Eloise and Angela, had been quite fun, and she enjoyed spending time with them. They were the same age her mother would have been. It turned out that when they were much younger, before her grandfather became Mage-King, they had often spent summers together with her mother and Sunni, and would regale her with stories of their various childhood escapades.

Angela's two daughters, who had made their debut a year before Delia, knowing that sometimes their mother and aunt's penchant for reminiscing could run terribly long, would enlist one of the younger ones (most often Ann-Marie) to create a distraction, then filch her from them. So by the time Eloise or Angela returned, Delia would already have been drafted into some excursion. Tabitha's husband, Cam, would observe and wink at her before returning to read his book. Tabitha merely smiled and observed as she ran her household. There was only one ruler in this proverbial roost, and that was Tabitha. Every member of the family deferred to her.

So as she relished this quiet time with nature, it came as a surprise when Jenkins, the staff member with the impervious stare who had refereed the first match she had played in, interrupted her meditation to hand her a calling card. It was from the mage who had been trounced by Talia and had escorted her home one evening. He wished to invite her and Tabitha's eldest two grand-daughters on a trip to the museum that Tabitha had taken her to. She was about to decline, but paused as she considered that perhaps Tessa and Shannon might enjoy such an excursion. Tessa definitely enjoyed art, and was always creating some pieces that had her in awe. She would love such a trip. Shannon would tag along because she liked socializing with people her own age, and the museum was one of the places where young mages liked to visit.

Yet, Delia was unsure as to whether she should accept this invitation. He was charming and handsome, and it was flattering that a candidate for the position of Mage King (she had gotten that scoop from Eloise) had deigned to invite her out; but there was something she couldn't put her finger on that didn't feel quite right. Luckily, at that moment, Tabitha had chosen to poke her head through the door. She seemed as if she had been scoping out a potential place to hide from her brood. Spotting Delia, her countenance smoothed, then relaxed, as she made her way into the room where Delia was seated. She gently shut the door, but not before Delia could hear ear-piercing shrieks from Eloise's ten-year-old twin boys and Ann-Marie's strident voice clamouring for them not to skate down the banister onto a floating cloud at the bottom. Delia didn't even want to know how the twins intended to skate down the spiral banister that connected the upstairs floor to lower one; for sheer inventiveness the twins were in a class of their own.

Nevertheless, Tabitha was just the person she needed to speak with concerning the invitation. Once she told Tabitha everything with regard to her entire dealings with this particular mage and gave her the calling card and attached invitation, she felt a bit lighter. Tabitha had grilled her exhaustively on her meeting with him, then when satisfied, looked thoughtful and remained silent for a few minutes. Given her wealth of experience in the social arena, Delia was sure that her guidance would shed some useful light on this situation. As far as she was concerned, she was a long way from the Merari dome, and though the lessons and the ball went a long way to improving her social graces, she was still out of her league when it came to dealing with this particular mage.

"It appears, my dear, that you have been singled out to potentially become the next Mage-Consort. A pattern which began with your grandmother may come full-circle with you. So it is now for you to decide whether to complete this circle or let your journey follow a different path."

On the strength of one walk and an invitation, Tabitha was ready to marry her off to this mage. Even that seemed like a stretch. Delia had seen for herself that Tabitha's house was one that overflowed with love, and both her daughters had married for such. Yet, Tabitha was a seasoned maharani, and Delia knew that she was someone to trust. However marriage, and on top of that to one who may potentially be the next Mage-King; even she was unconvinced. He barely even knew her, much less enough to marry her.

Tabitha had sensed her doubt and took pity on her. As she explained it to Delia, to her knowledge, this particular mage had not been in the habit of asking any other suitable female mages out to such excursions for a few years. Also, given Delia's pedigree and acceptance into their society, it was unlikely that he was offering a mere dalliance. Not to mention the fact that she had it on good authority that he was in fact to be the next Mage-King. So it was highly likely that he had already investigated her and received positive reviews.

He had already met her two grand-daughters and had never paid them the slightest interest beyond the perfunctory politeness. Yet, he was interested enough to discover that Delia was staying with her and issue such an invitation, knowing quite well that Delia was under her protection and that Tabitha had enough clout to make his soon to be newfound position disappear if he did anything untoward with regard to Delia. The fact that he did not wait until Delia was back home, and had sent the invitation there, was tantamount in their social circle to a declaration that he was courting her.

Tabitha then explained to Delia why she was probably seen by him as a suitable candidate. She was lovely, intelligent, and had an innate grace that drew people to her. The fact that her pedigree on her maternal side was top-notch weighed substantially in her favour. The last Mage-Consort had been well liked and respected, and Delia had the same air that her maternal grandmother had. She just needed time to mature fully. She had noteworthy connections, and quite a few would see it as an auspicious sign that the grand-daughter of the last Mage-Consort would step into that role once more. Last, but by no means least, her magical abilities would serve to complement his thereby suggesting that any future offspring they produced would be quite powerful.

By the time Tabitha had finished her explanation, Delia looked at her with newfound respect. She could see why Tabitha was chosen as maharani for quite a few years. Her assessment and analysis, given the information she had, was carefully formulated. It was not a romantic notion, but a candid appraisal. She had seen Tabitha in many different environments, but never once guessed at this level of depth to her. Delia was now profoundly grateful that she had confided in Tabitha. At least Delia would no longer be floundering in the situation like a proverbial lamb.

Kissing her lightly on both cheeks, Tabitha looked her in the eyes and told her that whatever her decision, she had her support. Then she quietly exited the room to a much quieter atmosphere than when she had first entered it. Delia had pondered over Tabitha's words a while before finally making her decision. She saw no harm in getting to know him better. A courtship did not automatically lead to marriage, and besides it was always good business to be on good terms with a future Mage-King.

After making her decision, she hastily scrawled a reply to his invitation, called Jenkins in, and requested that he deliver her note. Next, she found Tessa and Shannon and informed them that they had been invited to go to the museum. Tessa had been thrilled even though she had been to that particular museum so often that even she couldn't remember how many times she had visited it. As it turned out, there was a new exhibit by one of her favourite artists being displayed. So she positively glowed with excitement. Shannon, on the other hand, merely rolled her eyes at her sister and consented. She archly informed them that she would accompany them merely because she wanted to see what this mage had up his sleeve with regard to Delia. Since Delia was new to their circle, Shannon didn't want anyone toying with her, and was going to make very sure that his intentions were honorable.

The day of the museum trip dawned in a kaleidoscope of colors, and the household was teeming with excitement. He had called upon them promptly at the specified hour with two other gentlemen of his acquaintance to escort them to the museum. Everyone was paired off by the time they arrived at the museum. He was entertaining and funny, and kept her amused as he showed her the various exhibits. She found him charming, witty and very attentive. They got along quite well, and she made him laugh with her particular brand of insightful comments. Many mages there would stop to speak to him, and he would courteously make introductions before charmingly begging leave to continue his tour. Though she told him it was all right, he merely smiled at her and told her that he prized her company more.

She loved how his eyes crinkled at the corner when he laughed, and he had a way of looking at her that made her heart beat a little faster. By the time he had finished the tour he had insisted that she call him by his given name Alejandro. She had prevaricated. As they rejoined the other pairs at the end of the tour, he asked her if she and her friends would care to attend a play the next day that was being staged in the palace gardens. Shannon and Tessa had consented before she could get a word in. Apparently they had enjoyed the company of Alejandro's two friends. So she had merely smiled and resolved to have a discussion with the two of them when they got home.

The next day proved to be quite enjoyable, and like the pied piper he was, he managed to invite her and the others out for that entire week. By the end of the week, she had experienced many of Varga's entertainments. Alejandro had proved to be a good companion, and by the end of that week, she felt as if she knew him. Tabitha had merely smiled and observed. Unbeknown to her, Tabitha had paid a visit to Alejandro's residence and very politely and in no uncertain terms made very sure that Alejandro was quite aware that if he did anything untoward to her charge, she would personally see to it that he suffer the consequences. Delia had remained blissfully unaware of this exchange between the two, and had been quite happy to spend time getting to know him. By the end of the week she was hooked. She was in love for the first time, and there was a faint glow in her that made her look lovely.

Alejandro was finding to his discomfort that Delia had actually managed to affect him. It was true that he had started off courting her in a purely clinical manner because he found that she possessed sufficient attributes to make a good Mage-Consort. However, as he got to know her better, he found to his amazement that he genuinely liked her. She was like a breath of fresh air in his world of gilded politics. She was an innocent, but her intelligence was keen. She was lovely and her beauty seemed more exquisite each time he saw her. He was surprised to find himself eagerly anticipate their time together.

Strange as it may sound, he thought that he was probably falling in love. He had found that fact disturbing because he had not factored love into his plan. Before he had thought that falling in love with her would be detrimental, because it meant that she could wield a certain level of influence upon him. Yet, the more time he spent with her, the less he thought of it as a bad thing. Somehow in the rather short space of time she had managed to get under his skin. He actually wanted her as his marriage partner. He knew, however, that he had to make his move quickly if he was to succeed in marrying her. Her cousin and Ravi were due back in a week's time, and he doubted that they would look on his courtship of Delia favourably, given Thom's injury after the duel at the tournament.

So, after that first week of accompanying her to various places of interest, he had stepped up his campaign and proposed. She had been quite taken aback, but delighted. He had spoken to Tabitha and her husband, and had requested their permission as her temporary guardians for the marriage to occur. Tabitha had told him that though he had her approval, she could not give such consent, and would prefer that Delia's immediate family provide their consent. So dispatches were sent to Delia's father, Thom, Talia and Ravi (because Delia considered him to be a part of her family) with regard to Delia's engagement. By the end of the week, Thom and her father were in the Varga dome, while Ravi came back as soon as the exchange program was done.

*

PART TWO

<u>Two Weeks Later</u>

<u>Varga Dome: The Court Gardens</u>

Alejandro felt nervous. As he stood at the top of the pathway in front of those who had gathered for his wedding, he wondered if it was too late to elope. The palace gardens had been picked by his betrothed as the venue for the wedding ceremony and reception. He would have preferred it to be indoors, but Delia had been adamant. He was discovering more and more that Delia had a strong will beneath her adorably tranquil demeanour. Truth be told, he had been so happy that she had agreed to his proposal that he had been willing to indulge her in anything.

Hence the reason he stood alone facing the gathering, while his courier was sent forth to Delia's room to see whether she agreed to the marriage contract that had been negotiated. To be honest, he felt a little anxious. Although the terms had seemed reasonable to both of them, Talia was with her, and she had been none too pleased that her sister had consented to marry him. Flashbacks of her face as she blasted him in the tournament slipped unbidden through his mind's eye. If anyone could change Delia's mind, it would be her. Talia had made no pretense about the fact that she thought he was not right for her sister. Now he was left to idly wonder whether any bridegrooms had ever had their marriage contract rejected or re-negotiated at the actual wedding.

As he stood there waiting, he recalled the events that had led to this moment. Two days after his proposal, (Delia having told him this afterwards) there were still mixed reactions to his proposal from her family. Thom had been against the match, her father had thought it to be a good alliance, and Ravi was neutral. Heated arguments had taken place until Talia had arrived (at Thom's request). It seemed that Thom thought that he required some assistance, and had urgently cabled Talia requesting her presence.

His bride-to-be had been happy to see her sister, and had taken her around the dome. Delia had told him afterwards that Talia had listened, then told her that she couldn't help her decide. The decision was hers to make. She had admitted that she was predisposed to disliking Alejandro for what he had done to Thom. But she wouldn't stand in the way of her happiness. However, Talia had made her promise that she would come to her if anything went wrong.

Up until that point Alejandro had been willing to let bygones be bygones with respect to Talia. However, her last statement had prickled. How could she possibly think that he would do anything to harm his bride-to-be? Then he rationalized that Talia could not know the depth of his feelings that seemed to overwhelm his heart when it came to Delia. Somehow Delia had managed to secure a place firmly within his heart in a relatively short period of time.

Yet, Delia had been torn because for the first time in her life she did not have her sister's full support. This was her twin, her other half, the one she had always relied on, and Talia did not like her choice of a marriage partner. Delia had shared with him afterwards how lost and bewildered she had felt. She couldn't understand Talia's lack of support with respect to her choice. So she had gone into psychological warfare mode in an effort to convince them that Alejandro was indeed the right choice for her.

The culmination of her efforts had been a small intimate family supper she had planned so that they could get to know him better. Alejandro had to grimace at that particular memory, as he shifted uncomfortably while still awaiting the courier in order to know whether his wedding would proceed as planned. Delia had invited Tabitha and her husband as well, but they had been unable to attend due to a previous engagement. Privately, he had thought that Tabitha with her vast social experience knew what a disastrous evening it would turn out to be, and wanted to detach herself from any potential fallout.

His arrival had signaled the start of his verbal warfare with Talia. He had tried to be nice, but Talia had been deliberately impolite and blunt. Thom had served as Talia's right-hand man during the ensuing proceedings. Delia's father had tried to deflect them as best he could with good-natured quips and efforts to engage Alejandro in conversation as much as he possibly could without monopolizing him. Ravi had quietly observed, and his eyes danced in amusement at the verbal jabs that flew back and forth over supper. At one point, the night's proceeding threatened to degenerate into a replay of the duel at the tournament, but Delia had managed to diffuse the situation. He had left early and in a bad mood. Although Delia had refused to share what happened afterwards, he could only surmise that Talia had been unrepentant and probably made some particularly unflattering remarks about him. All Delia told him was that she had gone to bed soon after with a crushing headache.

He clearly remembered the morning after that dinner. He had awaken with one thought, and that was to make his intentions plain. He had turned up on Delia's doorstep early and found Talia, Thom, Dutra and Ravi already at the breakfast table. The butler had informed him at the door that his betrothed was still abed. He had not waited for his presence to be announced, but rather had stalked into the breakfast parlour and gave them all a piece of his mind. He had informed them that with or without their blessings he was going to marry Delia. He would have preferred it to be with their blessings, as it would please Delia but he had no intention of letting them run his life. He loved her, wanted to marry her, and if they could not accept it, then that was just too bad. The marriage contract had been prepared and would arrive shortly for their review. Furthermore, the wedding would be held in a week, and they were welcome to attend. With that he had spun around and marched out of the room.

He had been surprised to find Delia at the front door waiting for him. She was dressed in outdoor clothing, and her hair was slightly damp, as if she had been caught in a shower of rain. She had just smiled, then tip–toed and kissed him. He had been stunned, as it was the first time she had ever kissed him. It had made him ridiculously happy, and he had wanted another; but she had laughed and shooed him out the door. Her eyes had twinkled as she closed the door, but before she closed it fully she had told him that she had a lot of work to do if she was to pull this wedding off within a week. With that he had smiled, and had felt like dancing all the way to his own home.

True to her word, his betrothed had managed to arrange everything within the time limit. Somehow she had managed to get her family onboard (she never revealed how) and within the allotted time had performed a minor miracle. So as the courier finally made his way back to him with Delia's reply, he felt a sense of relief at her affirmation.

A few minutes later, the bridesmaids, Shannon and Tessa, made their way sedately down the aisle. His betrothed appeared soon afterwards slowly gliding down the aisle littered with petals. Talia walked behind her holding her train and managing to look composed. Yet his eyes were all for his Delia. She looked quite breath-taking in her red robes accented with gold, making his heart beat just a little bit faster the closer she came. His wife-to-be really was exquisite and he felt fortunate. As she joined him at the top of the aisle, he couldn't help but grin at the fact that she would soon be his for life.

The melodic voice of the head of the Kao drew his attention away from her as she begun the ceremony with a prayer to Mother Gaia. In her sermon she stressed the importance of treasuring each other during the marriage, learning to take the time to understand

and appreciate the other, and finally the value of compromise. Her sermon was thought-provoking, and certain parts of it nestled deep within him. She then led them to the exchanging of their rings and finally the sharing of a wedding drink between Delia and himself. He and Delia then endorsed their signatures on the wedding certificate, and with that they were officially married.

Before he had a chance to do more than squeeze her hand, her father, who had fairly beamed with pride throughout the entire ceremony engulfed them in an embrace. This was a signal to all to offer their congratulations. The reception that followed was lively, as Thom made the first toast. He noted that Tabitha's granddaughter, Ann-Marie, had chosen to stay by Thom's side throughout the reception. He had overheard Ravi and Laurence debating some obscure topic during the reception. Talia had been civil to him and happy with respect to her sister's joy. However, the most important person in the proceedings was quietly happy. He had caught a satisfied expression in her eyes that signaled her pleasure. As for him, well he had publicly held his wife's hand throughout the entire reception and had felt a sense of lightness within his entire being. They were now together, and he was looking forward to spending the rest of his life with her.

* * *

Chapter Six

'THE KAO ORDER'

<u>'Study Notes on the History of the Mage Civilization'</u>

PART ONE- First Millennia

Key Background Highlights
1. Creation of world by Mother Gaia and the subsequent creation of the Demigods
2. Creation of the Mage Race by the Demigods
3. Epic Battle between Mother Gaia and the Demigods
4. Aftermath: The Emergence and Prospering of the Mage Race.

PART TWO- Third & Fourth Millennia
1. Appearance of the 'espec'
2. Discontentment
3. Pursuit of an ultimate power source
4. Birth of the Kao Order
5. Secret Plan
6. Dark Prophecy
7. Massacre at the Feast of Duns
8. Creation of Present-Day Dome Cities
9. Emergence of Kao as part of Mage Council

PART THREE - Present
1. The Present Day Kao Order
2. Function and Duties of a Kao Member
3. Motto

<u>The Holy Citadel of Rhys - A Year Later</u>

Looking through her study notes, Talia thought that they appeared adequate. She had managed to cover all the salient points as she compared her guideline with the information she had garnered from the manuscript she had recently discovered. In her eyes, the manuscript had been a priceless treasure, as it outlined the history of their civilization and the Kao Order in a manner that kept her attention riveted. The manuscript had read like someone's journal; and for someone who had upcoming examinations, it was a blessing.

After Delia's wedding, she had returned from Varga and tossed herself wholeheartedly into everything dealing with the Kao Order. When she had first come to seek Sunni, she had been informed that Alyssa had also been a member of the Kao before the falling out with their father. Alyssa had opted to leave the order at the same time. Sunni and Alyssa had kept in touch through the amulet and the ring. These heirlooms had been handed down along many generations. Sunni believed them to be relics of the Demigods that had probably been bestowed unto their forefathers as gifts. Like Talia and Delia, Sunni and their mother had received these heirlooms upon turning twenty-one, with the same condition of passing it along to the first pair of twins that came along.

She and Alyssa had kept in touch over the years, and she had continued to check on them after her sister's passing. She would often look in when they were fast asleep or busy with some activity. Their father had probably caught glimpses of her when she popped in and out. Sometimes he would have conversations with her, believing her to be Alyssa's ghost. She never had the heart to explain to him, so she had merely listened. Yet, sometimes, she could swear that she too heard Alyssa speaking to her. Nonetheless, on her last visit there she had left her heirloom in the rose in accordance with Alyssa's last instruction to her. She had hoped that at least one of Alyssa's girls would seek her out, and had been glad when Talia had come looking for her.

Talia had been delighted to hear this story from her aunt. Sunni had kindly undertaken to mentor her with respect to the full scope of duties of a Kao member. Under Sunni's tutelage, she had learned all that she could, until she could almost taste what it meant to be a full-fledged member of the Kao. She had been even more pleased when Sunni had undertaken to train her personally. Then one day, a few months ago the head of the Kao had requested a meeting with her.

Half an hour spent with Mother Mizpah had left an indelible memory in Talia's consciousness. She looked like someone's elderly grandmother instead of the head of the most influential order of their world. However, as Talia soon realized, Mother Mizpah's benign appearance concealed a sharp mind and even sharper tongue. During their private tête–a-tête, Talia had felt the undercurrents of being subtly weighed and measured. Though she didn't have Delia's gift of empathy, she had lived with her twin long enough to recognize certain undercurrents. She had left that interview drained and uncertain as to the final outcome. Yet she had bolstered her resolve, and sternly told herself to finish what she had started.

Afterwards, Sunni had mentioned to her that she had made a formal application for Talia to be allowed full entry into the ranks of the Kao. She had noted her determination and believed that Talia would eventually become a valuable member of the Kao. So she had made her recommendation. Mother Mizpah had approved the application on the condition that Talia sit and pass the examinations that all Initiates were required to take.

Talia had been so pleased that she had been fast-tracked that she had applied herself even more diligently. Typically, one became a novice, then graduated to Initiate and then sat the examinations, and if successful became a Kao member. It was a process that normally took five years. If she was successful, she would accomplish it in two years. But she had to focus on mage history that was one of her weak areas. For the life of her, she could not see the reason why she had to study all this boring information about persons who had passed away so long ago. All the material she had read before had bored her to tears. Then one day, Mother Gaia had taken pity on her.

While delving through the ancient historical records in the Citadel's main library, she had made a wonderful discovery. Nestled behind two bulky and intimidating manuscripts she had found a slim but rather old and dusty account of the Kao's history and by extension their civilization penned by none other than her ancestor from whom the entire 'Tierney' line had descended. Sunni had laughing informed her that perhaps the reason so many in their lineage felt compelled to join the Kao was due to the fact that their great grandmother many times removed had been one of the original founders of the Kao. Thus, it seemed to be in their blood. Armed with this newfound knowledge, Talia had read the manuscript with a certain degree of reverence. It had read like a narrative which commenced with the period right after the epic battle between the ultimate maker of their world, Mother Gaia, and her errant children: the Demigods who created the mage race.

Her many times great-grandmother (whom she privately called 'Lila') had penned the rich history of their civilization, which had been forgotten with the passage of time, in a manner that held her interest. According to her, after the epic battle between the Gods, the mage population had flourished and grown into a great civilization known as Estrel. It had been a prosperous one, and the mages who made it prosper were said to have contained the best attributes of their Demigod creators. Though their power levels and abilities could never be said to rival those of their progenitors, they had still treated their natural world with the utmost care. The first mages to walk the world after that fateful battle had worked as a cohesive unit, and chose to share their magical abilities for the benefit of all.

To Talia, it had sounded like a utopia. As she read, she had found out that the reason why her ancestors had begun worshipping Mother Gaia was to express their gratitude. They had felt that it was only right that they should adore their ultimate maker for saving them from the cruelty of the Demigods. In their eyes, Mother Gaia had become the Ultimate God whose invisible hand guided all aspects of their world. Unlike their creators, her ancestors never even conceptualized being greater than this deity. Talia had snorted at how the passage of time seemed to have dimmed the memory of their civilization. Lila had spoken of the fear that the original mages had held with respect to the Demigods. Talia could almost feel Lila's remembrance in the words that were penned, almost as if she had been there instead of being born a few centuries later. It seemed ironic that in this modern era, the Demigods had been relegated to positions of legend and folklore. In fact, the Demigods' position as the original creators of the mage race had been mostly glossed over by the majority of their population, with the exception of those belonging to the Kao.

As Talia read on, she had discovered the existence of a race which had spontaneously appeared a few centuries later. It seemed that a few mages had children who had been born with no magical talent. At first these families considered these children to be abnormalities. They were considered to be 'special' and hence named 'the espec'. These children had been delegated menial tasks that did not require magic to occupy their time. As Lila described, and Talia understood it in the same vein that it had been written, it seemed as if the mages did not know what else to do with these members who could not contribute magical abilities to a society built on the sharing of magic for its growth and prosperity.

Within two centuries, it was noted that the 'espec' had managed to out-number those mages with magical abilities. From Lila's description, the espec were physically stronger, very fertile, innately cunning and increasingly discontented with the role that society had assigned them. Their discontentment had eventually grown into resentment towards the supercilious attitude displayed by those with magical abilities. Lila had found evidence amongst the journal entries of her parents' generation that the mages had looked down on them as inferior and had exhibited an almost overbearing attitude. It seemed that most had viewed the espec as servants, and disregarded the espec desire for self- determination and equality.

It was at this point that the tone of the narrative had changed, and Talia had been drawn into a decidedly more personal account of the ensuing events. It seemed that like the others who shared her particular gift of empathy, Lila had sensed escalating levels of animosity emanating from the espec. It had appeared to treble within months, and she had sought to warn others. Unfortunately, her warnings had fallen on deaf ears. Most of the other mages had scoffed at those like her with these types of magical abilities. Such abilities were considered soft and unreliable, unlike the more tangible magical abilities favoured by society for their consistency. Every time Talia read this passage she shook her head, as she thought how times had not changed. Delia and Lila would have gotten along famously and probably compared notes, had they known each other.

Talia's heart had gone out to Lila(for she imagined how Delia would have felt if she had been born then) as she heard the note of frustration that poured through the pages. It seemed that Lila had encountered others like herself in this quest to alert the general mage populace, and their stories had all been eerily similar. They had all been ignored as the rest of the population continued their pursuit to discover an ultimate power source to fuel their society. This pursuit had turned into an obsession amongst the mage populace, since the greatly reduced magical population had been straining their resources.

Ironically, the rejection of their warning had served to unite those mages with intangible and more mystical powers. They had met to discuss the situation, and a team had been born. They had refused to be deterred by the general attitude of the population, having recognized the potential danger. Their team would eventually be known as the Kao and its mandate was simple. Those belonging to the Kao had promised to protect and serve when the need arose. Although she had been elected as their leader, she had felt that another had been more worthy of the position. He was from an old but forgotten bloodline whereby one member in each generation had a rare gift of intuition that seemed almost otherworldly at times. However, for reasons unbeknown to her, he had declined to run against her.

At this point, Talia had smirked as she begun to suspect from Lila's tone and her own feminine intuition that a romance had been budding between that particular mage and her many times great-grandmother. Perhaps it was a certain softness in the manner in which she had written to describe him. It seemed that the two had worked closely in the Kao's initial plan of action to create hidden magical defenses that would automatically be activated in the inevitable uprising by the espec. They had worked in secret, and the majority of its members had been involved in some form or fashion. They had also enlisted the assistance of a select few outsiders with the expertise to fashion such a grandiose spell.

In order to buy some time to complete their work, the Kao had sought to allay the espec's animosity by interspersing a spell of calmness into the stream of magic that permeated their society. Lila described a society in which the entire society had been located in one area. All major cities had been located within a few kilometers of each other. The domes had not been created at this point in time. So this particular spell to calm the espec could affect the entire population within minutes, but could not be maintained indefinitely, as it drained too much power from the few empaths within their order. It was also suspected that the espec would eventually break free of such a spell.

The spell for the magical defenses had been rather complex, and to ensure that it was sufficiently powerful, some of the essence of relics rumoured to have been created by the Demigods were distilled and woven in to bind them. In fact, obtaining only the most powerful of ancient relics collected from all over the world and kept in the Holy Citadel of Rhys by necessity required such secrecy. These items actually had to be 'borrowed' from the Holy Citadel by one of their Members who ironically had one of the highest clearances in the Mage Council.

Like today, the Holy Citadel had been considered out of bounds for most of the mage population even in Lila's time. No espec had been allowed to go there because of the unpredictable nature of the ancient magic that resided there. The Citadel was rather selective as to who could enter its premises. It was a well-known fact that only a very small number of mages could actually enter the Holy Citadel confines without being transported elsewhere in the world.

So when the Kao operative had been informed by two of their experts utilized to create the spell that relics created by the Demigods needed to be retrieved from the Citadel, he had been extremely hesitant. Talia had commiserated with him as she read this part, for she had seen the Citadel in action when it was displeased. The Citadel was entirely its own entity, and brooked no threat to its good-self. Talia was not even surprised to discover that the operative in question was the one whom Lila felt should have been their leader. Her admiration for his courage had shone through her words and Talia had felt a keen sense of kinship with her.

Of course, her admiration did not prevent Lila from imparting a humorous description of the events that had Talia doubled in laughter. She had described how the operative who had removed the items had given into a foolish inclination and sought permission from the Holy Citadel first before removing the items. As he had told Lila afterwards, he had felt silly taking the time to explain aloud the situation to the Citadel and then seeking its permission. In normal circumstances, such an occurrence would be outlandish, yet within the confines of the Citadel it had felt like the right thing to do.

Soon after the relics had been obtained, the spells were completed. Thereafter, the relics had been promptly returned by the same operative in keeping with his promise to the Citadel. The spell had been created to work within the precincts of all the cities' walls, thereby leaving out the pockets of space between the cities. The Kao had decided that it would waste power to include these areas, since most mages tended to remain within the confines of the cities. They calculated that it was an acceptable risk before fashioning the spell to suit. So the Kao had turned to maintaining and sustaining a membership that would allow them to transmit the codes for these defenses throughout the generations to come.

Nevertheless, Lila had expressed her satisfaction that the Kao had managed to maintain total secrecy surrounding these defenses. The spell had been implemented throughout before the spell of calmness was removed from the magical network. It seemed that once the spell abated, the especs' aggression had trebled almost overnight. It was as if the espec had been awakened from a daze, and all the pent-up rage had been released. Fortunately, this anger had found an outlet in the worship of a new deity. A few enterprising individuals within the especs had founded a new religion that worshipped a deity in complete contrast to Mother Gaia. To the especs, this deity had miraculous powers, and they connected to it on a deeper level, more so than with the mages' worship of Mother Gaia.

These worshippers became rather fanatical, and sought to convert all espec to their beliefs. Lila and her group later discovered that those espec who had not agreed were disposed of through accidents. In the alternative, certain natural disasters that were to occur in later years were attributed to this deity becoming angry and destroying them for their unbelief. Within a short period of time, most of the espec worshipped this deity, and those who did not believe kept that disbelief to themselves for fear that they and their families would be disposed of. As Lila bitterly wrote, their followers had been careful never to interfere with any mages as they found them to be too powerful to be taken out without magic. They knew that if any of their followers were caught trying to destroy any mage, regardless of how cruel they were, the entire espec population would be jeopardized. So they had bided their time and waited patiently until the time to act was upon them.

In the meantime, the rest of the mage population kept pursuing their various spells and became less and less interested in following the ways of Mother Gaia. The only mages who still retained an abiding respect for Mother Gaia and its ways were the members of the Kao and other high-ranking officials in the Mage Council. The rest of the mages merely paid lip service, but few outside the inner sanctum of the Kao actually believed. The mage population had pursued their own individual quest for self-fulfillment through magic since the power levels necessary to maintain society seemed to them to be generated from an unknown source. Thus, it was no longer required of the mages to share their powers to maintain society.

Unfortunately, according to those who had recorded it on the ancient scrolls, this individualistic way of life was the pivotal instrument that would eventually lead to the downfall of the mages. It had been nearly twenty years later, on the fateful night of the auspicious but rare occasion of the Feast of Dus, that the worst fears of the Kao had been realized. The event was one whereby most full-fledged mages ventured outside all the major cities' walls to see the extraordinary birth of a star. As dictated by tradition, on this occasion the magelets and some adult mages had remained within the city walls, while the rest of the adult mage population journeyed outside the confines of their respective cities to designated areas throughout the world to witness this rare event. It was a pilgrimage that occurred once every thousand years at the birth of a star in remembrance of the creation of the mage race. It was therefore an honour to witness. Thus, only those who were fit and of age could participate if they so chose.

Most adult mages who had met the requirements were excited and behaved like magelets themselves. All the records and tales of ancestors who had made the last pilgrimage described the event as an unforgettable experience. For the first time in nearly a thousand years, all the cities had been virtually empty of adults. The designated areas had been within sight of the cities' walls, but just far enough to allow the respective cities' occupants to gather together, without being cramped and with a remarkably clear view for the event.

On that night excitement had been running high amongst all. They had joked and laughed, throwing playful spells at each other. It had been night by the time they had made their way through the gates and filed into their allotted places. The skies had changed all over their world from midnight black to amber with twinkling swirls of light. These swirls had no set patterns and looked like mini vortexes of colour and light. They moved in a diffused manner, filling the amber strip with unique patterns. As the patterns began to unfurl, the star was born; and for mages everywhere in the world whose tangible powers were linked to any element within the world, their powers became inactive as the power that began to flow from the birth of this star negated the other elements of their world. For the first time in their lives the majority of mages were left powerless, as their natural ability was subsumed within the flow of power from the star.

It was in that perfect moment in which the mages had been at their most vulnerable that the espec had launched their attack. Somehow, the espec had discovered that the birth of the star would nullify the mages' powers. They had assumed that the effect was one that would affect all the mages. Thereby, for the first time in the existence of the espec, they had an advantage over the mages, and they had exploited it with ruthless efficiency.

So, while everyone had been so enthralled with the incoming power, the espec had struck. The mages had for some reason failed to realize that a huge contingency of espec had been hiding and waiting for that particular moment when the typically powerful mages were left without their accustomed magic. The espec had been lethal and without mercy as they fell upon the mages with deadly weapons they had forged in secret. The attack had been so well coordinated that quite a number of mages had been killed before they could react. When they had attempted to defend themselves using their magic, they were cut down in the midst of their realization that their powers didn't work. So they had sought to flee back to the cities, only to find themselves blocked by the espec. Most of the survivors had then turned in the opposite direction. However, there were still those who chose to fight their way through the ranks of the espec. Amongst them had been the mages whose powers had not been rendered inactive by the star's birth.

It was with great irony that the members of the Kao had chosen this evening to host their own secret meeting within each major city wall, and had magically conferenced in the other Kao members from various cities throughout Estrel. The few empaths amongst them had been feeling increasingly uneasy and one had accidentally and unknowingly at the time come into contact with one of the leaders of the espec's faith. Her level of empathy had received a spike of anticipation with undertones of gleefulness intermixed with such a darkness that it had rendered her unconscious for a few minutes. It seemed that the unexpectedness of the meeting while she was recovering from an illness had left her natural defenses severely depleted.

Another one had a very dark prophetic dream that had accorded with a dark prophecy found in the sacred Book of Ahn. The origin of this sacred book was unknown, but it had been discovered in the Holy Citadel of Rhys after the legendary battle of the Demigods. Since only a handful of mages in Estrel could still translate it, and of that handful only one was trusted by the Kao, the process of comparing the prophecies had taken some time. In the end, by the time their meeting was called it was already too late to prevent the tragedy.

Nonetheless, all had not been lost, and they made their way to their respective city gates in an attempt to leave the cities' safety to assist their brethren. It seemed that those who had the intangible gifts that the mage community had once scoffed at were the only ones unaffected, since their magic did not depend on any natural element, but rather drew its essence from the mages themselves. However, as they quickly discovered, they were unable to leave the cities, as the hidden defenses put in place so long ago were activated when the espec within had attempted to launch a coordinated attack against those mages left within the cities.

It seemed that the mastermind behind this plot had allotted fewer espec to deal with those mages within the walls, since they were comprised mostly of the young and elderly. As designed, the magical defenses did serve their initial purpose well, since those espec who had attempted to attack the mage inhabitants within the confines of the wall, soon found themselves being transported to the regions of wildness in Estrel. Those espec who had witnessed their comrades disappear before their eyes huddled together and prostrated themselves in fear that they too would disappear into thin air.

So those Kao members who had intangible magics had made their respective ways to the best vantage points within the cities where their gifts would theoretically be able to transmit beyond their respective city's walls. It was a gamble, because they all knew that there were many unpredictable factors this night that would render their efforts to assist those caught outside virtually useless. Not only were they contending with the star's power interference, but the power activated from the hidden defenses could nullify their efforts as well.

Yet they had still tried, hoping and praying earnestly to Mother Gaia that they be able to do something that would help save their surviving families and friends left outside the walls. Their counterattack had consisted of attempts to jam the espec senses by creating hallucinations that would cause them fear and by heightening those fear levels through concentrated waves from the empaths. At first nothing had happened, and these mages had been left thinking that their powers had indeed been rendered inoperable. Then, one by one, the espec closest to the walls had begun to shriek in terror. Like a domino effect, the confusion spread outward from the ranks closest to the cities' walls until it made its way to those blocking the path to the cities. It seemed that though the hallucinations could only be projected up to a particular distance, those not able to see these hallucinations were still affected by the waves of fear being transmitted by the empaths. They had been further befuddled, as those closest to the walls of the cities had begun to attack the rest of the espec with their weapons.

Thus, at this point the espec had been faced with having to stave off attacks from within their own ranks, as frenzied espec attacked each other believing they were defending themselves from monsters. These attacks were joined by attacks from those few mages whose powers had not been nullified. It seemed that for once the mages' lack of respect for the intangible powers had caused the espec to underestimate them as well. Eventually the immediate area around the walls of each city and its gates were cleared of espec, who were now either fleeing in terror or fighting with espec they considered 'possessed.' Unfortunately, quite a few mages caught outside had been so preoccupied fleeing for their lives in the direction opposite to the cities that they had failed to notice that the way back to the cities had been cleared.

So as the mages with similar intangible powers neared the cities' walls, the mages of the Kao were able to communicate with them and urged them to let the others know that the way was now clear. They had also warned them that once within the city's confines they could not help the others, and emphasized that they were needed to guide the other mages home. It is to the credit of these mages that every single one of them complied with this request. Given their proximity to the other mages within the walls, they had been used as focal points to channel all the power that was available to the mages within, to amplify the hallucinations and waves of fear. This tactic had preoccupied the espec from harming the surviving mages, while other messages had been subliminally communicated to the fleeing mages to stop and come home. Those messages had been transmitted with a touch of hope and a sense of calm that would override the mages' fears.

Little by little it had worked, as the mages had stopped fleeing. Gradually, they had become aware that the espec were no longer blocking their way home. In fact, the espec had been preoccupied defending themselves from each other and some unseen entities. Thus encouraged, the survivors had made their way back home, assisting others who had fallen and were coherent enough to cry for help, but were unable to move without assistance. As Lila had stated woefully, it would never be known whether there had been survivors rendered unconscious who may have fallen amongst the bodies of the dead, as the mages had not been able to stop and search.

As the last of the survivors entered their respective city gates, those mages who acted as focal points made their way in as well. As they entered, the gates had magically sealed themselves. A flash of light from the star, having achieved its peak, blanketed the entire area; and when the light cleared the inhabitants of each of these cities looked over their walls in amazement. Gone were the bloody scenes of violence and the menacing espec. Instead they had been surrounded by an amber sky and appeared to be in countryside or beach areas. As communications via the empaths poured in from other cities, it seemed as if all the cities had been encased in domes and transported to varied locations around the world. Thus, this was how the mage civilization had first come to exist in domes.

After that blinding flash of light, the inactive powers became active once more. In fact, the mages' powers had been amplified. As some investigated using their magical abilities to explore their surroundings, they had discovered that though the cities were now located in beautiful regions, these regions were surrounded by mainly insurmountable landscapes. Thus the inhabitants could only live within the city confines or the definable open spaces, but it was impossible to leave or enter these regions by natural means. The mages themselves couldn't transport into other cities until they had specific locations. So each city had essentially been cut off from the other.

Another discovery had been made in the interim. The remnants of the espec had been transported elsewhere. Whether to the wilderness to join the perpetrators of the massacre or elsewhere, the mages neither knew nor cared. To be truthful, if any espec had been found within city walls at that point in time the mages might have destroyed them. Yet, as they soon discovered once the shock of the massacre had worn off, the daily necessities that the espec had performed for them had to be taken care of, and no one had a clue what to do. So they got on with the business of dealing with the menial but important tasks that the espec had performed. Grief and sorrow continued to permeate the very air of the cities as all the mages grieved for their lost ones. It was a disaster that had touched every mage family in the world.

The Mage Council held many emergency sessions following the immediate aftermath of the attack. It had been faced with a multitude of issues, amongst which was the immediate functioning and the establishment of communication between the respective cities. All the cities had been operating with a significantly smaller mage population. Once communications had been restored, they had investigated the hidden defenses that had been activated upon the attack. The Council had been in agreement that extending the ambit of the defenses of the domes that encapsulated each city to include the open areas was necessary. No one wanted a repeat of this tragedy.

It had been during one of these sessions that one of the council members had finally imparted the necessary information concerning the spells used for the defenses. He had also revealed the existence of the secret order to the other members, because he believed that it was time for the Kao Order to participate directly. The Kao had proven their worth, and he believed, should be involved in Council meetings without having to rely on subterfuge and other methods. One of the main reasons for his revelation lay in the fact that there had been no feasible alternative by which the dark prophecy translated from the sacred Book of Ahn could have been brought to their attention earlier.

Few prophecies were ever straightforward and most needed interpretation. Those with the gifts to interpret them were often times not the ones who had them. Thus, depending on the skill level of the interpreter certain elements, if not correctly interpreted, could distort the actual message. Not to mention the fact that there was no way for a prophecy to be pigeon-holed into an exact time-frame. Extremely gifted translators could predict an occurrence within a narrower time- frame, but that time-frame could still vary up to a period of a year or two. The unpredictable and problematic nature of this gift made most mages give it as wide a berth as possible. The mages on the Council were no exception to that rule.

However, there still remained an aspect within the translation of the prophecy revealed to the Kao that had alluded to a greater disaster that might destroy their entire world. It had been felt that the revelation would motivate the Council to support them by providing more mages suitably gifted in translation to help them make as accurate an interpretation as possible. As it stood, the Kao had been severely hampered by the secrecy that had shrouded their Order. The prophecy had alluded to a very dark period in their civilization that would come from within and be initiated by the events that had just occurred. Since the beginning of the Kao they had abided by one golden rule that of protecting the mage civilization.

So given that the event was fresh in the memories of all, the Kao had been willing to forgo their secrecy in order to prevent another such disaster which could be the doom of their world. The Kao had known the risk they would take by revealing their existence and that of the prophecy. Few mages held much credence in mystical abilities, and if the general population found out that their leaders had been guiding them according to some prophecy, there would be an outcry.

But this Kao member had felt that it was time for the Order to stop operating in the shadows and to start working hand-in- hand with the Council to advert any potential disaster. They had tried to live by their motto, but given the large number of casualties that had been incurred during the massacre; they had realized that they needed more persons involved in their efforts. He had approached Lila, and she had concurred with his decision. She had lost three siblings in the massacre and her conscience had continually bothered her concerning the decision not to include the open spaces in the making of the spell.

In Lila's mind, the revelation of their Order and perhaps alliance with the Council would hopefully enable them to better protect their brethren. So it had been with this in mind that he had revealed their existence. To further strengthen the Kao's credibility, he had promised them access to the entire defense spell that had been used for the cities' protection. However, this access came at a price; they had to listen to the Kao with regard to the prophecy. If the Mage Council, after listening to some Kao representatives and examining the defensive spell deemed, that it was not a crackpot cult, then its permission was sought for the Kao to operate more openly and in alignment with the Council to protect their society.

The Mage Council had been intrigued by the existence of such an Order in their midst. When the defensive spells and the prophecy contained within the Book of Ahn and confirmed by a more recent one were revealed, the Mage Council's intrigue changed to genuine respect for the work of the Kao. They now understood why the defense spells had only worked within the cities and had prevented the mages from leaving the confines of the cities. Those who had fashioned the spells had not forgotten about the pilgrimage. Given that it was made once every thousand years and that the espec had not been in existence at the time of the last birth of a star, it had been almost impossible to have foreseen and planned for such an attack outside of the cities. The Council had been impressed the most by the Kao representatives' willingness to bear the responsibility for this oversight. In a society that pursued only its own desires, the fact that such a group existed that was willing to put the well-being of their society first was extraordinary.

The Mage Council had been of the opinion that for such an order to be so concerned with their society's safety that it operated in secrecy for years without any assistance from the general mage population and with no regard for any reward deserved the Council's utmost respect. So the Council unanimously decided that the Kao was to be allowed a place on the Council and would assume in the open, a role which they had performed clandestinely for years. The Kao representative on the Council had been given the final say in all matters pertaining to the security of their population. When word of this got back to the majority of Kao members, they had been astonished. Some were a bit perturbed that their shroud of secrecy had been unveiled to the Council, while others had welcomed the free reign given to them by the Council.

Once the Kao Order had been recognized, the Mage Council and its new members had focused on rebuilding their society into one that was stronger and more self-reliant. Any and all remaining traces of the espec had been wiped clean, but the shared pain had lived on in the memories of all. At the first anniversary of the massacre, monuments that had been created in all the cities were unveiled to remember those that had fallen that terrible night. The defense mechanisms had now been tweaked so that whenever large groups went outside city walls they would be protected. If that fateful night taught them anything, it was that their society would no longer be driven by the selfish ambition of creating bigger and better spells. In its stead was a sense of guilt and fear that something like this could happen again if they did not take the time to be more considerate and mindful, and address all persons in their societies as equals.

As Talia finished comparing her guidelines with the manuscript that she had just re-read for the tenth time, she still had that sense of slight awe. What had stood out for her was the Kao's willingness to accept responsibility for their brethren. The original members had performed a duty, and in their eyes had failed to a large extent. Yet by their failure, they had learned and grown into a group that had lasted for centuries. Talia now understood that her need to protect was one that had truly been passed along their bloodlines. As such she would do all within her power to become a member, much like

Lila.

Her musings were interrupted by a knock on her door. She was a bit grumpy at being disturbed while she was digesting the information that she had read, but when she saw that it was Sunni at her door she smiled. Her aunt was always a welcome visitor. Yet, today her typically tranquil countenance held an elusive expression that Talia could not identify. Without any preliminaries she told her that Delia had come to the Citadel alone.

The word 'alone' had spoken volumes to Talia. Delia had been quite in love when last they had communicated. Something had to be very wrong for Delia to have sought her out alone. So she quickly rose to her feet and followed Sunni with great alacrity. The historical account penned by Lila flew from her mind as she wondered what had happened. Although Delia's husband was now the Mage King, Talia was certain that if he had hurt her sister in any way, she was going to make the blast at the tournament seem trite in comparison to what she would do.

* * *

CHAPTER SEVEN

' TROUBLES '

The Holy Citadel of Rhys

Seven Months Later

Looking back, Delia realized that the turning point for her had been the incident in the Citadel's garden. Her state of mind had not been of the best when she had left the palace some months earlier. Yet, thankfully her amulet had transported her to within a few feet of the Holy Citadel of Rhys where Talia had been. In retrospect, she was even more grateful for the gift that her mother had left her. She now knew that as long as the user of the amulet was somewhat functional and could fix their mind on a particular place or person for a few moments, then the amulet would take that person to the specific destination safely.

When she had arrived at the Citadel she had been emotionally distraught, and the guards, to their credit, had taken her to their supervisor immediately. They had been amazed that she had appeared within the ambit of the Citadel without any magical alarms being triggered. Ancient magic seeped deep within the very foundation upon which the Citadel stood, and perhaps this was what made it an entity unto itself. The Citadel was very specific with respect to any mages that it allowed within its hallowed space. The guards had witnessed her appearance within the outer courtyard a little beyond the outer door of the Citadel. When she had not been automatically transferred elsewhere, this had indicated to them that the Citadel was amenable to her presence. Therefore they had escorted her with the utmost respect to their supervisor, once she had requested an audience with Talia and Sunni.

The guards' supervisor, upon learning her identity, had sent a summons requesting Talia and Sunni's presence. As she found out in due course, the Citadel had been utilized as the remote headquarters of Kao for many years. The Citadel was older than the mages' civilization, having been created during the period when their creators still walked the planet. In fact, extraordinarily powerful objects and the sacred book of Ahn were still kept hidden within its confines. Thus, only the top tier Kao members and specially designated mages were granted access or even knew of its location.

Of this number, the Citadel selected those who would remain its occupants. The Citadel had a definite personality of its own, and no one was allowed to stay unless the Citadel itself gave its' permission. It seemed that the magic of the ancients chose its inhabitants, and unfortunate mages often found themselves transported out of the Citadel as they got the proverbial 'boot'. Attempts by these mages to find their way back proved futile, as the Citadel had a knack of hiding its presence. So the precious few who were allowed to live there, came to respect the Citadel as being their host, and their humble selves to be mere visitors. As a result, the Kao kept them there on a permanent basis and engaged them to work on translations, guarded the sacred artifacts of power (or rather kept inventory of them, since the Citadel had its own defenses) or provided support in some fashion.

Delia remembered how Talia had flown into the small room where the superior had left her waiting. Talia had such sprightliness to her that Delia would have sworn that she never touched the ground. Talia had changed, and she had appeared happier, even though her face had been full of concern. There seemed to be an element of being settled in Talia's psyche, as if she had finally found her niche in life. Judging from her sister's countenance, Delia had known the instant that she walked in that her sister had guessed that something was very wrong between her and Alejandro. However, her hug was all that Delia needed to realize that no matter the circumstances, her sister was always there for her.

So as if it was a story belonging to someone else, Delia had detachedly informed her sister that she had discovered that Alejandro had probably been having an affair with one of the female mages. Everything came pouring out as she told her how she had inadvertently discovered it. She remembered how calmly she had recited to Talia what she had discovered. She had been sitting in her favourite nook (the same one that had been their grandmother's). It held a loveseat hidden behind a brocade tapestry. Few persons in the palace knew of its existence. It was large enough to accommodate a private tryst, but what had appealed to her was its panoramic view. Just above the loveseat was a medium-sized window that looked out directly unto the mountains. She had loved sitting there when the twin suns were setting. The sky was normally awash with a brilliant array of colours set against the natural amber of the sky creating a truly beautiful masterpiece of nature.

Alejandro's feast had been scheduled for later that night. She had felt unusually tired, and a multitude of thoughts had been flowing through her head. So she had gone there to relax for a few minutes. Having gone from being a new bride to being the Mage-Consort within a few months of their marriage had been daunting. As Mage-King, Alejandro had assumed the responsibility for overseeing the progress of Estrel. All the mages within all five domes fell within his authority as Mage King. The only regions beyond his ambit of power were the Holy Citadel of Rhys and the outer regions that surrounded the domes. He was to serve for a lifetime or until such time as the Council deemed fit to designate another. As Mage-King, he had the deciding vote in matters in which the Mage Council was at a deadlock.

She had recalled how she had sighed as she thought of the numerous duties she should be attending to at the moment instead of dallying in her nook. As Mage-Consort she had duties to execute, but her primary one was to assist her husband. Thanks to Tabitha's assistance, she had become versed in mage politics and had her finger on the pulse of the Court. Any problems that fell within the scope of the running of the palace came to her. The palace staff had been tremendously helpful during those first few weeks. They had weaned her gradually into the workings of their world until she was considered competent. Then, they brought everything they could not handle to her. They liked how she dealt with them, and as a result would accommodate her inexperience. In return, she showed her appreciation for their support and diligence as often as possible.

She had recounted quite calmly to Talia how she would often share her day with Alejandro before they went to bed. She would tell him of all the quirky happenings that had occurred during her day. He would share his thoughts on certain matters that were before him. He seemed to like listening to her opinion on situations. He even opened up about his fears and misgivings allowing her to see his softer side. She had reassured him and even engaged in brainstorming with him on strategies to deal with the situations.

She had thought to herself then that she should have recognized that something was wrong when during the day he was distant. Yet, she had dismissed it as being part of his public persona, for during their private time together at night he would set aside this façade and just be himself. She had loved what she thought was his real personality more and more each passing day.

Delia had laughed emptily at how she who had the gift of empathy had been fooled. As she had told Talia, there had been no indication. In fact, sometimes he would even spontaneously surprise her with unplanned romantic dinners outside the palace. Other times she would receive little gifts during the day from him via his personal courier. Flowers and scrolls by her favourite authors were amongst her favourite gifts. They were little tokens meant to bring a smile to her face. In return she would pass little notes back that were guaranteed to make him smile.

He had sent her chocolate-covered strawberries earlier that same afternoon. She had been so tickled pink that she had gotten a new gown for that night's proceedings. She remembered what an elegant little creation it had been. It had made her look exquisite. She had even been planning to assist him in maneuvering two particularly difficult Council members into finding a compromise between their respective positions on a matter concerning trading in the Luz dome. She had felt that a soft touch was required, from what Alejandro had described to her.

If there was one good thing that had come from her marriage to Alejandro was that she had become quite adept at peacemaking between members of the Mage Council. Most of them had served on the Council during her grandfather's time as Mage King. They had respected her from the first moment she entered the palace. She knew that Tabitha probably had a role to play in this. Tabitha had been her confidante and had proven to be a valuable source of information. She had provided Delia with a dossier on each sitting member of the Council. Not everyone who sat on the Mage Council actually participated. The Kao member was often absent unless a matter dealing with security was being heard. However, Tabitha had been thorough, and had included a dossier on him as well.

Unfortunately, Tabitha and her husband had left on a sabbatical retreat for a year to the Saba dome. The rest of Tabitha's clan had been scattered throughout the other domes as well. Strangely enough, they had all gotten opportunities to live in other domes within eight months of her husband's ascent to Mage King. In addition to this, their father had recently requested that both Thom and Ravi visit Merari to investigate the properties of a new elixir that he wished to market. They had been there for approximately a month. So, essentially she had been on her own in Varga.

And then her life had turned topsy-turvy within the course of a few minutes, as two mages had chosen to gossip in front of her hiding spot. They had approached her hiding spot just as she was getting ready to leave. Not wanting to reveal its location she had stayed silent. She had recognized the voices of the two court mages. She didn't particularly like them, as they tended to gossip. However, it was from that conversation that she had felt compelled to investigate whether there was any grain of truth to what had been stated.

After they had moved away and she had felt sure that it was safe to leave, she had made her way directly to her husband's office area. She had gone there to seek Alejandro to confirm whether any of what she had heard was true, but he had been elsewhere. So she had done the next best thing and snooped discretely amongst his effects. In a secret compartment beneath his desk, she had discovered notes from a female mage that purported to discuss their various rendezvous. She had even found corresponding material that implicated her husband in such activities. What had hurt the most was the fact that her own notes that she would typically send to him every time he had done something nice had been neatly tied alongside that trash. As if they meant the same to him as those other notes.

She didn't know how she had managed to walk to her quarters afterwards in a seemingly calm fashion. It had been by Mother Gaia's grace alone that she had. She had felt betrayed. It had felt worse than when their mother had passed away. Her emotions had been churning, and her chest started feeling tight as if she couldn't breathe. So she had taken a bath and left her hair damp. She then knelt in her meditation area and tried one of the meditation techniques that one of her tutors had taught her. But the emotions had spilled over and she had not been able to maintain control. It was at this point that the oddest of things had happened.

Her hands, which would usually get a tingling warm sensation in each palm while she did the meditation had changed into something more. It had started off as the normal warm tingling sensation, then it had morphed. She had felt the warm tingling sensation change into circular motions as they built into an almost magnetic force which bridged both centers of her respective palms. Whatever power lay within that bridge had pulsed, and yet she had not been frightened. Then unbidden an image of Alejandro had flashed through her mind, and she had just reacted. She had taken that power and flung it at the picture of him that she kept at her bedside. She had not opened her eyes to aim. Nor had she moved from her position off the floor. Yet, with unerring accuracy and deadly efficiency, whatever had been within her hands had knocked his picture off her stand and shattered it into many tiny fragments.

It had been at this point that she had recognized that if she had confronted Alejandro then and there, she would most probably have attacked him and ended up either hurting him or herself in the process. For the first time in her life she was not in total control of her emotions, and it frightened her. So acting on instinct, she had packed a few essential items then dashed off some notes. One note was to Tabitha, the other to the Chief of Staff, then to Thom, and the final one to Alejandro. She had merely stated that she had been called away unexpectedly to see Talia. She was uncertain as to when she would be back, and she had left instructions that all urgent matters were to be addressed by the Chief of Staff. Alejandro's note had been brief, as she merely stated that she was going for a visit to see Talia. However, for the first time since their marriage she had not signed it 'affectionately Delia.' She had merely signed it as she did all her official correspondence 'yours faithfully, Mage Consort Delia.'

She had summoned one of her personal staff and told her that she was going to see her sister. She had then given her the notes to dispatch to the appropriate persons as well as instructions to close her apartment quarters until she returned from her trip. After the staff member had left, she had taken a cursory glance at her quarters then holding her amulet and bag, she had asked to be taken to her sister. The amulet had obeyed, and she had found herself in the ancient courtyard of the Citadel.

It was at this point of her story that she paused because of the entrance of their aunt. After fetching Talia, Sunni had left her to attend to her sister alone as she consulted her own superior. Sunni had requested a special dispensation from Mother Mizpah to allow her niece to stay. When Talia had shown up the first time she had done the same. For centuries, no non-Kao member had stepped foot on the Citadel's grounds. Yet, like Talia, the Citadel had made no effort to remove her from its presence.

As one of the top-tier mages within the Kao ranks, Sunni's mystical powers were considered valuable to the Order. Therefore she had been within her rights to request special dispensation. Given that news of Talia's win at the tournament had already filtered to those within the Citadel. Mother Mizpah had graciously consented as she considered that Talia had great potential as a future Kao member.

However, Delia as Mage Consort was a completely different story. As Mage Consort, Delia could never become a Kao member due to the rules of their Order. However, Mother Mizpah after some consideration had consented to her staying. Therefore, she could not in good conscience prevent Delia from staying. However, she did request that Delia be told that whatever she learned concerning the Kao or the Citadel during her time spent there was not to be disclosed to anyone.

When Sunni had walked into the room where her nieces were sitting, she had taken one look at Delia and knew that her niece was tottering close to the edge. Sunni had recognized the same remnants of power on her as she had on her sister Alyssa so many years ago. It had been right after Alyssa had broken off all ties with their father and had informed the Kao leader that she was leaving the Order. Alyssa's emotions had been spiraling out of control that night, and she had told Sunni that for the first time she was frightened of what she might be capable of. She had told her how her emotions had channeled a bio-magnetic energy that had pulsed from her hands. Sunni had examined her sister's palms and the energy around her, and knew that this manifestation could wreck her life. So she had hugged Alyssa that night and let her go. Now, she saw the same traces on Alyssa's daughter that she had seen on her sister that night, and she knew that she needed to bring this little one into balance.

So after introducing herself formally to Delia for the first time, she had promptly taken a hold of her and insisted that she be given an impromptu tour. Talia had been taken aback, because she knew from experience that Sunni's time was valuable to the Order. Yet, the slight movement of Sunni's head indicated that Talia was to come along. So Talia had complied and wondered to herself what was so wrong that made her aunt put aside her Kao duties to show Delia the Citadel in person.

* * *

CHAPTER EIGHT

'DOUBLE BLESSINGS'

<u>The Garden at the Citadel</u>

It was during the impromptu tour that the strangest thing happened in the rose garden. Delia had started feeling a bit faint, when a garden bench of branches, vines and flowers formed before their eyes between two ancient trees right in front of her. She had seen the glances that Talia and her aunt had exchanged, but she had been too astounded to take in any of it. She had never seen such spontaneous magic in her life. As she gingerly touched the bench, one of the branches gently pushed her into the seat; and the flowers that had formed part of it formed into a garland and offered itself to her. The seat even began to sway gently to and fro, rocking her as if she was a child it wanted to play with. She had felt warm and cherished and strangely unafraid of the wondrous magic around her.

At this point, Sunni had sought her permission to use a little of her own magic on her. At her acquiescence, Sunni had touched her lightly on her hand. As their skin touched, Sunni's power that gave her an inner glow flared to a brilliant light that had blinded even Delia's eyes. When she had opened her eyes again, the expression on Sunni's face was one of delight mixed with sorrow. It was in this idyllic garden that Sunni had told her that she was expecting twins.

Delia had recalled feeling as if her world had turned upside down yet again. However, this time a sense of love filled her.

She had felt the tears rolling down her cheeks as she sat in that garden seat made for her. She had wept until she had no more tears. By the time she had finished she had felt much lighter. Her cry had been a cleansing one, as if all the toxic emotions within had been dispelled in that one bout of weeping. To their credit, Sunni and Talia had not said a word. Sunni had held her while Talia had laid her head in her lap until she was done. Sunni had taken a good look at her afterwards. Whatever she had seen had reassured her, so she had merely nodded her head, then smiled. With that Sunni had left her to Talia's care and had promised to check in on her later.

Within days Delia had started showing symptoms of her pregnancy. The Citadel itself seemed to be in its glee as it catered to her every whim and fancy. Of the two, even Delia thought that the Citadel behaved more like the expectant mother than she did. It had even expelled a poor mage from the rose garden when she had begun to feel slightly irritated at his presence. Although she apologized profusely to him afterwards, he had given her a wide berth after that incident. All inhabitants within had recognized that the Citadel considered her to be its honored guest. It would publicly cater to her needs, since it appeared to take an interest in her unborn children. Unbeknown to her, speculation had been rampant amongst the Kao leaders as to the effect those children would have on their civilization. They had been the first to be born inside the Citadel since the time of the Demigods and it was clear that the Citadel would entertain no attempts to send her elsewhere.

Nonetheless, for now it was a constant source of amazement to her to feel the life growing within her womb. The accompanying twinges of back pains and the morning nausea of the first few months had been trying, to say the least. But the little kicks of communication from her unborn children constantly reinforced the fact that she would soon be a mother. Talia took to playing music for her, while the other mages, when not deterred by the Citadel, tried to amuse her. Sunni always dipped in on evenings and chatted about her childhood with her mother and grandparents. She had also brought along scrolls on parenting for mages, the 'Dos' and 'Do nots' of magical parenting. Delia and Talia had scores of laughs with respect to some of the 'Do nots', and wondered how Sunni had managed to get her hands on them.

When her delivery time came, it went surprisingly easily. Within a few minutes both babies had popped out of her into this new world. To her they looked like such angels. Her husband would have been proud to know that he had sired two male heirs. They were like bald wizened little men when they first came out. As time progressed they had filled out nicely, and little tufts of hair started to grow on their heads. Within a few weeks they demonstrated that their powers were developing at an amazing rate. It seemed as if they were multi-gifted, for different powers seemed to manifest themselves. The mages would pop in intermittently to either coo over them or test their power. It seemed that even to these wise and powerful mages they were considered miracles and treated with respect. It was as if the powers of the Demigods had been transferred to these wee ones, and some speculated privately outside of Delia's hearing that perhaps the Demigods had been reincarnated.

Whatever the case may be, the Citadel welcomed the little ones as if they were the Demigods themselves. It positively bloomed, creating gardens in the middle of the most unlikely places. It had boughs to fit the little ones in every nook and cranny one could find. The smell of fresh flowers and the warmth of sunshine seemed to shower each room that the twins were carried into. Even Delia thought that the Citadel would actually take over the care of her babies if she let it. It seemed that there was a lightness to the Citadel that there had not been in centuries. There was no place within the Citadel that was restricted to the twins. They were already a handful for ones who had only been around a few months. Their energy level was tremendous, and they tuckered out any mage who volunteered to keep an eye on them while Delia took short naps. Even Sunni found them difficult to keep an eye on for a prolonged period of time. They were always looking to explore their environment, and their spontaneous outbursts of magic could sometimes cause rather humorous results.

Delia thanked her lucky stars that she had been blessed to have an extraordinary babysitter in the form of the Citadel. She discovered this fact a few months after the twins' birth when she had left them asleep in one of the bowers and came back to find them no longer there. She had frantically questioned all of the mages, the Citadel had taken pity on her and had indicated their location to her by literally lighting the way to them via a soft ball of glowing light which floated in front of her. It had led her to a remote area of the Citadel that the other mages rarely ventured to.

The twins had been unharmed and were gurgling rather joyfully as they played together. Each of them had sported a bracelet made of a substance none of the other mages had ever seen before. All attempts to remove these bracelets from the hands of the twins had proven futile, and the power that emanated when more strenuous means were attempted frightened Delia. So in the end the twins had been left with the bracelets, and upon Delia's request, Sunni had a firm discussion with the Citadel as to removing the children without anyone's knowledge and giving them gifts of power.

The Citadel had sulked for a few days afterwards, and all the mages found themselves on the receiving end of its cold treatment. It would decrease the temperature in all the rooms that the children were not in at the time. Any and all spells that were being cast would backfire and simply be nullified. The rooms that held ancient relics that the mages were supposed to be guarding would disappear and reappear in another location. The last straw came when the Citadel decided to float the sacred book of Ahn that the Kao had guarded for generations through its corridors as if it was a toy to be played with. All attempts by the mages to retrieve the book proved futile, and it was a funny sight to see rather old and dignified mages reduced to physically jumping into the air in attempts to retrieve it. Talia, after withholding her laughter, had told the Citadel in no uncertain terms that if it did not give the book back she would take her nephews outside its walls for a week. The Citadel had dropped the book immediately, and after that left the mages alone.

Nonetheless, being here made Delia realize that she was still unique. Her husband's betrayal had undermined her new- found confidence. There was no ranking system within the Citadel. The Citadel made everyone aware that at the end of the day, regardless of how powerful a mage was, while they were within its sanctum they were all equal. Her talents for keeping a home came in handy, and the other mages quickly came to respect her for it. She made all their lives more comfortable. Her children were such a blessing to her. They made her grow beyond the person she had been, and she liked the person she was developing into. She had gotten back her balance. She was also stronger and definitely more confident. She wanted to be someone, whom her children would one day be proud to acknowledge as their mother.

As time passed by and the twins' first birthday approached, Delia decided that it was time that her husband met his children. As wonderful as they had all been, it was time for her to stand on her own two feet. Besides, the children needed to be brought up in an environment where there were other children. They also needed to be presented at the naming ceremony where all mages carried their children to be presented to the mage community. Sunni had somehow arranged to have her children slipped in amongst the others to be presented. The naming ceremony was one of the most important in a mage's life, as they were given their official mage names. They would be known by these names for the rest of their natural lives, and as such these names would be entered onto the 'Roll of Names'. It was a tradition that had never lost its importance. Mage families often brought their children to be named by the time they reached the age of one, when some of their lifetime powers manifested.

Talia had insisted upon accompanying her and getting her settled. Sunni's schedule had not permitted her to accompany them, but she had given Delia something just as precious. She had promised her that she would always look out for her great nephews, just as she had done for her nieces after their mother had passed away. Delia knew with every fiber of her being that Sunni would keep her promise until the day she passed away.

The Citadel had seemed to fall into a depression of sorts, and actually seemed to mourn the departure of the twins. It still kept a lightened atmosphere for the boys, but there was a definite feeling of loss that permeated the air. On the day of their departure, the boys had disappeared for a little while. Not having the heart to scold the Citadel, Delia and Talia had waited patiently for their return. When the boys appeared after a few hours, their bracelets had changed into intricate designs with a single jewel in each. Talia and Delia merely took the boys, fearing that the Citadel might take them again and delay their departure.

However, the boys surprised them as they simultaneously joined their powers to form a multi-coloured rainbow, complete with fluffy clouds, over the two trees where Delia had first learned that she was pregnant with them. The Citadel seemed to be pleased at their gift, and gave them another in return. In the courtyard where Delia had appeared before she even knew that she was pregnant, a portal had opened. As Delia peered through, she saw that it led to her quarters in the palace. All the mages gathered to see them off had stood around in awe, as none had ever known that the Citadel had the ability to do that. As they crossed through the portal into Delia's old room, the smell of flowers blooming and the warmth of sunshine seemed to go with them.

* * *

CHAPTER NINE

' REUNION '

Varga: The Palace

Her Royal Highness wishes to inform you of her return to the palace. Furthermore she humbly requests that she be given a day to settle herself. As such, she is amenable to meeting you in the Rose Garden located in the North-West quadrant of the Palace at 4 o' clock tomorrow afternoon.

Kindly find enclosed images of Your Royal Highness' new sons.

Yours truly,

Mage Consort Delia

After close to twenty months, his wife had returned unexpectedly. As with her departure, her re-appearance at the palace had been just as mysterious. No one in the palace could account for the manner in which she had returned. She had sent him the note immediately upon her arrival. He must have re-read it twenty times already. The almost after-thought manner in which she had penned a single line informing him that he was now the father of two boys had flabbergasted him.

She had never breathed a word of her pregnancy to anyone in the communications that she had sent throughout the time she was away. Yet, the images she had enclosed of their children indicated that he was indeed a father. His boys had inherited his cleft chin, cheekbones and hair, but they had taken his wife's eyes and dimples. To his prejudiced eyes they looked beautiful. His wife had given him a priceless treasure by continuing his line. Everything else faded away in comparison as he looked at the images of his children. His children! He liked how that phrase sounded on his tongue.

So he had sent a note consenting to wait another day to see his family, even though he was bursting with excitement. So he did the next best thing he could think of. By mid-afternoon, his children had everything imaginable that magelets of that age could want or need. Reproductions of his sons' images had been distributed throughout the palace and by later that evening, everyone in all five domes knew that the Mage King was the proud father of two baby boys.

As he fell asleep that night, he found himself smiling for the first time since Delia had left him. For so long, he had tortured himself with the reason for her departure and continued absence. Now, even though he had not seen her, it was enough for him to know that she was close by. He drifted asleep with thoughts of his two boys and what he should carry for them when he finally saw them for the first time.

*

<u>**The Next Afternoon**</u>

<u>**The Rose Garden in the North-West Quadrant of the Palace**</u>

As she sat in the garden a little before the appointed time, she watched her sons and smiled. They were watching everything from their strollers with great interest and gurgling in their own language to each other. She imagined that their conversation probably consisted of a running commentary on their new environment. They had been introduced to more people in less than one day than they had met in their entire life at the Citadel. They looked like normal little magelets. She just hoped they behaved that way when they saw their father. She was not prepared to give Alejandro a glimpse of their true power. Otherwise, he might challenge her guardianship of their children later on.

She knew that her children were extraordinarily gifted. However, she wasn't prepared to have them grow up as experimental subjects. She was going to follow in her mother's footsteps and do her utmost to provide them with a life as close to normal as she could. Her sons would choose their own pathways much like she and Talia had. As long as she had life she would give them that precious gift.

So while waiting on her husband, she had a firm talking-to with the twins. She had warned them not to display any magic before the mage they were going to meet. She didn't even know if they could understand her, but she had still tried. If Alejandro believed that his children had not started developing their powers as yet, or that they was so low at this point that they were not worth bothering about, then she stood a chance of being able to convince him to allow her to set up residence elsewhere and raise them on her own.

She felt his approach before she saw him. It was an odd tingling sensation of something familiar, but yet it gave her a sense of unease. She shrugged off that sensation and reminded herself that she was no longer that person he married. She was a lot stronger than before, and she had a bright and hope-filled future to embrace. Her children would grow into wonderful beings regardless of their power level. She would not see them turned into miniatures of her husband. She wanted them to become individuals who could hold their own in this world. They were special, no doubt about that, and she wanted to ensure that their uniqueness was preserved and treasured. If that meant deceiving her husband so that she could give them a normal life, then she was more than prepared to do so.

"Delia."

That single word, spoken in such a velvety smooth voice, sent tingles down her spine. She forced herself to take a deep breath and center herself as Sunni had taught her in the Citadel. Sunni told her never to react to a situation, take a deep breath first, try to center oneself, and then focus on the goal.

"Your Highness."

She sank into a deep curtsy as due his elevated status. She needed him mellow right now, and though he never stood on the observation of protocol, she would still adhere to it. Why antagonize him unnecessarily so early in this delicate game?

He chuckled a bit. 'Come now, Delia...there is no need to stand on formality between us. After all we're still married, and you are the Mage-Consort. Unless you're here to tell me that you would like to terminate that relationship and take my children as well.'

Well, well, he bypassed niceties and went for the jugular. She needed to tread carefully in her response. He had shed his public persona and was displaying his 'real' side. She had not expected it. It almost hurt to deal with this side of him. It was the side she had loved and that had ended up sending her into a spiraling emotional mess. She was saved from a response when the twins started tugging at her in an attempt to get her attention. Apparently they were quite taken with some small butterflies that were fluttering amongst the rose trees.

Alejandro's attention was also diverted as he looked at his children. Delia could see pride shining through his eyes as he gazed greedily upon his children. His features softened, and his lips curved into a slight smile, as one of the boys tugged her hand again. Delia sighed, for she knew from experience how persistent her children could be. As she glanced down at them, a random thought came to mind; butterflies were indigenous only to the palace region, and this was the first time her children were seeing them. The twins were always fascinated by nature. When they were at the Citadel they once made the garden bloom with all manner of flowers that had been extinct for centuries.

Oh dear, how could she have forgotten that! She needed to end this meeting as quickly as possible or move it inside.

'Please Mother Gaia, I'm begging you, let them not do anything in his presence…please Mother Gaia…please, please Mother Gaia!!!' She mentally begged.

'Milord, would you care to move this meeting indoors…I'm afraid that the children aren't accustomed to being outside this long, and the various changes in environment could take an adverse toll on their health.'

Mentally she asked Mother Gaia to forgive her small lie. The twins had never been sick a day in their lives, and they seemed to thrive in all types of environments, even more so in nature. She just needed them in a sterile environment where they would not do something unintentionally spectacular for ones their age. After this, she promised herself silently, she would make a list of places that were out of bounds for the children while they were at the palace.

Her husband looked at her in a bemused manner. Delia was definitely in her element as a mother. She even started making her way with the twins towards the castle before he even had a chance to reply. She had a confident attitude, and there was a firm purpose in her steps as she hustled them all indoors. She even had the audacity to turn around and indicate that he was moving too slow. He had to pause to chuckle a bit; it seemed that his wife had changed for the better. Her stay with her sister had given her some more backbone. He found himself interested in what else she had learned and how she had changed during her time away from him. As always, his wife piqued his interest. It seemed that she and her sister were the only two female mages to ever do so. Mother Gaia knew how much he had missed her.

He had tormented himself for months as to why she had left him in the first place. After six months without her, he had been ready to bring her back, but pride had held him back, and some matters always kept popping up, one after the other, which required his attention. Now that she was back, he fully intended to find out the real reason why she had left him without at least saying good-bye.

*

<u>Somewhere Close by</u>

Talia had to wonder what Delia was doing when she saw her hustling the children and the Mage-King right past her hiding spot towards the palace. They had agreed that Talia would not reveal her presence until the Naming Ceremony. So she had worn a disguise and played the role of the children's caregiver. This had enabled Delia to effectively keep all staff from her private quarters, using Talia's presence as an excuse.

So when they had picked this spot for the meeting between Delia and the Mage King, they had decided that Talia would remain within sight of the meeting just in case things went awry. Now, as Delia was barreling towards her spot, all Talia could think of was why was Delia straying from their original plan? For the love of Mother Gaia, the Mage King might actually see her from this close. Talia frantically dashed along another pathway that would put some distance between herself and her sister's rapid retreat from the garden. When they all got back to their quarters, she and Delia needed to have a serious chat about coordinating signals that meant a change of plans.

*

Indoors

Ah, relative safety! As she glanced back she saw Alejandro right behind her. She knew that Talia was probably going to lecture her afterwards on sticking to plans, but this impromptu decision was quite necessary in her judgment. She needed a space sufficiently private where they could chat. As her mind roamed the possibilities that could be used, she found herself drifting to the place where she had overhead the two gossips that fateful day. Well, it was time for her to face her memories again. She was stronger this time, and the twins were there to keep her focused. So with that in mind, she led him over to that fateful spot and made herself comfortable.

Once she was seated, the memories seemed to flood back instantaneously. She recalled it all. Yet unlike the last time, the pain wasn't there anymore. It was as if time and distance away from that particular episode in her life didn't impact her anymore. She must have smiled a bit, because Alejandro looked at her questioningly. So she obliged him.

"The last time I sat in this spot, I overheard two gossips speaking about your affair with another mage. Would you believe that wanting to prove this false, I went to your office to confront you! But you were elsewhere so I did the next best thing that any self- respecting wife could...I discretely checked through your effects.

Do you know what I discovered? I'll save you the time. The notes that I sent you hidden within your secret compartment at your desk alongside notes and other (sniffing delicately Delia wrinkled her nose)....material detailing your various rendezvous.

Can you imagine how much of a fool I felt in that moment?"

For once Alejandro was speechless. Never in his wildest thoughts, tormenting himself as to why his wife had left him, did he imagine that she thought he was having an affair. Of all the possible reasons he had played out in his mind, that one had never entered his head. He didn't know whether to laugh or cry. So he did neither. Instead he took her by the hand and firmly requested that she follow him this time.

As he escorted his dear wife with his children in tow, he knew that she kept giving him sidelong glances. He had not responded to her accusations because he knew she would never believe him without proof. Well, the proof was at the scene of the crime, in a manner of speaking. As he entered his office quarters, he indicated to everyone there that he wanted the room cleared immediately. As the last person left, Delia's helper, who had been taking care of the children since her arrival, appeared right before he was about to close the door. Delia had looked relieved to see this mage, and had been about to pass his children to this mage when he stopped her.

"You might as well stay for this, Talia. I would know your magical signature anywhere."

As she entered and closed the door, she removed her disguise and flopped into one of the chairs in an insolent manner.

"Good, this saves me the time. Really, Alejandro, could you have been more tacky? An affair within your first year of marriage...I thought that if our duel taught you anything, it was to never underestimate us Tierneys...That said, just give me the time and place that is most convenient to you, and we can settle what you did to Delia like the good old days."

"I'll even let you wear the face mask so that you wouldn't damage that pretty face of yours."

Alejandro could feel his fingers instinctively clench as if they wanted to wrap themselves around his sister-in-law's neck of their own volition. Instead, he stalked to the desk that had caused so much trouble, while mentally cursing his dear sister-in-law. After pressing the magical safeguard that would block his office from all external or internal spying devices, he opened the secret compartment and pulled out the notes and materials that had caused the problem. He also went to his bookshelf and pulled out a particular book. He passed both the materials and the book to Talia and Delia.

Then he sat down behind his desk, because he still didn't trust himself near Talia. He didn't want one of his children's first memories of him to be fighting with their aunt. So he gritted his teeth and explained that if she kindly turned to the book, she would discover that it was the cipher code that would enable her to translate the notes. The Viceroy had brought it to his attention a month before Delia had left him that there were some elements within the domes that had been instigating civil unrest and trying to disrupt their society. His so-called rendezvous had in fact been meetings with one of the Viceroy's operatives sent to infiltrate and locate the mastermind.

For more than two years they had been working on trying to contain and neutralize this unknown threat. The Viceroy and his team were no closer to locating the mastermind than they had been when it first came to their attention. All of their operatives sent in thus far had been eliminated. Whoever was behind this was extraordinarily good. He and the Viceroy had nicknamed him 'the Phantom'. He had managed to sow seeds of discontentment throughout the five domes. His following had grown stronger, and both he and the Viceroy suspected that it was only a matter of time before he struck.

The palace was rife with distrust and suspicion; and though he and the Viceroy had managed to maintain order, they both knew that any overt attack within the five domes could trigger civil unrest.

Delia didn't know how to respond to Alejandro. She felt like the wind had been taken out of her and her world just turned topsy - turvy. She realized that no matter how superb an actor Alejandro could be, he had just spoken the truth to her, and her perception had shifted. She wasn't about to just fall into his arms (although she was tempted) because she had the twins to think about. Glancing at the twins, she was relieved to see that they had fallen asleep. Apparently Alejandro's narrative held no interest for them. So she glanced at Talia, and silently asked with her eyes to leave her alone with him for a while.

Talia looked ready to argue with her, but she merely shrugged. Then turning to Alejandro she told him that she wanted to take the cipher and the notes to confirm his story. After letting him take a leisurely look at his children, she took the stroller and carried them to Delia's quarters where she could put them to bed.

"I don't think that saying I'm sorry can really cover this."

"No, it doesn't….Saying that you're 'sorry' does not make up for all the nights I couldn't sleep as I analyzed every moment we spent together, trying to find clues as to why you left me....Saying that you're 'sorry' does not make up for worrying about you all this time...Saying that you're 'sorry' does not excuse the fact that I missed the birth of my children and nearly a year of their lives. My 'own' children! Saying that you're 'sorry' does not excuse the fact that I am a stranger to my children right now....So saying that you're 'sorry' really does not cover it!"

"You're right. Saying that I'm sorry really does not begin to make up for the past. But it's a start Alejandro. You have a choice whether you are going to let the mistakes of the past hinder your future. Or whether you'll stay stuck in past hurts. It's your choice Alejandro."

"Just answer me this Delia, why? Why didn't you just stay and ask me? This could have been resolved so many months ago."

"I was afraid..."

"Delia... you should know that I would never hurt you intentionally."

"No Alejandro, I was afraid of what I may have done to you that night...That's why I left."

Alejandro looked confused at her last statement. So Delia sighed and made her way to his desk. As she propped herself against his desk, he took her hand and pulled her into his lap. So she rested her head on his shoulder and told him everything that had happened from the time she found the note.

*

Unbeknownst to the Mage King and his Consort, they had been observed in the rose garden by one of the Phantom's operatives. The arrival of the Mage Consort and her children heralded a change in the plans to be executed. The Mage Consort was a threat to their movement because from what he remembered of her, she had a knack for dispelling friction and improving open communications. She had to be eliminated before she became entrenched again in palace affairs. It had to be done quickly, because her arrival with her boys had already started changing the atmosphere of distrust that their group had so carefully sown over the last few months.

When he saw the Mage Consort lead the Mage King indoors with their children, he decided not to follow. She was the Mage King's weakness. He was sure of that. He needed to report to their leader. After seeing the Mage King with his family, he was definitely going to recommend that their strike plans be accelerated.

*

Sometime Later

Delia's Quarters

Talia had disarmed the security spells she had left in place before they had departed for their meeting with the Mage King. Then ever so gently, she had laid the twins down in their respective beds. When the little rugrats chose to sleep, it was never wise to wake them. They tended to be a cranky handful when their nap was disturbed. Once she was reassured that they were still in slumberland, she got to work on the coded notes.

By the time Delia walked into the quarters, Talia had already deciphered them and had verified with her Kao contacts that what was stated was actually true. As much as she didn't want to admit it, she acknowledged that she had been quick to misjudge the Mage King. She did not regret her decision to support her sister, but was grudgingly beginning to accept the fact that if she had been fair, she would have talked Delia into coming back sooner.

So when Delia floated into the quarters with a luminous smile on her face, Talia knew that she and Alejandro had made up. She was even humming one of her favourite tunes. Her sister was happy and that was all that mattered to Talia. So she decided to leave Delia to her happy thoughts and go visit the Viceroy. She wanted a clearer perspective on what was going on. She wasn't about to leave her sister and nephews alone and go back to the Citadel if there was any potential danger.

She also had an item from Sunni to deliver to him personally. Plus she wanted to assess for herself the general atmosphere beyond the palace walls. If it was possible, she also wanted to sneak a quick visit to see Thom, provided he was still in Merari. He had been traveling frequently between domes on business, but had tried to keep them updated as much as possible. So hopefully he would be in. She would just drop by unannounced at the home he had shared with Delia before her marriage.

*   *   *

CHAPTER TEN

' SECRETS '

A Little While Later
Museum

The Viceroy had opted to meet the Kao member at the museum since the best meeting places were sometimes those within plain sight. No one observing them would suspect anything other than two fellow art lovers discussing the merits of a particular piece. The museum was always hosting events, and he made it a point to go there twice a week and strike up conversations with perfect strangers. Therefore anyone observing him would assume that the Kao member was just another perfect stranger to him. He often met his Kao liaisons under this guise. Plus, he was an art connoisseur, so he quite enjoyed his visits regardless of whether he met a liaison officer or not.

Today the museum was displaying an exhibit by the new rising artist known only as Tessa. His sources had revealed that she was the grand-daughter of his old colleague Tabitha. He remembered the artist from the Mage- King's wedding, and hoped that she would be in attendance so he could ask her indulgence and commission one of her pieces for himself. He quite liked her style, and believed that she would eventually become one of the premiers of the art world. She gave a whimsical yet interesting perspective to her pieces that was appreciated by all art lovers. It was as if each piece had a part of her essence in them.

As he stood absorbing and thoroughly enjoying the various pieces in the exhibit, someone moved slightly behind him and gave him the secret phrase. He didn't bother turning, but gave the required reply. At this point the mage stepped to his side; and while seemingly pointing towards the piece that the Viceroy had been examining, began the conversation in earnest. The Viceroy was surprised to learn that the Kao member was a young female mage. Although she was disguised, something gave her away. She was relatively new as well, but had to be trusted implicitly by those in the top echelon, since they were the only ones who knew him as a Kao contact. The timing of their meeting came just on the heels of the Mage-Consort's return; and given the questions that he was being asked about the Mage-King's failure to identify the rogue known as 'the Phantom', he quickly realized that the young Kao was very well informed. She was intent on finding out all she could about the Phantom.

At first, he suspected that it was the Mage- Consort herself, then it dawned on him that there had been a sister of hers who had trounced the Mage-King in the showcase of that same year. The more he thought about it, the more convinced he became that it was indeed the Mage-Consort's sister. Once she asked if Thom Raule Rahmut de Arrea was in Varga, that confirmed her identity. Generally, her questions were intelligent and insightful. He began to wonder what the Kao would say if he requested that she be transferred to him to be used as one of his operatives. He was getting old, and he needed a successor. It seemed feasible. She had proven that she could handle herself against potential threats. She would probably adapt easily to Varga society, given her sister's return. He considered all of this as he answered her questions.

He was surprised to discover that the Mage-Consort had noted the change in the general atmosphere of the palace and its inhabitants since she had been away. She had only returned less than one day ago. He confirmed that someone had been eliminating his operatives and something rather nefarious was afoot; but all his attempts to uncover the source of it had failed. Misinformation was the order of the day and distrust was being sown amongst the inhabitants of the dome. His sources elsewhere spoke to him about the similar occurrence in the other domes. Whatever was coming was going to have a domino effect, and it was frustrating him no end that he didn't know by whom or to what end this mischief was being done.

Talia was thoughtful as she absorbed this information. She passed along the message and the item that Sunni had requested he be given. She had no knowledge of its contents. As he took it from her and perused it, his worse fears were confirmed. It was simple yet powerful: be ready because a change that would transform their world as they knew it was at hand. He was commanded by the Kao to keep the children of the Mage- King safe at all costs, because they held the key to their world's survival. With those words she departed. Anyone observing the Viceroy during that interlude would have seen him having a brief conversation presumably about art with a mage of indeterminate age or sex. They would have missed the whitening of his knuckles or the fact that he suddenly looked older than he had when he walked into the museum.

As soon as the Viceroy thought that sufficient time had passed so as not to appear suspicious, he made his way to his home where he did something he rarely did: he opened one of his best vintages and took a rather stiff drink. One thing he had learned when dealing with the Kao was that they were rarely wrong. As he examined the item, a note fell from it. He was instructed to give it to one of the Mage-King's sons when he felt the time was appropriate. In the meantime, he was to cut all further contact with them and destroy any evidence that he had been a Kao liaison. (Well, there went the idea of asking to transfer Talia to him to train). Dangerous times were ahead, and even the Kao was worried about its survival. For the Kao to be worried things had to be bad, so he took another stiff drink after that, then proceeded to plan. He needed to consolidate his assets and secure a place of refuge in the event that the situation went horridly wrong. He also needed to find out what he could about this imminent threat.

*

Thom's Residence (formerly Delia's home)

Talia had just let herself in via the secret entrance and bypassed all the security spells. Luckily, Thom had been a dear, and had insisted that both she and Delia know the spells in the event of either one of them wanting to use the house. Thom had been away, and by the looks of the place someone had been decorating in his absence. Thom had sent newsy communications to them, and had spoken about how Tabitha's grand-daughter Ann-Marie had taken a keen interest in his business ventures.

As Talia looked around, she suspected that the young mage (who if memory served correctly would be of age to wed by now) was keenly interested in Thom as well. Little knickknacks of hers were everywhere. She had been making her imprint, and poor Thom was probably still clueless. Talia had to chuckle a bit to imagine a little slip of a girl taking exuberant Thom in hand. However, from Delia's description of her and her family, she could only imagine how determined that particular young mage was. She sounded like someone whom Talia would get along quite well with.

Nevertheless, as she was here she had a few things to see about. Firstly, she needed to prepare an escape pack just in case things took a turn for the worse and they needed to leave quickly. She had not shared with Delia the information which the Kao had requested she pass along to the Viceroy. She had a rather unsettling feeling since meeting with him that time was no longer a luxury she could afford. So she followed her instincts and set about gathering items that would be extremely useful if the four of them had to survive in a hostile environment. She was thinking of outside the dome area, given the fact that the other domes would be the first place that would be searched.

Sunni had once told in the strictest confidence that a few Kao members had ventured forth and scouted the region beyond the dome and had submitted a relatively extensive report. The report had described rugged terrain with no way of getting there by magic, neither were there typical food supplies. There were certain areas that could be considered habitable, if one was extremely desperate. It was the Kao's ultimate back-up plan just in case anything terrible occurred. So she scouted Thom's home and took items that she considered necessary. Although Thom wouldn't mind her taking the items, she still left a note informing him. She also included directions to where she had secured his own emergency pack that contained instructions that could only be read by him. If anyone else attempted to read her instructions detailing how to leave the domes, the spell would automatically destroy itself. When she was done she stored all of the emergency packs in a safe place, then let herself out and made her way back to the palace.

* * *

Chapter Eleven

' LOSS '

<u>**The Naming Ceremony**</u>

<u>**Three Days Later**</u>

There was a strikingly beautiful dawn on the day of the Naming Ceremony. Both Talia and Delia had managed to watch the first glimmers of light on that day, as they had gotten up early to prepare for the ceremony. It was to be held at high noon in the Great Hall of the palace. Parents from all five domes would be in attendance to present their little ones to be named in this auspicious ceremony. This was the first major event in the lives of mages, since the mage population in essence welcomed the little ones to their community as they were connected to the collective communal power. The little ones would be magelets from this moment until they came of age to be recognized as mages.

This day was also auspicious in that it coincided with the birthday of one of the founders of the Kao. He had been a wise and well-respected individual who believed that it was the duty of each mage to make a difference to the mage world. He was one of Talia's personal legends, and she hoped that her nephews would indeed make a wonderful contribution to this world. She fully intended to instill his principles into their training.

Delia had opted to dress the twins in exquisite soft baby blue tunics with the monogrammed initials of both parents' surnames. The Citadel's bracelets worn by each twin looked quite fashionable with their outfits. Her attempts to curb their unruly hair met with a modicum of success, and they looked rather presentable. As a finishing touch she had anointed each one with her favourite scent, which was a hint of jasmine intermingled with mint and a slight touch of lilies. Her mother had been fond of that particular scent, and Delia seemed to have inherited a partiality to it as well.

After all the preparations were completed, Talia sat the twins down facing each other and crissed-crossed their chubby little hands so that each one held the other one's hands. The twins seemed to understand the solemnity of the occasion, and actually kept hold of each other as they waited expectantly for her to continue.

She had gained permission from the Kao to perform their rites over the little ones, and Delia had agreed. Few mage children had Kao rites performed over them. It was usually only reserved for the children or close relatives of high ranking Kao members. In this case, Sunni had sufficient status to permit the rites to be performed. The rites ensured that the children were under the protection of the Kao until they reached of age to choose their own path. Quite often these children either became members or served as liaison for the Kao order once they became of age.

Once the twins were ready, Talia lit a special candle she had brought with her from the Citadel, and began the rites. As she spoke the ancient form of greeting to Mother Gaia and requested that the twins be kept always on her pathways, she wove the ancient spell of protection over them, binding it with the magical essence of their bracelets. She had called on the essence of the bracelets firstly, because it had been a gift from the Citadel and therefore contained some element of that place; and secondly, she sensed that the Citadel had meant for it to be used for their protection.

Her ceremony merely formally bonded the twins with the gift of the Citadel. They were already linked, and as such the spell merely reinforced the link. Personally, given the Kao's warning to the Viceroy, she wanted her nephews to have the strongest protection available, and be it as it was, the Citadel was still the only place where the ancient and purest forms of power still existed. So, if the Citadel chose to give the twins gifts that were virtually un-removable by some of the most powerful mages in the world, then she would gladly use that gift to reinforce their protection.

Sunni had told them that she had done the same ceremony for Talia and Delia when they were younger. Alyssa had opted to do a private Naming Ceremony for them instead of being included in the general one of that year, hence the reason most had been unaware that the previous Mage-King had two grand-daughters. She had used her connections and pulled a few strings to ensure that it had been kept as quiet as possible. She had done everything in her power to ensure that their lives would be as normal as she could make them, and that included organizing a private Naming Ceremony.

Once the rites were completed, Talia and Delia prepared themselves for the actual Naming Ceremony. Talia had decided that she would attend as herself: aunt of the twins and a member of the Kao. She would present the children as Delia was required by protocol as Mage-Consort to be placed next to her husband. Even though their children were being presented at this particular ceremony, they were still the respective heads of the mage ruling elite, and as such were required to perform certain duties. It was the one event of the year that all mages, regardless of status, were able to meet the ruling mage elite. It was a tradition that had been passed down since the inception of their society. It was a way of remembering that they were still part of a communal whole, despite the fact that they were located in different domes. The new ones' essence was added to the whole of the communal power base, thereby enabling them to be linked magically with the entire mage population.

As soon as they had finished their own preparations, they were surprised by an insistent rapping on the outer door of Delia's personal quarters. Talia didn't sense any imminent threat, so Delia bade the person enter. She was surprised when Alejandro entered bearing some trinkets for his children. He had been sending gifts to Delia and the children since his meeting with Delia. It was a mixture of wooing his wife and trying to make up for not being a part of the twins' lives from the beginning. He had sent the twins everything a child their age would like or need. Delia had been touched by his thoughtfulness.

In fact, the outfits the twins were currently dressed in had been sent by him. He had not asked that they be worn to the naming ceremony. He had merely said that he thought that the colour might suit them, and hoped that Delia might be able to use the outfits one day. Delia had found the tunics beautiful, and after much consideration had chosen them for the twins to be presented in at the Naming Ceremony. Of course, she had gone out and purchased a gown in the same exact shade as the twins' tunics, so that she and the twins would match.

What surprised her when she saw Alejandro enter was that he too was dressed in the same exquisite baby blue as the twins. Hence, the entire family was decked out in matching colours. Alejandro had a boyish grin when he saw her and the twins in the same colour. His grin died when he caught sight of Talia in her official Kao uniform of emerald. He obviously hadn't known that Talia was going to be present at the Naming Ceremony. Delia wanted to head off an argument between the two before it even started, so she thanked him for all the gifts he had sent. She also told him that Talia would be presenting their children on her behalf, since she would fulfill her duty as Mage-Consort for the occasion.

Alejandro was a bit torn at having his wife with him during the entire ceremony or having his sister-in-law present their children at the Naming Ceremony. There was a loophole which permitted Delia to present the children once the ceremony had begun, but he needed to verify it with the Protocol Officer. Until then, he opted to bow gracefully to the inevitable, and managed a brief greeting and nodded a small measure of thanks to her. Talia just inclined her head in acknowledgment, then proceeded to organize the twins to leave. Thus dismissed, Alejandro gallantly swept into a courtly bow and asked Delia if she would care to accompany him to the Great Hall where they were to be instructed by the protocol officer on their respective roles. Delia agreed, and he told her that he would await her just outside the door. She smiled, then proceeded to kiss her children good-bye (while running through a mental checklist to see that they were in order) and then hugged her sister. When she was completely satisfied that they looked quite presentable, she sailed out of her quarters to meet Alejandro.

*

<u>Sometime Later</u>

<u>Great Hall</u>

The Protocol Officer turned out to be quite nice, if somewhat harassed by the numerous details that accompanied such a ceremony. He was a nervous little mage who, as it turned out, was a real stickler for detail. He walked them through the entire procedure from beginning to end. The Viceroy was there as well, since he was to present the little ones to the Mage-King and Mage-Consort, and they were to formally announce to the gathering the names of the children. According to the arrangement, all the mages would gather in the Great Hall. Promptly at high noon, the assembly would be called to order. They would stand until the Mage-King, his Consort and the Council entered the room and were seated in their allotted areas to the front of the assembly. When they were all seated, the Kao Council member would give the blessing before the Mage-King formally opened the proceedings. After that, the Viceroy would request that those presenting the little ones stand and recite their pledges to ensure that the little ones became beneficial members of the mage community. The Viceroy would lead the recital, while the others would repeat it. At the end of the recital, the adult mages holding the children would step forth midway to where the Viceroy stood, which was exactly center between the ruling elite in front and the general mage populace.

The Viceroy had to announce the name of the adult with the child, then the Mage-King and Consort had to indicate that they should approach. When they were in front of the royal mage couple, either the Mage-King or Consort had to announce their names to the herald located on either of their sides. The herald would then announce the chosen name of the little one to the entire Great Hall. A selection of names had been chosen by the Kao Council, and it was at the discretion of either the Mage-King or Consort to pick the one that best suited the little one being presented at the moment.

Alternatively, the royal couple also had the discretion to choose a name that was not within the given selection. The last Consort (Delia's grandmother) had an unerring ability to choose the most appropriate name for a given child, and would whisper her choice to her husband if he looked lost. In fact, she had chosen all the names, and her husband had merely gone along. The Protocol Official looked hopefully in Delia's direction as if trying to will her grandmother's knack onto her.

After the herald announced the names, the adult mages would then turn towards the rest of the mages in the Great Hall and hold out their children to be welcomed into the community. They would then be escorted back to their respective seats by an official. After the last mage child had been presented, the Mage-Consort would close the ceremony with a few words. Then the ruling elite would file out first, while those who presented the children would sign on the little ones' behalf in the Great Book recording the names given to them at the ceremony. Afterwards everyone would assemble in the palace gardens for refreshments and a bit of socializing.

At this point, Alejandro asked if it would be possible for Delia to present his children alongside her sister. After some consideration, the Protocol Officer decided in favour of his idea. Delia would move from the head position once her children were brought forth and join her sister. When the children were presented, she would accompany Talia back to the general section and remain there until she had to close the ceremony. The Protocol Officer seemed to have an epiphany at this point, since he started to smile gleefully. As a way of staying true to the spirit of the ceremony, she would close from within the ranks of the general section, instead of being escorted back to the front. He couldn't think of a better way to incorporate the true essence of the tradition than by having one of the highest-ranking members of mage society close the ceremony within the gathered community.

Delia's stomach clenched at having to close the ceremony but given the fact that she would be able to present her children, she would willingly do it. The Protocol Official had given her the prepared speech that the Palace Speechwriter had written for her. Delia took a deep breath to center herself, then found a quiet corner and started to learn it by heart. By the time she had run through it three times, she was prepared. None too soon, for a few moments later, they were escorted out to the interior chamber to await their summons to the Great Hall. She was pleasantly surprised when Alejandro kissed her on the sly when none of the other Council Members were looking, and told her how wonderful she was. He even slipped his hand into hers discreetly, and continued to hold it even after they were all summoned to the Great Hall.

<u>High Noon in the Great Hall</u>

The Great Hall was resplendent with spells which made the hall shine irisdescently. The walls had a soft golden glow to them, and the various tapestries which had been used for this festive occasion brought a touch of elegance to the oft imposing Hall. The high vaulted ceiling of the Great Hall had been spelled to display past scenes from previous Naming Ceremonies. These scenes flowed one into the other, and quite a few were of maglets who would later become important members within the mage community.

An elevated platform of marble was located in the front of the room and had a raised dais for the Mage-King and his Consort, with additional semi-circular seating arrangements on either side of the dais for the members of the Mage Council. Although the area for the Mage-King and Council members was decorated in white, the soft golden hue from the walls created a halo effect that seemed like a frame for the stark white. The participants, family members and others who wished to attend, were located at either side of the Great Hall. Everyone was dressed in their most beautiful robes, and the Great Hall was filled to capacity, since the general ceremony occurred once a year, and magelet births were becoming fewer in number as the years went by.

Once the ceremony began, the Mage-King and Consort were the last to enter the Great Hall and to be seated on the dais. As planned, one of the Kao Council members gave the blessing, which was followed by Alejandro's address. The recital which followed was memorable, as in unison all the mages of age within the Great Hall pledged to protect and ensure that the little ones present today would become beneficial members of society. When the time came to present the children to be named, Talia and the twins were the first to be led forward.

As they approached the Viceroy the twins were quite taken with him, for Talia found herself suddenly bereft of the twins as they floated right from her arms and straight to the Viceroy's. It wasn't as if a spell had been used for them to float to the Viceroy; the twins merely rode the air on their own cognizance, and upon reaching the Viceroy gurgled at him in delight, each vying for him to hold them. Talia was dumbfounded at this; the twins to her knowledge had never done this with her and Delia. The Viceroy had been surprised as well, but one look at them and his face softened, and he took one in each arm. The instant he complied with their gurgled command to be held, a soft glowing light began to emanate from the three of them, creating a shimmering cascade of light and colour which enfolded the Viceroy, the twins and Talia.

Talia felt goosebumps rise on her skin, for she remembered a similar experience when Thom had been injured and Mother Gaia had healed him. As the light began to warm her skin she dropped to the ground in obeisance, as she recognized the divine presence of Mother Gaia in that moment. As she dropped to the floor, she heard a quiet voice which had a somewhat musical lilt to it, yet the message was clear: ***"Protect them!"*** The message was repeated, then the light faded. As Talia glanced up she saw a dazed expression on the Viceroy's face. He was still in awe that Mother Gaia had chosen to appear to them. He had been unable to drop to the ground, as he had held the twins; but he recognized the otherworldly layer of power as the shimmer of light and colour had started emanating. It had felt protective and good and he felt humbled and blessed at the same time.

The twins were able to bring Talia and the Viceroy back to reality, as they started gurgling and pointing impatiently towards their mother. As Talia and the Viceroy looked around, they noted that everyone seemed unaffected by the display. It took them a moment to realize that what had occurred had not been witnessed by anyone else in the Great Hall. Although the others had been present, they had obviously not been privy to Mother Gaia's direct intervention. It seemed as if time had frozen for everyone else but those involved. Nevertheless, once Mother Gaia's power faded, both the Viceroy and Talia's senses and powers had been replenished with a little extra boost, which put their power levels above their typical peak levels. They were thoroughly energized and ready to perform at their best at a moment's notice.

The Viceroy and Talia merely exchanged measured looks that held an unspoken pact between them. No matter what occurred, they would both act as protectors to the twins until they died. Talia had learned that Mother Gaia often worked in mysterious ways; and if Mother Gaia had decreed the Viceroy to be one of their protectors, she wasn't about to question why. So they continued with the ceremony as if nothing of consequence had just occurred. She trailed behind the Viceroy while he held each twin in the nook of an arm and walked the distance to the front where the Mage-King and

Mage-Consort were located.

Delia and Alejandro bade the Viceroy approach with their children. When the twins saw their mother, they stretched out their arms for her to take them. Apparently, the little rugrats weren't about to float to her as they had done with the Viceroy. So she rose from her position and walked towards the Viceroy. He had been informed of the change by the Protocol Officer, so he gladly relinquished his hold on the precious bundles. As he was handing both to her, one decided that he wanted to go back to Talia, so he stretched out to her, and she took him. He was like a miniature version of what she imagined Thom was like when he was younger. Delia had to smile at that, and then it came to her.

She told Alejandro their names, and he nodded his consent. Delia supervened the herald and turned to the general crowd as she presented **Thom Raule Shulto-Tierney de Ramos** to them, and Talia followed closely as she presented **Ravi Luis Shulto-Tierney de Ramos**. Once the twins were presented, the Viceroy went back to his position, and both sisters were escorted back to the general mage area. All the mothers present at the ceremony smiled as the Mage-Consort joined their ranks.

The Protocol Officer had probably been oscillating as to whether to make her come back to the front or not; but once he saw all the mothers smiling in response to the Mage-Consort's becoming part of their ranks, he patted himself on the back for his change of plans. He had forgotten to inform the head of the security detail of the change, but he didn't think that it was a major issue. So the ceremony continued as planned until the last child had been named and presented.

While the last mother was being escorted back to her seat, sudden flashes of light filled the Great Hall, stunning everyone into silence. Most assumed that it was part of the Ceremony but when they noticed that the flashes had connected with members of the security detail who had been posted prominently in the crowd, and these mages dropped to the floor writhing in agony, that split-second silence changed to pandemonium. Mages began to scream, as it seemed as if out of nowhere mages dressed in black appeared within the crowd and started to attack the security mages, using the crowd as a cover. Quite a few swarmed towards the mage elite located to the front, throwing spells at them as they ran. The remaining security detail within the Great Hall automatically split their forces into two, one to meet the immediate attack and the other to get the mage elite to safety. Unfortunately, they were ambushed by the doors, as more of the attackers poured in at those points.

The twins had saved Talia and Delia from the same fate as the mages in the security detail, as their protective shield went up an instant before two bolts of light whizzed towards them. The bolts were deflected off the shield and back unto their respective senders. When Talia realized that they were under attack she had erupted into action, as she pulled Delia and the twins away from the general crowd closer to the walls. She hoped that the golden glow would interfere with their attackers' aim. The twins' shield couldn't be sustained for all four of them continuously, so Talia ordered them to protect themselves only. She wasn't sure they understood her, but she didn't want them wasting their powers unnecessarily.

The Viceroy had joined their group the instant he deflected a bolt that had been aimed at him. He had deflected it, then kept moving as quickly as he could to reach the twins. There had been a split second where he could have made the decision to head to the front of the room that was more heavily guarded by security mages, or to help Talia and the children, who he realized were relatively unprotected from their position. He chose to honor the unspoken pact he had made with Talia earlier. He was relieved to see that Talia had moved her group as close to the walls as possible. Once he joined them, Talia signaled for him to lead the way, which placed Delia and the children in the middle, and she brought up the rear. The Viceroy knew the Great Hall intimately. He knew where the general exits were as well as the hidden ones. He nixed the general exits in favour of locating the closest secret escape exit.

Whoever was attacking seemed to be intent on their little group, because bolts kept whizzing at them. Talia was doing a commendable job at deflecting most. One or two managed to get by her, but luckily didn't hit anyone from their group. They had reached the hidden exit, and the Viceroy was trying to locate the trigger mechanism which would reveal the exit, when seven attackers surrounded them. They had decided to use the personal touch and fight in close quarters. Talia and the Viceroy turned to deal with them, while Delia frantically tried to locate the trigger mechanism from behind them. She was crouched low against the wall, with her body as a shield between the twins and the mayhem.

Talia dispatched two of them quickly and quite efficiently as Sunni had taught her some tactical offensive measures used by the Kao. The third reassessed her and gave her a bit more of a fight before she took him down. Three had opted to rush the Viceroy at once, and he had tucked and rolled disabling them from a crouched position on the floor. He took them down quickly. Unfortunately, as he was doing so, and Talia was handling the third, the last managed to slip past and was fighting with Delia. Delia was no match for him, but she fought valiantly as she tried to protect her children. In the process, she managed to trigger the release mechanism which revealed the exit. When the attacker saw the exit revealed, he redoubled his efforts and got Delia in a choke hold.

She had almost passed out when Talia came bearing down on him. She relinquished the use of any spells at such a close range, and started using combat techniques taught to her by one of the instructors at the Citadel. She aimed for his knees; and a well-delivered kick to the back of his knees, which was followed by a few punches to his face, forced him to drop Delia. She was able to crawl to her children. Unfortunately, the attacker started firing spells at random. The extra spurt of power that Mother Gaia had bestowed unto Talia earlier came in handy as she dropped him to his knees with one of her spells. He had a brief moment to throw a bolt before he slipped into unconsciousness.

Unfortunately, his last bolt found a successful target, as blood blossomed on Delia's once lovely blue dress. At first, Delia just stared at the red spot that started to get bigger, then she crumpled to the ground. Talia felt her heart stick in her throat as she saw her sister fall. She felt Delia's pain, and knew that the wound was a life threatening one. When she got to Delia's side, she felt Delia's life force slipping away. The twins were safe, but had started to wail once they saw their mother crumple to the ground. They knew something was wrong with her. She wanted to stop and see if she could do a power transfer, but common sense dictated that they get to somewhere a bit safer, as the Great Hall was now a battlefield between the attackers, the mage security detail, the Council members, the Mage King and those mages who were protecting their children.

Talia didn't want to leave Delia in the Great Hall, but she was realistic enough to know that she would slow them down considerably. Nevertheless, she wanted her sister away from the hall, so she slung her across her shoulders and grabbed one of the twins. She couldn't hold both while carrying Delia, and she knew that the Viceroy would recommend leaving her sister in the Great Hall. She made sure the other twin was in the Viceroy's arms before she passed through the exit which led into a narrow corridor. She was halfway through before she realized that the Viceroy was not behind her. She deposited Delia on the ground and laid the twin next to her, and ran back to where she had entered the corridor. The exit was shut again, and from the muffled sounds, it sounded like a battle was raging. She couldn't find the trigger to open the exit, and after a few moments gave up and went back to Delia and the twin she had.

The exit led them into a narrow corridor which opened into what turned out to be the gardeners' lodging near the palace walls. Once Talia had scouted the area and realized that the fighting had not reached there as yet, she found a contraption that made it easier to carry Delia and the twin. She borrowed the gardener's robes and pinned up her hair, trying to pass as a young man. She covered Delia and the twin with a few sheets then made her way to Thom's home. The Viceroy was on his own, and she sent a prayer to Mother Gaia that he would honour the pact and protect the other twin.

Talia had managed by some pure inventiveness on her part to haul Delia and the twin into Thom's residence without being detected. Once there, she laid Delia on the couch in the parlour and put the twin to sit right next to her. As she tore away part of Delia's tunic to where the wound was, she realized that Delia's injury was not one which could be healed by her. So she tried the next best thing, she tried to transfer some of her power to her sister in the hope that it would give Delia enough power to survive until she got trained healers to attend to her. Once the power transfer was complete, she waited a few moments. Delia became conscious for a few seconds.

In those few seconds, she hugged her son. She asked Talia where little Ravi was. Talia told her quickly that the Viceroy had him, but they had gotten separated. Delia asked her to make sure that Ravi got her heirloom from their mother. She smiled faintly as she told her that this was one journey she couldn't make with her. As she held little Thom's hand, she wiped the tears that were running down his face. She whispered to her son not to cry. She told him she wanted him to listen to Talia, be a good boy, look out for his brother, and always remember that they were the best part of her. With that, Delia slipped back into unconsciousness.

In a few minutes, her hold on her son's hand grew limp, and Talia felt the life force as it left Delia's body. She pulled little Thom into her arms and wept for her sister. She would have stayed so indefinitely, but for little Thom tugging her hair and pointing towards the travel packs she had pulled out from their respective hiding places. Hugging him, she got to her feet, changed him into something appropriate for travel in rugged terrain, then took off Delia's heirloom and penned a note to the Viceroy. She put the note and heirloom on top of Delia's body, then pulled the bell which would summon Thom's staff to the parlour. Once she heard them approach, she kissed Delia's forehead, gathered little Thom and her travel supplies, and departed.

When the staff arrived in the parlour, they were shocked to see their former mistress laying still on the couch with her favourite piece of jewelry on top of her, with a note attached. There was a small baby-blue tunic next to her. Once they realized that she was dead, they staggered in disbelief and shock. One of the older ones took the note and heirloom and held them in keeping for the Viceroy. They had been hearing strange reports of fighting taking place within the palace, but seeing Delia's body here confirmed it. The staff immediately sent word to Thom, and to the palace. They found no trace of who had gotten Delia to the house, but they suspected it was her sister. Once they got over the shock, they began to prepare her body and wait until either their master returned or the Mage-King came.

*

Earlier at the Hidden Exit

The Viceroy had seen Talia disappear into the passage and grabbed one of the twins, when another contingent of attackers came at him. He had a split second to close the release mechanism to prevent them from following Talia when they attacked. Luckily, the twin he held took offense to being attacked and threw up a protective shield around them which prevented any of the attackers' bolts from hitting them. As a result, the Viceroy was able to draw them away from the hidden exit and towards the middle of the Great Hall. He ended up in the midst of the Hall, and having located the Kao member on the Mage Council, made his way to him.

The Kao member was cut off from the other members because he and a few of the remaining security mages had chosen to protect the frightened parents and their magelings from harm. The Mage-King and the others were drawing the bulk of the fighting towards them and away from the parents. Having noted all this in one glance, the Viceroy moved quickly, dispatching any attacker in his way. Once he got to the Kao member, he relayed the information to him. The Kao member relayed this information to the rest, then ordered the Viceroy to secure the child before he stepped to the front of the room and started blasting indiscriminately at the attackers. The attackers stopped worrying about the parents and started attacking him The Mage-King and Council members stepped in to assist him as they realized he was trying to draw the attackers' attention.

The Viceroy used this diversion to blast a spell at two of the nearest hidden exits. Once the exits were revealed, he motioned the frightened parents to make their way through them. The attackers ignored the parents who were rushing towards these exits in favour of attacking the Kao Council member and the mage elite still remaining in the room. By the Viceroy's assessment, none of the magelets had been hurt, and the bulk of the fallen mages consisted of the attackers, security detail and a few Council members. A few moments later, a large contingent of what appeared to be mage security entered the room and managed to subdue the rest of the attackers. The Viceroy used this distraction to get to the Mage-King and let him know that Delia had been injured, but Talia had managed to escape with the other twin.

*

<u>A short while later</u>

<u>The Great Hall of the Palace</u>

" Your Majesty, there's a messenger here from the former residence of your wife…he says that he has an important message to deliver to you personally."

Alejandro's heart, which had been troubled with fear for his wife and child's safety since the attack, seemed to beat a little faster. They had been separated during the attack, and she had disappeared from the palace with Talia and one of their boys. The Viceroy had been holding his other son and had managed to keep him safe.

" Bring him to me…"

" Yes, Your Highness!"

*

<u>Shortly After</u>

<u>Delia's Former Residence in Varga</u>

The instant his son had crossed the threshold of Delia's former residence, he began to wail. He had refused to leave the Viceroy's arms since the attack, and had been relatively quiet until they had entered Delia's home. Then he had let out an agonizing cry that had sent a jolt of fear back into Alejandro's heart. Alejandro had exchanged a quick glance with the Viceroy, then quickened his gait. A staff member handed them a note from Talia before they could enter the main parlour. In it she explained that his other son was fine and with her. There were other items in the note but he didn't have time to finish it. He walked into the formal parlour. He saw a bevy of staff kneeling around the reclining couch, and on that couch lay Delia in the blue dress that she had been wearing earlier at the ceremony.

Somehow his legs managed to carry him to the couch. He knew before he even got there that his wife had passed away. As he felt his wife's cooling forehead his knees buckled, and he fell to the ground beside her. She looked peaceful, as if she was merely taking a nap. Yet the red stain on her dress indicated that this sleep was more permanent in nature. Everything around him seemed to fade away as he rested his head on her chest. There were so many things he would never be able to say to her. He thought of all the time together they had lost and now she was lost to him forever.

He felt his son being placed next to him on Delia's body. Somehow he knew that his son was clasping his wife's neck because her arms could no longer hold him. He heard his son whimper softly as he felt his mother's skin grow colder to the touch. Then he felt his son's hand pulling at his hair, and looked up. He saw Delia's eyes looking at him mournfully through his son's face. For the first time since his wife and children had arrived at the palace, his son indicated that he wanted to be held by him.

Obeying an instinct as old as time, he pulled his little one into his arms and started rocking him gently. He didn't know how long he just sat there with his son; but while holding him, he found his purpose. He was going to make sure that he eliminated the Phantom. He knew that wherever Talia had gone, she would keep his other son safe. He and the Viceroy would protect this son. However, this might mean that he would have to display a lack of interest in this son if only to keep him safe.

With his mind made up, he summoned the Viceroy, who had ushered everyone out of the room while he and his son grieved together. Giving his son to the Viceroy, he quietly and quickly explained what was to be done. As he read Talia's note fully, he realized that she had left instructions that he was to give his son Delia's amulet upon his attaining the age of twenty-one. She had also written down Delia's last words to her sons. He indicated that the Viceroy leave the room with his son, as he wanted to say his goodbyes to his wife. Once they had left the room, he told his wife everything that he had not gotten the chance to say to her in life.

When he walked out of the parlour a short while later, he saw his son curled up in the Viceroy's arms. He saw Delia's eyes watching him from his son's face; and unable to bear it, he turned and walked away.

* * *

CHAPTER TWELVE

' AFTERMATH '

"Ripples of death

Flow outward through time

Changing the world"

-Haiku by Keri

Nine Years Later

Aftermath of the Attack

"Ravi Luis Shulto-Tierney de Ramos! Get down from there immediately!"

Ravi, otherwise known as R.L to his friends, sighed as he heard the Viceroy's raised voice. How could someone expect to have fun with the Viceroy and his cohorts constantly keeping an eye on him?

"Don't make me tell you again, young man," warned the Viceroy.

Reluctantly, R.L relinquished thoughts of flying down the banister at full speed. Although his father was the Supreme Overlord, R.L rarely saw him. His upbringing had been left to the Viceroy, who had become his unofficial adopted uncle. The Viceroy had been known to discipline him on occasion when he had behaved very badly. Although the Viceroy never spanked him, R.L hated the quiet thoughtful manner in which the Viceroy would outline the options for his punishment when he misbehaved. He much preferred being spanked to the clever methods the Viceroy thought of to punish him for his naughtiness.

He wondered who had ratted him out. He had made sure that none of the Priory members were around before he had climbed to the top of the banister. The Viceroy had warned him since he was little to stay clear of all members of that group. He had complied, since he didn't like them. The Priory was the one responsible for many of his favourite people disappearing from the palace.

He had once asked the Viceroy why the Priory made people disappear. Instead of telling him that he was too young to understand, the Viceroy had sat him on his knee and told him what had happened when he was still a little magelet. According to the Viceroy, it had begun with the pursuit of someone known only as the Phantom. In the beginning the Phantom had been responsible for the disappearance of some of the Viceroy's agents. Then, during the Naming Ceremony, there had been a surprise attack. His mother had been injured while the Viceroy, who had been holding him at the time, had been separated from his aunt and brother. Although the Mage King had succeeded in winning the battle that day, it had come at a cost. R.L's mother had subsequently died, and Talia, his aunt, had disappeared with his brother.

As a result of the attack, the Mage King had declared martial law, and subsequently became known as the Supreme Overlord. However, the efforts to weed out the Phantom had proven futile. The Phantom and his unknown followers had increased their attacks, and would strike at random thereafter. They had killed many mages and magelets in these attacks. Then one day, eight years ago, they had managed to capture a member of the Phantom's group by accident. He had been attacking an unarmed group of mages when help had arrived at the scene sooner than the attacker had expected. They had managed to knockout and capture the mage. Unfortunately, it turned out that he was a member of the Order known as the Kao. Upon learning this, rather than believing that he was probably a rogue within the Kao Order, the Supreme Overlord had ordered that all Kao members and their known associates be rounded up for questioning.

The Kao Order had been the protectors of their society for generations. So the Order had been displeased with the Supreme Overlord's command, and had tried to negotiate with him for an internal investigation instead. Then the unthinkable had happened. At a high level meeting between the Supreme Overlord, Mother Mizpah (the head of the Kao at that time) and other high ranking officials of the Kao, there had been an assassination attempt on the Supreme Overlord's life by two of the officials in attendance. Mother Mizpah had sacrificed her own life in order to save the Supreme Overlord's during that assassination attempt. The attempt had merely confirmed to the Supreme Overlord that the Phantom was indeed a rogue Kao operative.

It was at this point that the Supreme Overlord had ordered the complete dismantling of the Kao. A new order known as the Priory had been born in the aftermath. It had been led by a former member within the Mage Security Services. He was known as the Protector, and he had set up his order in complete contrast to the Kao. For starters, the Priory was completely loyal to the Protector and the Supreme Overlord. Those chosen to serve within its ranks had no affiliation with the former Kao Order. The members were selected from all levels within their society, and none of them adhered to the teachings of Mother Gaia.

Almost overnight, the Kao went from being respected members of society to being virtual outcasts. Known members were ruthlessly displaced and their assets confiscated. Public notices were sent out throughout all the domes encouraging mages to turn in family members who belonged to the Kao, in order to avoid being labeled as conspirators and having their assets seized as well. The Protector was only too happy to oblige, and launched a campaign whereby the members of the Priory sowed discord and disharmony amongst the mage population, utilizing disgruntled members within the mage security to perpetuate their goals. They also started lecturing daily from pulpits, trying to indoctrinate the masses into obedience.

Through a twelve month steady diet of this misinformation and propaganda assisted by disgruntled mage-security members who were now Priory members, information was leaked and twisted with the sole purpose of sowing discord amongst the Phantom's followers. Eventually the Mage Council had been disbanded, and the Supreme Overlord's position consolidated. The Priory received its due reward for its efforts, and was established as the pre-eminent order within society. The Protector was made special adviser to the Supreme Overlord, and his position was second to none. Those disgruntled security members who had been instrumental in creating the situation were promoted to positions of power, while others were given the option of resigning or being fired. A few opted to resign, while the others found themselves downsized. The entire political and social structure of their society underwent a transformation, and few even realized how drastic the change had been. Change had come, and the general population had followed the plans of the Protector like lambs to a future which was fraught with uncertainty.

Those mages who did not agree with the new regime were forced to flee to the outer regions beyond the dome. They were effectively cut off from the rest of the mage population, and had to survive as best they could. As time went by, the number of refuges grew, until whispers begun to circulate within the general population that a settlement had been set up to accommodate those unhappy with the present regime. None of the Priory members knew the location of this settlement. It seemed as if an underground resistance had been formed to assist displaced mages who had incurred the displeasure of the Priory. No one knew who the members were, but the Priory suspected that it was being run by members of the Kao. All attempts at infiltration were thwarted. The Priory did not know how they operated, nor did they discover the method by which the mages were transported to the outer regions. After a while, the number of mages seeking refuge dwindled, and life for the others returned to some semblance of normally. Yet the Phantom still remained at large, and the attacks continued.

R.L had listened to all this and stored it in his memory. He had been puzzled by one item, that of Mother Gaia. His tutors had only given him the bare details about that deity. He didn't understand what it had been like for an entire Order to worship this deity. Yet, for some reason he knew that this deity was real. He couldn't explain how he knew it, he just did. The Viceroy had told him of his personal experience with the deity. Mother Gaia was the embodiment of all things within their world. It was neither female nor male, though it was called Mother. It was the divine being that created all within their world, including the creators of their race. The Viceroy had been weighing how much more to tell him, then decided against saying more. He did, however, arrange with his namesake, Ravi, to tutor him further with respect to many items, including Mother Gaia.

With Ravi lessons were always fun, since he made everything take on a different dimension. Ravi had started tutoring him soon after his talk with the Viceroy. Ravi would teach him five months of the year, then disappear for another five months. During the five months that Ravi taught him, he learned all sorts of nifty things that he later found out were pretty advanced for his age. For the other five months, he would attend school with the other magelets like himself whose parents were high ranking mage officials. He was normally bored to tears during those five months, and would usually find himself in mischief.

This was one of Ravi's alternate five-month periods. His two-month vacation starting next week, and he would be allowed to go to his grandfather in the Merari dome. He loved visiting Grandpa Dutra. The Viceroy would normally accompany him on these vacations and Ravi would join them with his brother Thom. It seemed that Ravi would split his time between the brothers, teaching one for five months and the other for five months. At the end of his five-month stint with his brother Thom, he would bring Thom along with him to their Grandfather's manor in Merari. In this way, the brothers would be able to see one another for part of each year. This had been an ongoing arrangement for the last five years.

No one other than his grandfather, Ravi, the Viceroy, Thom and his aunt Talia knew of these visits. Aunty Talia never accompanied Ravi and Thom on these visits. To the world (his father including) Thom had disappeared with his mother's sister on the day of the attack. Given that Aunty Talia had been a Kao member and as such was now hunted by the Priory, everyone involved thought it best to keep it secret. No one would suspect the Viceroy or Ravi of being anything other than proper mage officials, given their rank. Both the Viceroy and Ravi had sworn him to the utmost secrecy. He had willingly complied, because the highlight of his year would normally be the time spent with his brother.

His father never paid any attention to him, much less spent time with him outside official functions. On those occasions, his father would absently enquire into his health and well-being. Yet, he would always ensure that R.L never wanted for anything. When they were together, his brother would always enquire into these meetings with their father. R.L would try his best to describe their father to him, but would usually have little to say. He hated disappointing his brother. Yet, Thom never pressured him. Instead, he would fill him in on his Aunty Talia and Great–Aunt Sunni. R.L could hear the note of admiration in Thom's voice for these two ladies, and wished that he would be able to meet them one day.

Nevertheless, during their vacation time together, they would normally roam the woods alone and play all sorts of games as they tested their powers. They did so in relative safety, as both Ravi and the Viceroy had installed security spells that would block any type of intrusion during the period they were there. To R.L, that idyllic two-month period with their grandfather made up for the entire ten months they spent apart.

So although it was with a somewhat reluctant air that he got off the banister, jettisoning any further thoughts of flying down, he did so with a light heart. Nothing could dampen his spirits at the moment, for he was going to see his brother soon. He was about to bother the Viceroy for what may have been the hundredth time concerning their trip when he caught a look in the Viceroy's eyes that bespoke something more serious. His heart sank a little as he saw the sadness. It was then he learned that his grandfather had passed away and that his vacation was now cancelled indefinitely. It seemed that his father wanted him closer to home.

PART TWO

<u>Somewhere in the Outer Regions</u>

Talia couldn't believe that it had been nine years since Delia had died and she had arrived at the outer regions with little Thom. When she had arrived that first day years ago, she had met a few Kao members who had been there to replenish supplies and do further recon of the region. When she had brought news of the attack, two had left immediately for the Citadel, and returned months later with grim news. The one known as the Phantom who had been responsible for the attack at the Naming Ceremony and other attacks since then had increased his attacks. Martial law had been instituted, and one of the followers of the Phantom had been a Kao member.

They had also delivered enough supplies to last a year until she could find alternatives in the region. Sunni had entrusted a private and confidential message for her eyes only with one of the returning Kao members. The message had been succinct and to the point: under no circumstances was she to return to the Kao or the domes at this time. Sunni told her that something was afoot, and that certain elements that had infiltrated the Kao making her return with the Mage-King's son a very bad idea. She confirmed her suspicion that the Phantom was indeed a Kao operative, and that Mother Mizpah was worried about the ramifications it would cause for the survival of their Order. As a result, both Sunni and Mother Mizpah agreed that Talia was to be effectively cut off and left to fend for herself. Sunni had apologized for this in the message, but it was the only way to ensure their safety. Those who were there were to remain there indefinitely. They had been banned from contacting mages in the domes or the Citadel. She also instructed Talia to disguise Thom and herself, as well as assume aliases.

Talia had destroyed the message afterwards and complied with Sunni's instructions implicitly. She had gotten the others there to call her by her middle name, Ramona, while little Thom was now referred to as Novo, which was part of his maternal grandfather's name. They had become accustomed to the names within a few weeks. This turned out to be a blessing, because as Sunni had warned, things got a lot worse in the domes. Refugees flocked into the region with the assistance of the underground Kao network once the Priory gained control, and a settlement burgeoned. The underground network formed by the Kao had been organized to ensure the safe passage of their true members as well as any noteworthy mages who they deemed worthy to be secure.

Most times, the mages who had been secured had been a step away from being arrested and carted away by the Priory because they refused to conform to the new order. Persons such as the maharani, her entire family, and luckily Thom who had been visiting with them at the time they had been extracted, had been among those who had been secured. Others had not been as lucky and quite a few of their extractions had met with failure, as the Priory was able to swoop down on their targets before the Kao could get to them. Overall, the Kao's successful rescue rate was about fifty percent.

Upon the arrival of the maharani, her brood and Thom, Talia had met with them and warned them not to jeopardize her alias. They had agreed, and things had gone smoothly. Although those who were relocated to the outer region were screened vigorously to ensure they were in no way connected to the Priory or to the Phantom and his followers, Talia thought it best to err on the side of caution. Tabitha and her entire family had been saddened at Delia's passing, but had been happy that at least one of Delia's sons was there. They adopted Novo into their brood much as they had done with Delia and had taken him under their wings. Talia had allowed Tabitha free input into raising Novo, and both Thom and Tabitha's husband, Laurence, had become father-figures to Novo. Ann-marie had finally lured Thom into marrying her, and Novo had three mother-figures in his life, plus an extended family that saw to his needs and happiness.

Tabitha and her brood also proved to be a force to be reckoned with as they aggressively molded the new settlement into a unique dome of sorts. Tabitha had grouped the refugees and assigned them various tasks which ensured their collective survival. The settlement now had an independent and steady food and power supply, thanks to her husband's efforts. It had been hard work, but Tabitha had taken her skills organizing debutante balls and managed to pull the best out of every single one of them. She had a knack for inspiring one to achieve their very best.

Sunni's arrival as one of the last surviving members of the Kao echelon had heralded a new focus on protecting their autonomy. The entire Kao echelon had been taken one by one by the Priory operatives, until she was the last one left. She had been lucky in that she had been at the Citadel when the last few were taken captive. She had left the Citadel once she heard the rest had been taken. Although the Priory did not know the location of the Citadel, nor would they be able to access it, the now captive Kao echelon members could. So she had gathered the last of the remaining Kao within the Citadel's confines and headed for the outer regions. She had ensured that the Citadel would not let any Priory member enter. She had spoken to the Citadel about what had happened and then bade her old friend good-bye. Ever since the twins' birth within its walls, she no longer viewed the Citadel as an inanimate place, but oddly enough as a friend. The Citadel had understood, and when she looked back as her group departed, she had witnessed it raising a shield which had encompassed it in its entirety.

Sunni and the last remaining handful of Kao from the Citadel had managed to create strong defenses around the settlement, much like the ones in the Citadel. She had also instituted an informal security force within the settlement to keep order as well as a place whereby grievances could be adjudicated. Eloise, (another of Tabitha's daughters) and two others sat as adjudicators on matters that came before them. Tessa had channeled her artistic talents into creating functional yet creative areas for the children to be taught. She was also one of the teachers in the school that had been set up to accommodate the magelets. The settlement flourished until it became a mini dome, the only difference being that it consisted of refugees who had escaped from the Priory's ruthless claws.

It was within this environment that Novo grew and flourished. He was about six feet in height, and incredibly handsome. Yet one never focused on his features but rather the power that emanated from him. His powers had outstripped the others at an early age, and the only one who was able to teach him was the one known as Ravi. Ravi was an oddity at the settlement: he was the only one allowed to move back and forth between the settlement and Varga, and always brought news and other tidbits. The Priory was never able to detect him as anything other than an eccentric mage, and left him alone. So he would spend five months of each year living at the settlement, and then accompanied Novo to Merari for two months. During those two months, Novo would spend time with his grandfather and brother.

Talia would have loved to see little Ravi in person, but the risk was too great. So she contented herself with news about him from Novo upon his return to their settlement. Little Ravi, or R.L, as Novo liked to call him, seemed to have everything material that a little boy his age could want. Yet, even Novo wished that R.L could come live with them. When asked why, he shrugged and told her that he thought that R.L would have been much happier living with them. That comment had weighed heavily on Talia's heart for quite a while. However Sunni, in her infinite wisdom, had told her that it was better to have one of Delia's children than none. If they were to take

R.L away, Alejandro would leave no stone unturned to get back his son. He had merely allowed Talia to keep one since he knew that she would keep him safe from the Phantom and other threats. However, he still needed to have an heir apparent. If they took R.L, then the entire settlement would be at risk. Talia had accepted her aunt's wise advice and left it alone. Yet, a tiny corner of her heart kept a spark of hope that one day R.L would be able to come to them. So in the interim she merely waited.

Hearing a knock on the door, she bade the person enter. It turned out to be Sunni. Much like that first time when Delia had first come to the Citadel, her aunt's serene countenance bore an indefinable element. As she relayed the news she had received from the domes via their network of intelligence, Talia's heart fell. Her father had passed away and R.L was to spend the summer with Alejandro. The first thought that came to mind was how she was going to break this news to Novo.

*

<u>A week later-Merari Dome</u>

<u>Dutra De Novo's Funeral</u>

Alejandro stood near the front of the casket in which his father-in-law's body was encased. Not surprisingly, Dutra's funeral had turned out to be well-attended. Most had liked his father-in-law, for Dutra had proven to be an affable and decent sort of man. He had passed away quietly in his sleep as his spirit had gone to rest with his wife and daughter whom he had loved so well in life.

As Alejandro glanced down at his son, his heart went out to him. R.L was staring at his grandfather's remains with a solemn expression. His features were well-schooled, but Alejandro knew that his son was on the verge of crying. Yet, like a trooper, R.L doggedly kept a stiff upper lip throughout the entire proceedings. He wondered idly how close Talia and his other son were to the proceedings. He had felt the prickling of awareness that told him that Talia was near. He knew that she wouldn't have come without his other son.

When the ceremony came to a close, he walked aside a bit to speak with the official who had presided over the proceedings. As he idly glanced around, he saw his son hugging another boy around his age. His glance would have moved on, had not a warning bell been triggered. As far as he knew, R.L had no close friends. According to the reports he received from his teachers in school, he was a loner. Therefore, it was not in keeping with his character to allow anyone to comfort him. The only persons R.L was close too were the Viceroy and Ravi. Making his apologies to the official, he tried to make his way through the crowd to his son's side.

Anticipation coursed through his veins as he got closer. Then the Viceroy stepped into his path and blocked him momentarily. When he got a clear view again, the boy had moved away from R.L to a female cloaked in a veil, like most others there. As the boy glanced up, Alejandro felt his heart stop as he saw Delia's eyes looking back at him. Talia must have sensed that he had realized that his other son was there, for lifting her veil slightly, she looked at him fully and inclined her head. Then holding his son's hand, she disappeared with him from within the crowd of funeral attendees.

Alejandro felt like howling with frustration at that point. So close. He had been so very close to having both his sons together. As he reached R.L, he saw the change that his brother's appearance had wrought. R.L's countenance was lighter, and there was a smile in his eyes. He seemed to be clutching something, but had put it in his pocket when he saw his father approach. Halting in front of him, Alejandro merely looked at his son. Surprisingly his son had stared right back at him in a direct manner that almost dared him to question him. Taken aback, Alejandro realized in that moment that his son had secrets that he was not privy to. So ruffling his hair, as R.L had done so long ago to him when Delia had died, he merely said the first thing that came to mind.

"Let's go home, son…"

* * *

CHAPTER THIRTEEN

"Deeply I slumber

Meet me there brother

Dream me hither"

-Haiku by R.L, Son of the Overlord

Ten Years Later
Varga Dome

Galine was dreaming of the past. Her dreamscape journeying had started off at the point when she had first come to Varga nine years before. Her subconscious had slipped her in to this specific entry-point in the dream portal of her mind. For it seemed as if it wanted her to delve into her past memories. As she had often told R.L when instructing him about the dream portals, dreaming wasn't an exact science like the other more tangible powers. Few mages had this gift, and even fewer could consciously try to create portals. So when R.L had asked her if it was possible to create dream portals where two different individuals could meet, she had been intrigued. Most just scoffed at those like her, but he had sought her help. As a result, she had developed a better understanding of her gift and its uses.

Yet this particular dream of hers had brought her to a pivotal turning point in her life. As she looked on, she saw her younger self hurrying down a pathway in the dream. She had just arrived in Varga a few weeks before, during the two-month school break. Her grandmother, being the Viceroy's older sister, had requested that he keep an eye on her while she completed her studies in Varga. Since no one in their family dared to say 'no' to her grandmother, Galine had found herself assisting her great-uncle in small personal matters in her spare time after she was settled. In return, he had been training her in different aspects of court protocol and other skills which he thought necessary for her to know. She had been raised in a much simpler environment, and he thought it prudent to polish her skills while still obeying his sister's directive. Both had found their bargain satisfactory, and as a result she had become a welcome visitor to his household.

She had been running late that day. She had been making a mad dash up the pathway in the back garden that led to the backdoor when she had collided with someone. It was her fault, really; she hadn't been looking where she was going and she was laden with some freshly baked goodies from the mage-baker. The Viceroy had a sweet tooth, and she had taken the time to stop off to pick up a few of his favorite pastries in the hope that it would temper his imminent lecture concerning her tardiness. She had planned on sneaking in through the back entrance and preparing a tray of his favourite tea to go with the goodies as a form of apology. As it was, when she bumped into the person, everything went flying; and before she could land flat on her back in a most unlady-like position, she had been steadied and her goodies saved from falling. Ironically, she was more grateful that the goodies had been saved than she was that she had been saved from the fall.

As she turned to thank her deliverer, she found herself gazing into the most beautiful eyes she had ever seen. His eyes seemed to pierce her soul, and for a moment she was tongue-tied. The stranger had taken pity on her and smiled, looking faintly amused at her momentary inability to speak. He was around her age, and really good-looking. Then he had smiled, and his eyes had crinkled at the edges, making her heart beat just a little faster. Galine smiled as she saw her younger self captured in that moment with the then stranger, standing as if both of them were the only two persons in the world. She saw the instant when reality had come crashing back. As she recalled, it had been the chiming of bells in the distance that had shattered the moment. The bells had signaled that the Priory were on patrol. She didn't want to be caught out of doors when they started, as they were notorious for taking in those considered to be 'loitering.'

She had instinctively shuddered at the sound of the chiming bells, and with more haste than was deemed appropriate (especially given that he had saved her goodies from an untimely end) she had thanked him, took her items which he had saved, and flown down the pathway, sailing through the Viceroy's backdoor. Her younger self hadn't spared him another glance. However, as Galine looked on in her dream form, she caught a glimpse of his reflection in one of the window panes. She must have seen it then, but it had never registered with her. He had been staring at her younger self in a contemplative manner that indicated that his interest had been sparked.

As Galine followed, she caught up with her younger self in the kitchen hurriedly preparing a tea tray. Once the tea tray was piled with his favourite treats, she had gone in search of her great-uncle. She had found him in his study, and had started apologizing as soon as she entered the room, only to discover that he had company. His company turned out to be a mage of a nondescript age. She had curtsied in deference to him, for she had felt a sentience of the presence of great power. It was as if some part of her inner being had suddenly been jolted into a heightened state of awareness. That awareness had been altogether different from the one she had experienced earlier with the stranger in the back garden. This stranger produced a higher awareness in her being, as if she had been in the presence of a divine one. Galine saw her younger self barely hearing the Viceroy's introduction. Her great–uncle had introduced him as Ravi, who was a rather good friend of his who frequently visited him whenever he was in Varga.

She recalled how she had to make a few attempts before she was able to find her voice. She had offered to fetch him some tea as well. Thankfully he accepted her offer, and she had been able to escape to the kitchen. Within the confines of the kitchen, she managed to pull herself together. It was the first time in her life that she had been so affected. It was as if his mere presence had triggered her in some indefinable way. Yet, one thought kept reverberating through her. She had to stay close to him. He was a part of a puzzle that was essential, and she didn't know what that puzzle was. She didn't question how she knew this. She just accepted it.

So, in an effort not to appear gauche, she had resolved to act perfectly normally and treat him as he appeared: a mage who happened to be acquainted with the Viceroy. She had written down her encounter in her diary later, but at that point she had played the role of normal to perfection. Thus, she had re-entered the room, served him some tea with some goodies, and replenished the Viceroy's tea plate. She knew from past experience that when the Viceroy had company, she was to attend to other matters. However, he surprised her and bade her to stay and have tea with them.

As Ravi and the Viceroy spoke, she had been fascinated by the depth and breadth of their knowledge. The sheer intelligence and frankness with which they dissected matters ranging from politics, to religion, to even the mundane kept her riveted. She had been unaware of the passage of time until Ravi had decided to bid them adieu. She had been reluctant to see him leave. Her heightened awareness of him was still there, but it was manageable. Surprisingly, Ravi seemed to have taken a liking to her during that time, and gruffly told the Viceroy that she was worth keeping around and he hoped that next time he popped in for a chat, he would have the pleasure of her company again. Galine had felt herself blush. He had just laughed at how red her face had become, and had proceeded to ruffle her hair as if she was a wee magelet before leaving.

The Viceroy looked at her thoughtfully after Ravi had departed, and asked her a few brief questions. She didn't know what he was seeking, but she answered him as best she could. He seemed a bit surprised at her assessment of some issues, but conceded room for her perspective as he mulled over her answers. It seemed as if he was assessing her worth with respect to something important. Once he appeared satisfied, he told her to run along. As she was leaving, he requested that she come earlier, as they had some serious work to do. She was a bit surprised, but it meant that he had weighed her and found her suitable for his purposes. So, she had smiled cheerfully and waved good-bye as she sailed out the front door.

As she had walked back to her quarters at the palace (where she resided with other students from different domes as part of their training) she had contemplated the events of that evening. Her senses were still heightened after her encounter with Ravi. It was almost as if she had been asleep for a long time and had been awakened from this sleep. The feeling never wore off, but it had become more manageable as time went by. She had been mentally invigorated by the animated discussion that had taken place between the Viceroy and Ravi, and the subsequent queries put to her. All in all, it had been quite an interesting evening, and she remembered how much she had looked forward to her next visit. The Viceroy's approval meant that more was now to be expected of her.

It was at this point that Galine was abruptly awakened from her dream journey by an incessant and cacophonic shrieking which seemed to emanate from down the corridor. She didn't have time to process what her dreams had wanted to reveal to her. Instead, she found herself tumbling out of bed in search of the source of the noise. As she stuck her head out the door, she saw that others had been awakened as well by the caterwauling. Venturing down the corridor, she came upon the source of the shrieks. It turned out to be two female mages engaged in a physical tussle that had them rolling around the ground, while trying to pull each others' hair out. Galine just shrugged and left them. The situation just spelled 'R.L'. She had warned him that the batch of new trainees was proving to be a bit immature and easily infatuated.

Admittedly he had scrupulously adhered to her advice, and took care not to engage any of the trainees more than was politely necessary, especially after the episode five years ago when he had been sixteen. Yet, each year without fail, at least a few younger trainees became infatuated with him. That was one of the main reasons that Galine kept their friendship extremely secret, and did not associate with him outside the confines of her great-uncle's home. She wasn't about to have her sanity and peace of mind jeopardized through a mere association with him. However, this did not prevent her from quarrelling with him in the privacy of the Viceroy's home whenever such incidents occurred. He would merely shrug and have her laughing at the absurdity of it. If Galine hadn't known that he never actively encouraged the trainees and preferred older more mature mages for his liaisons, she would have been harsher on him. Their friendship had never crossed that romantic boundary, and had always been strictly platonic.

As it was, she knew better than to wade into a full fledged fight between two moonstruck females, especially when she suspected that the individual in question had not encouraged either one. Luckily, one of the others had stepped in and parted them. Samantha, one of Galine's contemporaries, upon hearing the cause of the caterwauling, had laced into them with such an acerbic diatribe that the two in question had just hung their heads in shame. As Samantha passed her door, she just shrugged and shook her head, to indicate that the tussle had been for the usual reason. Since Galine was now fully awake, she decided to get a start on her day. She wasn't due to have sessions with her instructors until mid-afternoon. So she was free to drop in by the Viceroy and make sure that his home was in a state of readiness for his arrival later that day. He had been away for a week and Ravi, the Viceroy's friend whom she had met so long ago, was currently in residence. Ravi had a tendency to stay with the Viceroy for five months then travel to another dome for another five months. He always seemed to get a wanderlust after staying in Varga for five months. She knew that the only reason he stayed so long was to tutor R.L. As it stood, the end of Ravi's five months stay in Varga was approaching, and she could sense his anticipation to be off.

She and Ravi had actually become friends of a sort. Although the Viceroy was her mentor, Ravi still held a special place in her life. She kept close to him, and he had taught her quite a bit. It was also through her visits to her great-uncle that she and R.L had become friends. He had been the one with the piercing eyes that had prevented her from falling that day long ago. He was also the only person that Ravi chose to tutor during his five months. Sometimes she had been allowed to sit in on these sessions. It had always been enlightening, and through these sessions she had realized that R.L was truly gifted. Of course, it wasn't until much later that she had discovered that he was the Supreme Overlord's son.

It had actually been at a banquet where the trainees for her year had been formally introduced to the court mages. At the time it had ranked as one of the grandest affairs of her lifetime. She had been jittery with nerves just before it had begun. One by one the trainees had been announced by name and been formally introduced to the Supreme Overlord before pledging their allegiance. When the time came for her to curtsy before the Overlord, she had found the nerve to look up to the dais. The Overlord was quite distinguished-looking, but seemed rather cold, as if the joy of life had been withered away until it was so miniscule as to seem nonexistent. He had inclined his head regally, which was a sign that she had been acknowledged and could move on. It was while she was rising from the curtsy that she saw R.L garbed as befitted his position as son of the Supreme Overlord. Although R.L's features had been schooled into a serious expression as befitting the occasion, his eyes had told a different story. He even had the audacity to wink at her before she had moved on.

She had been steaming over what she viewed as his deception that entire evening. She had felt like a fool in not recognizing him. The older trainees had told tales of him until she had pictured him as a bit of a self-centered rake whose twin purpose was to party and prove his prowess with half the female mages in Varga. She had limited him to only half the female population since the other half was either old enough to be his grandmother or young magelets. During the times she had met him, he had shown a completely different side to the tales she heard of the Overlord's son. He had shown her that he was kind, intelligent, had a quirky sense of humour, and was an honorable person with a distinct sense of duty. She had been getting accustomed to him, and had even toyed with the idea of inviting him to one of the yearly fairs held in Varga, when his identity bombshell had been dropped on her.

To his credit, he had sought her out the next day at the Viceroy's home. She had been rather polite, but distant. Their association had gone on like that for more than a year, and a half until she found herself in a spot of trouble she could not cope with, which had been instigated by mages unknown. He had not interfered directly, but she suspected that he had assisted in its eventual solution. Then one evening they had blown up at each other. She couldn't recall what they had argued about, but after the argument their friendship had gotten back on track. So much so, that she had even sought her grandmother's help in perfecting the dream bridges just so that she could teach him more.

She had first shown him how to use dream portals to communicate privately when they were much younger. Almost all of the mage population had forgotten the existence of this method of communication. However, Galine had come from a long line whereby this had been passed along for generations. She had seen his dream catcher talisman, and had inadvertently mentioned that it was one way to fuse a dream bridge. He had been intrigued, and had badgered her until she had shown him how to create one based on what she had learned from her grandmother. She never enquired as to the identity of the mage he was communicating with via the dream bridge, though she suspected that it was someone he loved dearly. So after their argument she had taught him how to further perfect the dream bridge. Since dream bridges were supposedly non-existent in the eyes of the typical mage world, only R.L and the person he communicated with could access their dream bridge. The person could be as far as the outer regions and still be able to meet him via dreams in their private dream bridge.

So as she swept in through the front door, she was surprised to see both Ravi and R.L already there. When she had walked in they had been discussing something in a serious tone. She had made her presence known, and was about to go to the kitchen to fetch something to eat. Her stomach had decided to choose that moment to remind her that she had not eaten since she had awakened. R.L merely excused them both from Ravi's presence and led her towards the kitchen. She smiled, because she knew that he was well aware of how cranky she was liable to be when hungry. Ravi had shrugged at both of them, because he had been on the receiving end of her bad-temper a time or two before.

R.L chose the moment that she was brewing tea to make his request. She knew R.L's birthday was approaching (half the new trainees were already planning on doing something for him) but he surprised her by politely asking her if she would like to accompany both Ravi and himself to his paternal grandfather's manor in Merari for a few weeks. His grandfather's manor had thorough safeguards against intrusions, so no one would ever know she had been there. She looked at him suspiciously, as if trying to gauge whether he was inviting her for a liaison. So he had hastened to add that there was someone he wanted her to meet. He further went on to state that she was perhaps the only real friend besides the Viceroy and Ravi that he had ever had. The Viceroy was unable to come due to other commitments, and he had obtained a pass for three mages.

There was no way she could deny him his request after that. It was the first time he had looked vulnerable to her, as if he had just put everything he had on the line. So she followed her heart and agreed quickly, then proceeded to fix breakfast for all of them. She found herself humming for the rest of the day as she planned for the trip. R.L didn't know it, but her spirit had been restless, and she wanted to seek somewhere new for a while. R.L had just handed her the perfect opportunity to do just that.

R.L had told Ravi that Thom (otherwise known as Novo) would meet them as planned. The dream bridge between the brothers was still functional. He had created it with Galine and Ravi's help all those years ago right after their grandfather's passing, and it had served as their link throughout the years. It was Thom who had given him the idea at their grandfather's funeral. He had given him a dream catcher talisman. R.L had been toying with it when Galine had unwittingly provided him with the method of communication. The rest had been history.

Their dream bridge had replaced their vacations together, and had been a constant in their lives. Without it, R.L would have felt trapped in a gilded cage. Although he had painstakingly garnered a reputation a shallow playboy, he had done so to prevent others from delving too deeply into his true personality. He had succeeded admirably, for he was often reprimanded by the Protector. The Viceroy, knowing him quite well, had merely warned him to tone down his smoke and mirror act and to use more discretion in his choice of rules to flout. So R.L had complied.

When R.L had created the dream portal, he had shared it with Ravi. He had wanted Ravi to teach Novo how to use it when he went to see him. Ravi had been delighted, for he had looked at it as a way of killing two birds with one stone, in a manner of speaking. Even he had forgotten about the dream portal method of communication. So he promised on the condition that when he taught R.L something, R.L would later communicate it via the dream portal to Novo. This way they both learned at the same rate. So he had willingly agreed. When Ravi was with Novo, his brother would communicate the lesson via the dream portal to R.L. The twins were each others' training partners, and soon surpassed even Ravi's expectations. As a result of this unorthodox training and communication, R.L became less unruly and if one truly made an effort to know him, a truly exemplary mage.

Now as they approached their twenty-first birthdays, Ravi had gruffly told them that they no longer needed his services. In his opinion, they knew what they were about and didn't need him anymore. Both brothers had hastened to reassure him that they would be lost without him, but Ravi had merely laughed at their vain attempts to keep him as their mentor. Both brothers had been downcast for a few weeks, until Novo had latched upon a brilliant idea. What better way to thank Ravi than by creating something that he would love and presenting it to him in person at their grandfather's manor in Merari? In this way, they would be able to celebrate their twenty-first birthday together.

R.L had to consider how he was going to get away from Varga, when an idea came to him. It would soon be the twentieth anniversary of their mother's passing, and what better way to commemorate it than by visiting the place where his mother had been brought up? Ravi had been on board, and had suggested that he invite Galine. He knew that R.L liked her tremendously, and he also knew that she could keep secrets quite well. R.L had smiled at this. So with a light heart he had patiently awaited her appearance. As she walked into the room she looked slightly cross. Judging by the earliness of her arrival, he suspected that she hadn't eaten as yet. He hid a smile, because he knew that she just might turn him down.

No one ever knew what to expect from Galine. Most female mages in her age bracket would quite literally jump at the opportunity to spend time with him. It would boost their status, and quite a few were looking to snare him into marriage. Yet, Galine had the knack of displaying a winsome combination of wisdom beyond her years and girlish enthusiasm. She was one of those rare mages who seemed to be immune to his charm. So taking a deep breath, he excused them both from Ravi's company, and led her to the kitchen to make his request.

* * *

CHAPTER FOURTEEN

' A PROPHECY '

PART ONE

<u>Merari Dome</u>

Be it ever so humble...there's no place like home!

The old saying was true… 'be it ever so humble… there was no place like home.' Although it had been many years since he had last visited his grandfather's manor, his sense of belonging had not diminished with the passage of time. He was, simply put, 'home'.

R.L's spirit had felt lighter and freer than it had in many years. A part of him had rejoiced at the mere act of crossing the threshold, almost as if his return to his mother's birthplace had healed a missing piece of him.

He suspected that the other missing piece of him would soon be made whole when he was reunited with his brother. However, for now he would wait.

As he waited for his brother, his thoughts turned to another place he had once known as home. Even though he had been very young, he remembered an old-fashioned castle of sorts. Not an ordinary castle, but rather, one that could communicate with Novo and himself. It had sent them all over its environs to play. When they had been tired, it would rock them gently to sleep in the bough of a tree in a very special garden. He recalled how safe and cherished he had felt within those walls.

He would have been inclined as he grew older to believe that it was just a figment of his imagination. Yet, the bracelet that he still wore had been a gift from that very castle. Each year the bracelet had expanded to fit him snuggly. He never took it off, and he wasn't sure that he could. He had worn it for so long that everyone had accepted that it was something his mother had enchanted for him. Most memories of his mother made him smile.

He never told Galine that her penchant for wearing the fragrance of a hint of jasmine intermingled with mint and a touch of vanilla reminded him of his mother. If he did, knowing her as he did, she would probably stop wearing it on the few occasions that she deemed worthy enough to apply it. Mother Gaia knew that those occasions were only too few and far between. She was unlike any female he had ever known, and somewhere deep within him, he knew that she was his life mate.

She never encouraged him. In fact, she scarcely paid him any sort of feminine interest, aside from the first day they had met. She never tried to impress him, and quite frequently would ignore him when she had a task at hand. Then to top it off, she would turn around and ask him why none of the other male mages paid her any attention. He had declined to inform her that he had made sure that they knew that she was off limits. Unfortunately, that didn't prevent her from trying all sorts of schemes, such as virtual dating and other methods. So he would wait patiently, then sabotage each and every one of her attempts when he found out. He did admire her persistence in trying. Just when he thought she was contented, she would do something to rock the proverbial boat.

This was one of her lull periods, and past experience had taught him to make sure he paid extra attention at this time. So he had asked her to come along with him to his grandfather's home. She had taken charge of the domestic aspects of the household as soon as they had arrived. She had been enchanted with the garden when she first spied it. His grandfather had once told him that his maternal grandmother had created it as a way of leaving her stamp on their lives. Galine had told him it was like an oasis of calm when compared to the hectic pace she had to keep in Varga. She had wanted to bask in it as long as she could. So it came as no surprise when she had taken to puttering around in it during the early hours of the morning and relaxing there in the late evening.

Ravi had just shaken his head at both of them. He had told R.L one day that Galine was one of those persons who had to be told. After that, he had left them to their own devices, and would traipse through the woods each day. R.L had taken to accompanying him on these walks, as Ravi had the knack of turning even the simplest of outings into a useful lesson.

Then, in the wee hours just before dawn of their third day, under the cover of darkness, Novo arrived. A frisson of awareness had jolted R.L awake. He had gotten out of bed and gone downstairs to open the door. Sure enough, he had seen a figure approach steadily along the pathway. That other missing piece of him finally clicked into place as he recognized his brother. Novo had sensed him as well, because his face had been turned in R.L's general direction until he caught sight of him.

Their reunion had felt so right. Once more, blood of blood, who shared the same genes that had been passed down through many generations, were together again. They had stared at each other for a long moment before they had finally hugged. That hug had fused that piece that had been missing so long into one, and R.L knew without asking that his brother had felt the same.

They must have spent a few hours talking in the kitchen after they had raided the pantry and found some delicious pastries and hot cocoa. Sunrise came, and still they talked. They tried to fill in all the gaps they couldn't have when they met in the dreamscape. Novo showed him images of their extended family, and had R.L rolling in laughter at some of the exploits of Tabitha's clan. In exchange, R.L told him of the Viceroy and the daily goings-on at the palace.

He spoke of his interest in Galine, and Novo just smirked. It seemed to amuse his brother greatly that the one girl R.L liked was the only one who paid him not one iota of feminine attention. Good-naturedly he told his brother that perhaps she might like him instead. R.L had merely smiled, while simultaneously sending Novo a warning glance with his eyes. Novo's eyes had merely gleamed in amusement, which held a promise that he would return to this topic at a later time. Nevertheless, for now, he gracefully left it alone, and let R.L smoothly change the topic to their father.

Novo felt a twinge of sympathy for the loneliness that he picked up from R.L's tone. His brother had been raised as the heir apparent to their father. R.L did not know what it was like to be embraced by a loud and often boisterous family. He had everything at his disposal, but lacked the genuine caring from mages who loved him for the individual that he was and not who he represented. Privately, Novo was now doubly grateful for the Viceroy and Ravi's influence in R.L's life. Luckily, all was not lost! Novo had concocted a private plan to bring R.L back to the refugee camp. By Mother Gaia's grace, R.L was going to meet the rest of his family before he had to return to Varga.

He had started formulating his plan when R.L had met him at their dream bridge last time. He had approached Sunni, Talia, and Tabitha with his proposal. He knew that his family longed to see R.L in person. So it had simply been a matter of wearing down their resistance. He kept emphasizing how wonderful it would be to have R.L in their midst. Tabitha's eyes had gleamed at the prospect of having Delia's other son with them, while Talia and Sunni had been more cautious. However, he had eventually won them over when he stressed that he would make sure that R.L returned before he was missed. Sunni and Talia had exchanged an indecipherable look at that point which he had merely shrugged off as being their 'Kao signal'. Then after a private discussion they had agreed.

Upon his departure, Talia had approached him and given him a scroll. She had told him that it would unfurl on his birthday at the exact hour of their birth. She made him promise to keep it safe until then. She had made him swear that both he and R.L would be present for its opening. He had taken it with great solemnity, and agreed wholeheartedly. He didn't tell her that Sunni had beaten her to it with respect to giving him instructions. Sunni had asked him earlier to retrieve an item of great importance. The gravity in Sunni's voice as if the fate of their world rested on this item had imbued him with a sense of resolve. Sunni didn't place her trust in others lightly. So hand downs, Sunni's request had been the more pressing.

Thus, by the time he filled R.L in on his plan for him to visit the refugee camp, his quest to retrieve an item of great import and the birthday scroll, his twin was suitably impressed. At that point, Galine and Ravi had made an appearance. They looked half-asleep. They had probably been drawn to the sounds of merriment emanating from the kitchen. As Galine walked in, and stopped in amazement, blinking her eyes to ensure that she wasn't seeing double, Novo took a good look at her. She wasn't gorgeous by their society's concept of beauty. She was cute by its standards, and had a quiet assurance about her that gave her a dignified air. Her eyes shone with intelligence. Yet, he sensed that she was not all that she appeared. She was an enigma, and he could see why his brother was fascinated with her.

For Galine's part, it had definitely been a déjà-vu moment for her, as she saw the brothers alongside each other. She had identified R.L when he had gestured towards his brother and brought him forward for a formal introduction. She had always thought of R.L as being handsome. Yet, Novo made her heart beat just a little faster. It was funny how he affected her, because R.L and Novo were identical right down to their piercing eyes.

However, Novo had an air about him that made her think instinctively of a live wire vibrating with energy. In contrast, R.L's intensity was more laid back. It was still there, but so under wraps that she was surprised at times when it came to the forefront. Unlike R.L's eyes, which would suggest a wicked sense of humour at times, Novo's eyes were warm and inviting, as if beckoning one to become his friend or more. She could just imagine what havoc turning both of them loose amongst the other trainees would cause.

Ravi, on the other hand, just grunted at both of them and told Novo that it was about time they were both in the same place at the same time. He also warned them not to even think about trying any shenanigans. His gruffness was underscored by his hugging them both and wishing them a happy birthday. He further spoilt his warning by bidding them go find something to do while he breakfasted. So off they went, arm-in-arm, while he and Galine had breakfast in peace. They could hear the brothers speaking to each other at a rapid pace as they went upstairs to store Novo's things.

Ravi knew from experience that Novo wasn't about to go to sleep anytime soon, even though he had arrived quite early.

Galine, on the other hand, as soon as she was sure that the twins were safely out of earshot, lit into him like a bee scenting honey. Ravi ignored her until he finished clearing the last morsel off his plate. He was only surprised that she had waited patiently until then. It was well-known that the Overlord had two sons, one of whom had been missing since the attack at the Naming Ceremony many years ago. It was public knowledge that the Overlord had issued a reward for anyone who could bring him his other son. Rumours had abounded a plenty as to the whereabouts of his other son. Yet, to this day no one had been able to produce the missing son. He knew Galine smelled a story, and she was aware by his previous statement to the brothers that he knew a great deal more. She had interrogated him gently at first, then with a great deal more persistence. He had merely given her non-committal answers which held not one iota of information. He made his escape to the woods soon afterwards, leaving her to her own devices.

*

Meanwhile in one of the bedroom chambers

Novo had just asked R.L for the time whilst he unpacked. When he realized that it was almost time for the scroll to open, he asked R.L to close the door. As he pulled out the scroll, it begun to hum a sweet song as it unfurled itself in a shimmer of light. They heard

Talia's voice emanate from the scroll as she wished them both a wonderful birthday. In her message to them, she told them about a legacy that had been passed down from one generation to another, until it was now their turn. She told them about the special ring and amulet that had been given to their mother and her on their own twenty-first birthday. As she explained the significance of these possessions, she added detailed instructions concerning their use. She emphasized the secrecy that being the current holders of these precious gifts entailed. She also indicated that the ring and amulet were to be passed onto the next pair of twins to be born to either one of them. With that, the scroll disintegrated.

Novo and R.L looked at each other before diving to retrieve their respective heirlooms. Talia had given Novo the ring along with the scroll upon his departure. He had tossed it to the bottom of his duffel bag. As he emptied his duffel on the bed, he spied the ring as it gently landed on the mattress. It was too small for all but his little finger, and he promptly put it on.

R.L had been given the amulet by the Viceroy before his departure as well. The Viceroy had told him that his aunt had indicated in a note many years before that he was to be given his mother's amulet on his twenty-first birthday. At the time, R.L thought that his aunt had wanted him to retain a keepsake of his mother. So he had taken it and left it nestled in a case containing his personal items. Unlike his twin, he merely summoned the said case from the adjacent chamber simply by calling it.

Once they both had their respective gifts, they looked at each other then tossed a coin to decide who would go first. Novo won the toss, and his first experiment was to the woods behind the manor. When it was successfully completed and he returned to the bedroom, R.L then gave his a try. They continued experimenting with their legacies well into the afternoon. Like generations before them, they enjoyed the process of mastering their gifts. When they finally felt assured that they were quite competent in their usage, they swore never to take them off until they passed them along to the next generation of twins.

*

Later that evening in the garden

Galine was surprised when R.L and Novo joined her in the garden. She hadn't heard them approach, but had just looked up and seen them both looking down at her. She had gone to the garden to think for a while after Ravi's hasty exit earlier that morning. Then she had ended up weeding and pruning as the ground called to her. Novo had spoken first. He had told her in an endearing fashion that he was looking for something one of his family members had left behind. It was supposed to be hidden in the garden, but he was perplexed as to exact spot it had been left. All he had to go on was that it was hidden within the center of a particular rose within this garden. The garden was filled with roses at the moment that had spontaneously flourished when R.L had crossed unto the property. Even more had bloomed upon Novo's arrival.

Galine had been in the process of pruning the ones that had bloomed earlier that morning. She pulled out weeds and made sure that the protection spell that she had reactivated around the garden was still working. Essentially, she had merely reinforced the dormant spell she had come across during her time spent in it. The spell seemed to inhibit natural threats to the flourishing of this garden. Hence the reason the garden continued to survive without care. Whoever had cast the spell had been powerful because, even though that mage had since passed on (judging by the dormancy of the spell), the fact that it still lingered in the essence of the garden despite years of no one's care, spoke volumes as to the power level of that particular mage.

By Novo's description of the particular rosebush, she surmised that it must have been one of the original plants in the garden. She had a feeling that it was probably the one from which the spell was cast. If it was, it would make the search relatively simple, since they would just need to follow the strands of the spell to its center. The Viceroy had taught her how to do this type of search. Closing her eyes, she opened her 'feel' senses, which would direct her. Different mages had different ways of doing this type of search. It all depended on one's gift.

For instance, some could 'see' the patterns of the spell and follow the strands like a map to the point from where it had been cast. Others could touch an item which had been spelled and be able to find the point of casting. She operated a bit differently from the others. She was able to locate the origins of the spell by a sense of 'feel', which was really another modus of intuition. To her, it was becoming still and then using this form of intuition to sense her way to the spell's center. In this instance, from Novo's description and the time she had spent in the garden, she was able to lead them to the particular rose bush fairly quickly. It was as if this particular spell was tugging at her, wanting to be found, since it had developed an affinity to her when she had recast it.

This particular rose bush had one particular rose which was spectacular, on closer observation. The rose was hidden from the view of any casual passerby. One had to actually be looking intently at that particular rose bush to see the rose. Galine had been in the garden quite a bit and she had never observed it. Privately, she thought that the spell caster had deliberately cast it that way. When Novo and R.L saw the rose, they just glanced at each other. Novo then touched the center of the rose gently. After a moment, as if it approved of his touch, the rose's center expanded until Novo's entire hand could go through. Novo did so and sure enough, was soon pulling something out from it. That something was invisible to them in the light of the garden. So after thanking the rose for yielding its treasure (it seemed to be the right thing to do), they proceeded to the manor.

Once inside, the thing turned visible, and revealed itself to be a pouch. Upon opening the pouch, Novo was able to extract a book from it. It was a slender book which was bound with a red cover. It had a clasp on the side, and a funny symbol none of them had ever seen on its cover. It was while they were trying to open the clasp of the book that Ravi walked in on them. When he saw what they had in their possession, he stopped them in their tracks and confiscated it from them immediately. As he ran his hand along the slender volume, the book begun to hum, then rose from his hands and released its clasp before settling itself on the center table of the parlour.

Everyone except Ravi looked on in surprise. In hushed tones, Ravi told them that they were never to reveal this to anyone other than to the person who requested its retrieval. Novo told him of Sunni's instructions. He hadn't expected to find it upon the first day of his arrival. However, Galine's assistance had made it remarkably easy. Ravi smiled at Novo's comment. He told them that this book had been searched for by many for quite a long time, and no one had been able to discover its whereabouts. Only one mage in Estrel knew its exact location, and the fact that she had sent Novo to retrieve it, spoke volumes as to her trust in him.

At this point, something had clicked within Galine's mind. This had to be the sacred book of Ahn. As legend had it, this book was discovered by a group of mages who had managed to survive the great battle between the Demigods and Mother Gaia, at the Holy Citadel of Rhys. Somehow she had expected it to be bigger and more distinguished in appearance. This was the book of legend that contained prophecies as well as other things. It was as old as the mage civilization itself. Yet, to look at it, one would have been lulled into believing that it was a simple ordinary book. Now that they knew what the book was, Novo, R.L and herself approached it with much more reverence than they had displayed before. It proved remarkably well preserved for one of its reputed age.

Once they were gathered around it in a semi-circle, the book elevated itself slightly. It then turned its pages until it reached a page three-quarter way towards the end. The writings were neat and done in an old fashioned type of calligraphy. A mage, or perhaps Demigod for that matter, had probably penned this book. The writing was in gold, and the pages were of a darkish material. Surprisingly, there were illustrations to accompany the writings. As she slowly deciphered the writings, she was surprised.

It spoke of the beginning of their world and the darkness that had helped transform a being called Ge. According to the writings, someone would unwittingly call the darkness from its sleep and it would blanket their world once more, unless the children of Ge stopped it. However, it went on to say that the children of Ge could only be restored by the chosen ones at the place of remorse with the help of the lost one. As prophecies went, this one was gibberish to her, and she told her companions such.

Novo, R.L and Ravi looked at her in astonishment. It didn't occur to her that they couldn't read the book. For some reason she had expected Ravi to be able to. Ravi had her repeat what it had said word for word at least twice, as he recorded her translation of it. He looked a bit disturbed when she repeated the phrase that the children of Ge could be restored by the chosen ones with the help of the lost one. It was as if that particular phrase had personal significance to him. After he had recorded her translation, he told them that in his experience the prophecies in the book of Ahn proved surprisingly accurate, and time was usually of the essence when the prophecies were revealed. So if they didn't mind, they had to leave immediately for the refugee camp. Ravi told Novo that he would vouch for Galine, since they had no time to send her back. Nor did he want to, given that she could translate the book. So without further ado, they were packed and off to Novo's home within the half hour.

* * *

CHAPTER
FIFTEEN

This new world we know so well.
By Ge's transformation of the old world of darkness
we all came to be.
Beware!
The sweet slumber of this old entity shall be
disturbed once more. A great foe of the ruler of this
new world shall unwittingly put us all at great risk.

Unknowingly he shall call upon the remnants of
dark
into Ge's new world,
causing the old to collide with the new, thereby
reversing all that is known.

Yet, all is not lost.
Hope lies with the restoration of the children of Ge.
To do so, let the chosen one seek them at the place
of great remorse. When the time is right, they must
look to the one lost so long ago. Otherwise, the
world shall be no more!

Refugee Settlement

The journey to the refuge settlement was surprisingly short and uneventful. Ravi had contacted some operatives he knew, and two guides had been sent for them before the evening sun begun to fade. By the time Estrel's twin moons reached their zenith, their group had arrived safely within the confines of the refugee settlement. No one amongst their group could identify the route by which they had come. The guides had requested their consent to blind the collective senses of the group in the last stages of the journey. Thus, for the last leg they had been virtually handicapped and totally dependent upon their escorts to guide them through.

Their group had been welcomed by Sunni, Talia and Tabitha upon its arrival. R.L had been embraced by them, like a prodigal son who had finally returned home. Tabitha had begun to fuss over him as soon as Talia and Sunni had relinquished him to her care. Novo merely looked on and grinned at his brother's overt discomfort at his family's attempt to welcome him. Once the twins were safely dispatched into Tabitha and Talia's eager care, Sunni took Galine and Ravi to a gazebo of sorts where others were gathered. The gathering there consisted mostly of women. They were seated in a circle, with one spot available towards the entrance of the gazebo. As Sunni presented Galine and Ravi to the group, the mages gathered there welcomed them. Ravi had given the Book of Ahn to Sunni earlier for safekeeping. She hadn't wanted to reveal its location even to this group, and had requested that Galine tell them about the prophecy that had been revealed.

According to Sunni, these were the survivors of a special branch of the Kao known as the Circle. They were mages whose powers were indefinable according to the traditionally known ones that existed in their world. As Ravi bowed deeply to them, he spoke.

"Esteemed members of the Circle, I come bearing tidings of a prophecy revealed by the Book of Ahn. I have taken the liberty of recording its translation unto this parchment… I have little else to add to the contents. However, I am at your service should you have need of me."

With this, he floated the parchment to the member closest to him. As she gently plucked it from the air, she merely touched it, and without appearing to read it, inclined her head to the others. As a collective, they all nodded.

"We have but one question for you Master Ravi… do you know the location of the place of remorse?

After a momentary pause, Ravi shook his head. The Circle appeared satisfied that he was being truthful and indicated as a collective that he was allowed to leave.

Sunni then brought Galine forth since she was the one who had interpreted the prophecy. When Galine approached the Circle, all the mages within raised their left hands in one accord towards her to indicate that she may join them. Galine glanced at Sunni for guidance on this, but Sunni had merely shrugged and indicated that the choice was hers. So Galine had squared her shoulders, then took her place with them. However, she chose not to face them. Instead, she chose to face outwards towards Sunni as she repeated her narrative ending with what had been revealed. Her choice of facing outward, rather than to them, indicated that though she had joined them for the moment, it was through necessity, and she was not going to join them permanently.

Galine felt the pores of her skin raise of their own accord as soon as she entered this space where the mages were seated. She wasn't cold, but she felt a sudden chill wrap around her, while her equilibrium felt off-balance. She instinctively thought of the time when she felt as if her head was full of cotton for a full week, but she had displayed no symptoms of being ill. In this case, it was more like a probe, instead of being besieged. Instinct on her part told her that she was found to be acceptable, as the chill changed to a welcoming warmth. This warmth lulled her pores back to their normal state.

It seemed as if this particular group would welcome her into their fold. Given that she was still struggling between denial and acceptance of her own powers, joining them would mean that she would have to acknowledge and accept that she was a bit different from normal mages. It would also mean being exposed to a realm of possibilities that would surpass her comprehension.

It was one thing to imagine and discuss possibilities in theory. It was quite another to discover that certain possibilities discussed in a purely theoretical setting actually did exist. Perhaps it was a hunch on her part, but she had an inkling that the world in which those of this exclusive circle operated was one which defied any known boundaries and rules. It meant that those of the circle were left to define their own code of conduct. Depending on the level of ability of a particular member, this could cause severe problems, especially if that member opted to go rogue.

None of these thoughts showed in Galine's expression as they ran through her mind while she recited the prophecy to the Circle. Yet, one dominant thought remained uppermost in her mind. She liked puttering around in normalcy, and found it quite enjoyable. She wasn't about to relinquish it to delve into a mysterious world fraught with unknown dangers. That wasn't meant to be her path at this stage of her life. Of that she was assured. Her Creator had a use for her, just as it did for each member that sat in the Circle. She doubted that their Creator would bring into being such powers if there weren't a higher plan involved. Nevertheless, she was not inclined to develop and enhance whatever power it was that made those of the Circle welcome her.

By her action of sitting outward she had politely opted out of joining their exclusive group. The Circle had graciously accepted her refusal, but she knew that they were not to be deterred. By silent communication, they merely indicated to her that the invitation would always be an open one. Yet, there was such intentness in their focus on her that she felt it even as she left with Sunni. She felt uneasy. So much so, that she didn't even realize until afterwards that she was clutching Sunni's arm in a death grip as she walked away.

*

In the meanwhile

R.L and Novo had been shuttled off to Tabitha's home, since it had more space than Talia's place. Over the years, Tabitha's original brood had gradually left the nest. So Tabitha and her husband had decided to turn their home into a sort of 'half-way' lodging where new arrivals were kept until they were sorted out with accommodations of their own. This was in addition to accommodating any visitors that came from the domes.

Since Talia aka Ramona, hadn't wanted to let R.L out of her sight, she had prevailed upon Tabitha to let her stay over. Of course, it was a longstanding practice that Novo had his own room by Tabitha's, even though he lived with Talia. Novo was a part of Tabitha's clan in all ways that mattered. The fact that he wasn't blood related mattered little to them. He was a child of theirs, and love made them accept him as such. Novo never realized how much he had taken it for granted until he saw R.L's dazed expression at being coddled and pampered by Tabitha, Talia and Laurence. They were still welcoming him in the wee hours of the morning, whilst everyone else was still asleep. It was as if he was a prodigal child that had finally come home.

For the first time since his mother's death, R.L felt like weeping. He had been denied that sense of belonging and affection that came with being a part of a family that truly cared. He knew how to navigate the artificial world of court like a pro; he was the most sought-after male mage in the Domes; his every whim and fancy would be seen to once requested. Yet, R.L never felt as loved as he did that night ensconced in the room right next to Novo with his aunt, brother and self-adopted grandparents surrounding him. They would have spent the entire night talking if Novo had not shooed them out. Tabitha had been prepared to argue but Novo had stood his ground and told her flatly that she could fuss over R.L as much as she wanted in a few hours. With that, he had propelled them all outside and told them that he was staying with his brother just in case anyone had any bright ideas of sneaking back. Novo had looked pointedly at Tabitha and Talia, who had both snorted at him.

R.L was torn because wanting to laugh at the expressions on Tabitha and Talia's faces as Novo closed the door on them, but kept a straight face. He could hear the soothing tones of Laurence as he led the ladies back to their respective rooms. To be quite frank, he was overwhelmed at the obvious affection and goodwill by people who were virtual strangers to him. Talia had known him from the time he was in his mother's womb and had been there when he was a babe, and still she had continued to love him throughout the years.

Tabitha and her husband had adored his mother, and on the

strength of that love had watched over her child. Their love was so all-encompassing that it automatically included R.L without question. R.L never felt as cherished in his life, as he did from the time of his arrival. He felt a sense of complete happiness just being in the presence of his brother and extended family. Novo understood without words exactly how R.L was feeling, and just let him alone to deal with his emotions. R.L was experiencing the world as it should have been if they had not been separated. As he closed his eyes he fell asleep with a smile, for he knew that his brother had finally found another home.

At the lookout

Ravi couldn't rest. He rarely did, since he had no need for it. The prophecy kept reverberating in his head. Specifically, it was the part about the chosen ones seeking the help of the lost one to restore the children of Ge that kept bothering him. Only a handful of persons, mage or otherwise, were aware of the story of how Mother Gaia became the divine being it was known as now. It was a story spoken of now only in whispers, in the most ancient of places of this world.

The only ones able to pass on the story of the being known as Ge would have been the Demigods or Mother Gaia. The Book of Ahn always bothered him because he never knew who its author was. Over the course of years, whenever he had occasion to deal with it, it was always surprisingly accurate. He often wondered whether a Demigod with the gift of prophecy had written it, or Mother Gaia.

He didn't have the gift of interpretation necessary to decipher the book so he always had to rely on others for the translation. Some Demigod he turned out to be.

He had spent such a long time within the ranks of the mage population that his prior life seemed as if it had belonged to someone else. In a way, that life had belonged to another, one who had since learned the lesson of humility and of being the last of his kind. Or so he had thought, until this prophecy had revealed otherwise. He was torn between being relieved that he was not the last of his kind, and worried whether his brethren had changed. As he delved into his memories of that past life, he recalled the day when the creation story had been told to him by Mother Gaia as a very, very, very young Demigod.

He had always had an enquiring mind, and he had been trying to figure out the concept of creation. He knew that everything in this world, including himself, had been created by his parent. However, he had been stumped as to who had created his parent? He had puzzled over that one for a while before tackling Mother Gaia for the answer. He had chosen a few of his playmates to accompany him to her favourite spot. Upon finding her, he had asked her directly that question that had him stumped.

In those days, Mother Gaia had assumed the form of a slightly larger female version of the Demigods. In reality, Mother Gaia had no gender. She just appeared in the feminine form because their world associated 'mother' with 'female'. So, when he had asked her this question, she had gotten a far-off look in her eyes and had remained so still that he had been almost convinced that she wouldn't answer. When she finally started, she described her origins in a very distant manner, as if she was a third party to the tale. She had told him that there had been a world older than this one. That world had begun with a deep empty expanse which had no form. Prior to the creation of this new world, there had existed two eternal beings who had merely slumbered. One of the eternal beings had been the darkness.

Nestled within the fabric of this darkness there had slumbered another eternal being of light known as Ge. The darkness that enveloped Ge had been a formless void that wrapped Ge in a cocoon of darkness. It had done so until the moment that Ge had gained consciousness. At that point Mother Gaia had paused in her story to make sure that he and the handful of others who accompanied him had understood what she had shared with them thus far. They had all nodded their assent. So she had continued.

She had described the moment in which Ge had awakened as one of the most pivotal point in the life of their new world. She spoke of Ge stretching and expanding within this cocoon of darkness, until its rays of light begun blending with the very fabric of this cocoon. This blending had triggered a gradual metamorphosis within the void. By blending the essence of light and dark, the void had changed into something new and wondrous. As Ge became more animated, the more rapid became the change. Until a new world was born, and life was created in the expanse that had formerly been an empty cocoon of darkness.

Upon achieving a state of full consciousness, this 'being' known then as Ge underwent a transformation from its original state of light until it achieved a new form. When Ge's new form emerged from its transformation, all creation welcomed this new creature. Ravi could still remember how engrossed he had been in the story. He had waited with eager anticipation for her to confirm what he suspected, that Ge had transformed into Mother Gaia. She had taken one look at his face and started laughing in that tinkling voice of hers.

Ge had indeed turned into Mother Gaia, the Divine and Ultimate God of all life, whom he knew as his parent. He had been troubled as to how she had known of the beginning if she had been unconscious. She had explained gently that some part of her had always been aware. She could not describe how she knew, only that she did. It was an awareness that transcended reasoning.

Her narrative had raised other questions in his curious mind. He had asked her what had become of the darkness that had contained her within its fabric and had aided her transformation. She had explained to him that part of the darkness was within each of them. Her essence had combined with its own substance to create something new. However, another part of the darkness had rejected this change and escaped to a place beyond the reach of the transformative process.

The darkness was not of itself bad, it was just a void that lacked everything that made this world what it was. It lacked emotions, needs…it just existed. She did warn him not to call it from its resting place, because it would engulf the world as they know it. She had emphasized that although the darkness did not have motives as the Demigods did, and did what accorded with its nature, it could still bring their world to an end.

Ravi had been about to ask who had created the darkness and the light known as Ge, but his parent had lightly swatted his behind and indicated that he should go play. He had never gotten around to asking her that question. He had grown older, and other interests had taken its place. Then, like the rest of his brethren, he had gotten arrogant and careless.

The Demigods had always known that when Ge had first been 'born', so to speak, as Mother Gaia, she had explored this world that had inadvertently been created through its awakening. She had noticed a pattern whereby all life within this world was procreating and producing young ones like themselves. Mother Gaia had none to call her own, and wished to complete this world with her own offspring. So after much thought, Mother Gaia had proceeded to lovingly fashion her own offspring, combining part of her own life force with that of the life force of this new world which still had an element of the void contained within its essence.

As the shapes of her offspring took form, she had whispered words of power over them and life began to infuse their beings. One by one, they came alive, much to her delight. As the last one gasped its first breath of air, she had welcomed her children into this world by enveloping them in a shroud of light and whispers of love. She had told them the story of their birth since their infancy, and it had always been one of his favourites.

Unfortunately, as time passed, the Demigods had changed from adorable, carefree, playful children whom Mother Gaia loved and cherished. They had turned into spoilt miniatures of their Creator with an awesome amount of power. They had constantly wreaked havoc in the world by their temper tantrums, bickering and fighting. Mother Gaia had given them free will, but did little more than admonish them, then make them set the place to rights. He and his brethren were always contrite after her admonitions, and for a while everything was peaceful. They would be happy for a while, then all hell would break lose again as one of the Demigods, for want of another word, 'acted up.'

This pattern had continued for eons, and after the first few eons, even Mother Gaia stopped intervening, in the hope that the Demigods would develop without her interference. After all, they were the most powerful beings, aside from herself. Ravi had supposed after much reflection later in his life that she had wanted them to mature. She was probably hoping for them to learn temperance and wisdom. But one eon faded into another, and still they had fought. There was always some strife with regard to who should be the leader within their group. Mother Gaia had never quite understood why her children felt the need to have a ruler, since she saw all life as equal. She couldn't really ask, as it had been eons since her children had stopped speaking to her because she had opted not to interfere in their petty squabbles. So instead, Mother Gaia, being the divine being that she was, kept a discreet but constant tab on her little ones.

As time passed, the fights became more vicious and vindictive in some instances. This pattern had continued until finally a clear winner emerged as their leader. This leader was one who had been born in the middle when the Demigods first came to life. He was powerful like all her children, but brutal and arrogant. Yet he managed to keep the others in line, and peace reigned under his rule. In fact, the Demigods had seemed to flourish under his rule. Eventually, they had even started to advocate for children of their own. It seemed that like their maker, they too felt a genetic need to procreate.

So they had experimented, and eventually managed to create miniatures like themselves. These were the first of the 'mage' race that would continue to populate the world even to this day. These mages lacked the power levels of their makers, but had all of her children's attributes. Unlike Mother Gaia's parenting style, the Demigods were very much involved in the lives of their offspring.

However, for some, this involvement constituted abuses of the worse kind. As events would have it, one day, a Demigod had destroyed one of the favorite mages of another Demigod. That Demigod had became so highly annoyed that he had wiped out a few mages of the one who had destroyed his own mage. From that time on, mages became like pawns to be destroyed if their respective Demigod protector had a feud with another.

Then one day the inevitable had occurred, and the fragile peace that the Demigod ruler had tried so hard to maintain was destroyed. It had started off innocently as one of the many rows between any two Demigods. Then it had managed to escalate into a full-fledged war that divided the majority of Demigods into two opposing factions. The Demigod leader had himself joined a side. Of all the Demigods who had walked the world since they had been created, only seven of them refused to participate in this war, and had attempted to broker a pact of peace. They had been ignored, and both sides had started destroying mages as if they were toy pieces, in an effort to best the other side. The mages had become like pawns, and their anguish had been heard throughout the world.

The wanton acts of destruction that the Demigods had done through the eons paled in comparison to the purposeful decimation of their own offspring as if they had no value. To Mother Gaia, these acts of her children crossed that intangible line from the realm of light into a realm of darkness. Her heart had probably wept at the evil that her children had come to. So in the midst of the battle she had appeared and demanded the immediate cessation of the destruction of the mages.

She had ceased to interfere in their affairs for such a long time that her appearance had come as a surprise. Some Demigods on both sides had arrogantly laughed in her face and had told her to go back from whence she came. She was duly informed that she had no place in this matter and to stay out of their business, as was her normal modus operandi. One particularly offensive Demigod told Mother Gaia to leave, for the time in which she could have meddled in their affairs was long past.

The sheer audacity of challenging her authority and supreme will in this world was the last straw. Never, in all its eons, had Mother Gaia witnessed such blatant disrespect and conceit on the part of her children. Their relative immortality had made them arrogant. As she looked upon the faces of her children, her heart had turned from them. No longer were they the offspring that she had lovingly created. They had become monsters capable of such cruelty that in that instant, Mother Gaia probably vowed to destroy them all.

Ravi never knew for certain what had triggered the battle between Mother Gaia and his brethren. However, he still remembered to this day, how horrific it had been to behold. The Demigods who had always seen their beloved parent as an indulgent, oft absent figure had been caught by surprise. The swift transformation by Mother Gaia into a terrifying divine being with no mercy on a rampage had shaken them all to their core. All the Demigods who stood against Mother Gaia in that initial meeting and in their arrogance had sought to fight individually had perished in the attempt. The shock that they were not invincible and that their immortality could be taken away by their maker had been a rude awakening. For the first time in their existence, the Demigods had felt truly terrified.

Those who had been able to escape the initial onslaught had retreated to higher ground. They had formed an alliance to make their last stand. Of all the Demigods left, the seven Demigods who had tried to remain neutral throughout the initial strife between the opposing factions had refused to join this alliance. Instead, they had made the decision to flee and hide from Mother Gaia's rage. It was more than fear that fuelled their decision.

They had known that they could not stand against Mother Gaia in her rage. On a deeper level, it had felt wrong to fight their parent when they believed that their brethren were in the wrong. They had believed that Mother Gaia's anger was justified. So, they had chosen the less valiant option of fleeing in hopes that with time, their maker, when calmer, would forgive their transgressions.

For those who had chosen the valiant option of combining their powers and making a stand against their irate parent, little could be said. Ravi recalled how terrifying the battle had been from a distance. There had been earthquakes, floods, fire, and lightning storms. In fact, all manner of disastrous elemental disturbances had been seen. The mages that had survived the Demigods' decimation had been scared out of their minds. The mages had felt the constant shaking of their world, and saw billowing thunderstorms with vicious flashes of lightning cover particular regions for days on end. They had been unaware that Mother Gaia in her infinite wisdom had created an invisible sphere which had served to protect them from harm while the battle raged. She had probably not wanted to see her grandchildren destroyed by her children through an act of spite or carelessness. By so doing, she had preserved the future of their world.

On the last day of this immense battle nothing was really known, except that a deafening sound was heard, then an eerie silence followed. In that eerie silence it seemed like everything in the world stopped; the wind, the flowing of the rivers, even time itself stood still. Then a soft golden light spread forth from the place of the battle until every corner of the world was touched by warmth.

It was Mother Gaia seeking for any of her children who had not been a part of this last stand. As the light pulsed throughout the world seeking any Demigod survivors, she seemed to have sensed none. It was then that a mournful keening sound that broke everyone's heart was heard. Mother Gaia had emerged the victor, but the cost had been heavy. Since that day no Demigod had ever been known to have walked through their world again.

Ravi had told this story to R.L and Novo when they were very young, and he had done so with great flourish. Of course, he had excluded himself from the story; but as with most boys, Novo and R.L had been spellbound, and had hung on his every word. They had plagued him with questions for weeks after. He never thought that any of his brethren had survived. Now, he was forced to rethink that notion. He very much doubted that his brethren had changed. Given his experience with his brothers and sisters, he was of the opinion that the mage world would be better off dealing with this eminent threat on their own. The Demigods may prove to be an even bigger problem than the darkness. So, with that in mind, he resolved that he would do everything in his power to stop his brethren's return.

*

Meanwhile, at Sunni's home

Galine had chosen to stay with Sunni, and had been placed in Sunni's spare room. After seeing that her guest was comfortable in her new quarters, she had turned her mind to mull over the situation with the group. Even she had felt her pores raise as the members of the Circle had raised their hands to Galine. She remembered how the tiny hairs at the back of her neck had stood on end, as she had felt them watch Galine intently as she had accompanied her out of the group's presence. Sunni felt it prudent to keep this little one away from them. Judging from the death grip Galine had on her arm as they took their leave, she had an inkling that Galine had sensed enough to be afraid.

Exactly what her fears were, she chose not to share. Yet, Sunni had understood that by indicating that Galine be allowed to sit with them, the group acknowledged that she was like them. So it begged the question. What gift did this little one have that made this remnant of the Circle deem her worthy to join? Since it was rather obvious that Galine wasn't going anywhere near them of her own volition, she figured that she ought to monitor her and run interference if she deemed it necessary.

The meeting with the Circle had brought to mind her sister. Like Galine, Alyssa had been asked to join the Circle that had existed when the Kao had been the pre-eminent order. She had joined, but as time passed, she grew more and more distant. Sunni had walked in a few times to find her sister huddled in the corner of a room weeping for no apparent reason. One day, within a year of her joining, her sister had turned her back on everyone and walked away. It had been right around the same time that she had fallen out with their father. She had cut ties with the Circle, the Kao, her parents, even Sunni...and started a fresh new life. It was only much later that she had contacted Sunni and then others from her family. She never discussed what had happened when she became part of the Circle; and to the best of Sunni's knowledge, her sister had lived out the rest of her life in relative peace and happiness.

It wasn't that the Circle was bad in and of itself. It was just that its members could do things that would make ordinary mages very nervous. Even the most powerful of mages with talents that were considered normal couldn't fathom these eerie talents and hence felt a bit uncomfortable if they came into contact with these odd talents by accident. As a result, the members of the Circle tended to stick to their own kind, or alternatively kept such a low profile of their talents that no one would suspect that they were different. Nonetheless, Sunni wasn't about to let Galine be pressured into joining them if she didn't want to. The Circle was not a group any mage should enter into lightly, even if the Circle was the only group with the knowledge to further develop the peculiar gifts of a particular mage.

Turning her mind to the prophecy that had been delivered, it seemed obvious that the twins and Galine were the chosen ones. That being the case, Ravi would be a worthy guide in assisting them in figuring out who the lost one was. The Book of Ahn would only have revealed itself to the chosen ones. This worked out well, since it would provide Galine with a way to stay out of the orbit of the Circle for the time being. Now it was just a matter of waiting for the Circle to give them a location of the place of remorse. This particular Circle was anything if not brilliant in solving such problems. With that, she extinguished the lights and went to bed.

* * *

CHAPTER SIXTEEN

' THE PHANTOM '

At the Secret Lair of the Phantom
Luz Dome

The subordinate shifted uncomfortably before him, even though the news he brought had been good. His lack of response and silence had disquieted the mage. He could almost see the beginning of fear emanating from him. He had not made it this far as leader of their group for so many years without earning his reputation. As 'the Phantom' he had struck fear into the hearts of many. He had come a long way from his humble beginnings. Now, he was ready for the final move in the game that he had been playing for so long. If he accomplished it successfully, he would displace the Overlord as ruler once and for all. A new era would be born, and he fully intended to be the one to lead it.

Ironically, he had the Priory to thank for his plan. He had taken great pains to ensure that his followers had infiltrated the Priory on all levels. Then one day it had paid off. One of the lower-level members of the Priory had accidently discovered a hidden room in his great-uncle's home during some renovations. This news would not have been of any interest but for the fact that the said great-uncle had been reputed to have been a disgraced member of the Kao. He hadn't merely been disgraced, he had been a member of the most elite branch within the Kao, known as the 'Circle'. According to the member, it seemed as if his great-uncle had been booted out after it had been discovered that he was involved in something that violated the tenets of the Kao Order.

Luckily, the member's superior had been one of his followers. He had deemed it noteworthy enough to make further investigations while downplaying its import to the member. His investigations had unearthed the fact that the great-uncle had been arrested in the first wave after the Priory came to power. Some of the journals he found in the room had made reference to the Circle, but more importantly it had made to a spell that was powerful enough to transform their world. He surmised that whatever this spell was, it might be able to unify the domes once more.

Unfortunately, according to the entries, one of the other Circle members had discovered what he had been dabbling in and reported him to the Council before he could complete his work. Although that member had been relatively young, she had enough connections for the right persons to listen to her. When he had found out, he had retaliated against her. She had chosen to leave the Kao soon after. Unfortunately, that had not been the end of it, because someone on the Council had not let the matter drop. Instead, he had been banned from their group altogether, and his fellow Circle members had turned against him when they discovered what he had done to the one who had reported him.

Thereafter the entries had been full of bitter anger over the banishment, but it had also delved into the spell he continued trying to perfect. He had wanted the ultimate revenge against those of the Circle and the normal mage world by extension. He had theorized that the spell should be able to set all things back to the way they originally were. The complexity of the incomplete spell was extraordinary, and it was at this point that the member's superior knew that the Phantom would be intrigued.

To be honest, when the member's superior had reported it to him, he had been disinclined to bother with it. Then he had read the spell. It was so far beyond what he had ever encountered that he knew that its maker had been a genius. Never before had he run across such a spell. Though incomplete, if it did manage to reverse the spell that had created the domes in the first place, he could finally grasp the reins of power from the Overlord once and for all.

So he had set about canvassing his expansive network of followers, as he sought those who could be used to complete the spell. Eventually he had put together a team, and they had worked on its completion. Years had passed before they had a breakthrough. One of his followers working in the prisons had found the mage who had created the original spell. He had been known only as Prisoner 345, his official name having been lost when the original prison records had been destroyed.

It was by luck that Prisoner 345 had fallen ill on his follower's watch, forcing him to enter his cell. Upon entry into the cell, he found all of the walls covered in symbols. The markings had been so strange that he had reported it to his own superior, until the information had finally made its way up the hierarchy to him. It seemed as if the 'great-uncle', while rotting in the cell all these years, had completed most of the spell, but was one piece short of completion.

He had arranged for Prisoner 345 to be released; and once healed, had set him to work. Prisoner 345, or 'Nok' as he was asked to be called, had agreed wholeheartedly. He wanted to see his life's work brought to completion. Plus, he wanted the added bonus of destroying the Overlord's son. He had discovered that the Overlord's son was the grandchild of the one who had gotten him booted out of the Kao. His eyes glazed with hate and malice every time he spoke of her. Since he couldn't make her suffer, he fully intended for her child to pay the price.

As 'the Phantom' and leader of a sizeable following, he hadn't really cared what Nok wanted, as long as he got the spell done. Besides, the Overlord's son would have been eliminated anyway, as he would always be a threat to his new rule. So he had agreed to the bargain. Now, according to the news that had just been delivered, it seemed as if Nok had managed to complete the spell at last. The timing seemed almost opportune.

The anniversary of his attack on the Naming Ceremony was in three days. To commemorate the event, the Overlord had ordered a ceremony for those who had fallen. It was intended that a memorial for those who had died on that day be unveiled. How sweet it would be to finally gain control on that particular day. In fact, it would be terribly easy. After all, who would suspect the Protector as being 'the Phantom' whom everyone had been chasing these last few years? Who indeed?

* * *

CHAPTER SEVENTEEN

A day Later

The Varga Dome

There were times when being the Overlord was not all that it was cracked up to be. He had managed to create an empire in the time he had been elected Mage-King. He was the ultimate ruler of the mage population. Yet, dealing with that odious little mage known as the Protector wore on his nerves. The Protector had sent him a memo concerning the inclusion of a special item in the ceremony tomorrow night. It involved a spell that promised to be very special to their world. It was a mere courtesy on the Protector's part, so he had merely sent a response duly noting the inclusion.

His sons had turned twenty-one a day ago, and he had to face the fact that he had not been much of a father. R.L had opted to go stay by his maternal grandfather's home in the Merari dome. He still hadn't been able to locate his other son after all these years. He suspected that Talia had taken his son to the refugee camp that was rumoured to exist. No one in his employ had ever been able to discover its existence. Yet, those who had 'disappeared' over the years must have gone somewhere. They certainly were not within any of the domes.

He had found himself conversing with Delia in times like these.

Sometimes it was as if she was just on the periphery of his world. He had many regrets in his life, amongst which he counted the time they had lost together when she thought he had been having an affair. She had been a truly wonderful person, and he had been too busy maneuvering court politics and chasing 'the Phantom'. He had tried after the death of Delia's father to be a better father to R.L. He made sure that R.L never wanted for anything. What he could not give him in terms of his time, he compensated for in material terms. If he was honest, at times he had been a bit jealous at the close relationship that the Viceroy had with his son. However, it had begun to bother his conscience more of late.

Perhaps it wasn't too late to try. After all, the Phantom had limited the number of his attacks over the last few months. If he left now, he could spend some time with R.L. The Empire could survive a few days without him. Thus, having made up his mind, he issued a missive to the Viceroy telling him that he was in charge for a few days. As he tidied up loose ends before he headed to Merari, he felt considerably lighter than he had in years. He felt Delia's presence with him, as if she too was pleased that he had finally taken the gauntlet to salvage a relationship with his son.

A Few Hours Later: Merari

There was no sign of R.L or Ravi anywhere on Delia's father's property. He had arrived at the manor and found it empty. Surprisingly, the manor had allowed him access to its grounds. He probably had Delia's presence to thank for that. Otherwise, the security spells in place would have prevented him from entering. He had left his attendants in the city, since the manor was not situated far. His attendants had objected strenuously, but he had remained adamant. He wanted to spend time alone with his son without anyone underfoot. They had pleaded that one of them accompany him, but to no avail.

A sense of unease crept over him with the appearance of no one. So he spelled the manor to reveal the activities of the recent past. When he saw both his sons in the foyer area accompanied by Ravi and a female mage of slight stature leave the manor in their travel clothes he became incensed. As time regressed further, he saw them all surrounding a book as the female mage read it to them. Unfortunately, with these spells one couldn't hear what was being said, but could merely see. Judging from the manner that Ravi had handled the book and the awe on his children's faces, instinct told him that they had found the Book of Ahn. He had been so absorbed in the spell that he never heard the tell-tale creak behind him that ought to have warned him of imminent danger. The last thing he felt before drifting into unconsciousness was sharp pain behind his neck.

*

Nightfall at the Refugee Settlement

Sunni didn't know what to make of the message that had come from the two operatives that had been left behind at the manor to wipe clean the past events that had taken place there. Yet, she had followed their instructions precisely, and had an area set up to hold a powerful mage. The first inkling she had as to the identity of the mage they had captured was when Talia had grasped upon seeing the unconscious mage's face in the moonlight. It seemed as if the Overlord had decided to visit his son for no apparent reason. Even the Viceroy had been unaware of his plans, and as a result had failed to warn them. The operatives left at the manor had seized the opportunity to capture the Overlord and bring him there for safe-keeping until they could figure out what to do.

Sunni felt the beginnings of an enormous headache. Every single person in the settlement had a good reason for disliking the Overlord. He was both directly and indirectly responsible for their being cut off from the rest of society. Many had lost loved ones and had their lives torn apart because of what the Priory had done. Even Talia was upset at having him here. There was little to be done until he regained consciousness. Until then, she would post some of her most trusted people to watch over him.

*

Dawn at the Refuge Settlement

Somehow the word had gotten out that the Overlord had been captured. Hence, before Sunni even had a chance to breakfast that morning, one of the guards had sent for her to disperse the unruly crowd that had gathered ready to lynch the Overlord. R.L and Novo had been luckier. Tabitha had waited until they had arisen and breakfasted before informing them of their father's presence at their settlement. She had sent them along to where he was being held with a basket of breakfast items for him. The boys had exchanged surprised looks, then obediently submitted to Tabitha's fussing over them as they proceeded to follow her instructions. However, R.L could tell that Novo was excited at finally meeting their father after so long.

On the way to the holding area, they ran into pockets of disgruntled mages reminiscing about their lives prior to their being marked by the Priory. Novo and R.L had merely kept on walking until they got to their destination. The guards had let them in at once, but had checked that it was only food that was being delivered. R.L could tell that Novo was curious to meet the mage who had fathered them. Although Novo had quite a few father-figures to help him in his development, meeting his 'real' father was probably to satisfy his curiosity.

When they both entered the holding area where their father was kept, the expression which flitted across his face as he saw both of them together was akin to relief. Other expressions flitted across their father's face as he struggled to comprehend that in his captivity he was at last able to see both his children together. However, the last expression of unexpressed joy on their father's face made his children realize that there was more to their father than they had previously given him credit for. Even R.L was surprised, and for an instant felt a bond with his father. Novo didn't know what to make of the mage in front of him. So much of what he had heard about him had been gotten second hand. Now that he was actually in front of him, there were so many questions he wanted to ask him.

When R.L indicated that they had food for him that seemed to snap their father out of the state he had been in. For the first time in his known life, R.L experienced his father yelling at him. The entire area surrounding the designated holding spot must have heard their father's voice; all activity seemed to come to a halt as all strained to listen to the irate tones of a rather upset father. Word had been sent to Tabitha and Talia, who came running to the holding area immediately. It was then that shrill voices were added to strident male tones.

The verbal battle went up a few notches until it finally ended up in a shouting match between Talia and the Overlord. It was only when Sunni was called in yet again to the holding area that the shouting match ended. It was without a doubt the first time that anyone had ever heard of the Overlord losing his composure. If R.L hadn't been a witness to the spectacle, he would have dismissed anyone's claims that his father had been involved in a verbal spat. His father was the quintessential mage without a heart, or so he had thought until he saw the screeching match between his father and aunt.

Yet, after the shouting match had finished, everyone felt considerably more relieved. The Overlord went from being a distant figure to being just a mage with faults just like every single one of them. One of the points raised during the course of the shouting match was the Overlord's anger that Talia had kept his other son and never once contacted him to know that they were alright. Talia had rebutted that he had never bothered to raise the one son that had been left in his care, because he had been too busy creating his precious empire. An empire that had destroyed countless lives, as well as sacrificed the Order, that had protected the mage civilization for generations.

The point she had made concerning the Kao had been a sore area with their father, for he had lit into her like a riled creature. For some reason, he blamed the Kao for hiding his son from him. Talia told him in no uncertain terms that he was being foolish to hold on to such notions. It had degenerated into a shouting match from that point, and the twins and Tabitha had stood by in amazement, as two usually calm mages tore into each other. Many festering misconceptions on both their parts emerged during that shouting match. By the time both parties had finally run out of steam, everyone present had a better understanding of the history between both parties.

The shouting match had relieved the tension on all sides. At this point, the Overlord went from being an imposing iconic figure driven to create an empire to an actual mage who was considerably more approachable. As Sunni questioned him as to his reasons for being at the manor unattended, he smiled wryly at this point. In what appeared to be an unusual bout of candor, he told her while looking at both his children, that he had come to the realization that he had not been much of a father to R.L. He had thought that perhaps there was still time for him to become a friend.

After Delia's death, his priority had been making their world safe once more. As a result, he had abdicated most of his fatherly duties to the Viceroy. However, now that his empire was built, it had dawned on him that he didn't know much about the son he had with him. That had forced him to take a look at his life and re-evaluate it. His visit to the manor had been a spur- of-the-moment decision, and he had wanted to surprise R.L. As he smiled deprecatingly, he probably wouldn't be missed for at least a day with the Viceroy in charge. His presence would be missed for the ceremony scheduled for that night. Especially since the Protector had planned a surprise spell just for him.

Sunni had registered the Overlord's comment about the Protector's surprise spell instantaneously. One of the operatives she had working within the domes had been recruited by the Phantom's followers for his expertise in complex spells. Through the comments made by his immediate superior, a man known as 'Nok', during one of his less lucid bouts, the operative had reported his suspicion that the one known as Phantom was quite possibly none other than the one known throughout the domes as the Protector.

The suspicion had made perfect sense to Sunni. She had never understood why the Viceroy had never been able to capture the mage responsible for the attack on the Naming Ceremony. She had put her own people on the matter as well, because she had held the Phantom responsible for Delia's demise. Like everyone else, she had merely passed over the possibility that the Protector was the Phantom because he had not aroused any suspicion over the years. He hadn't seemed the type. In addition to which, he had been a new member of the Kao at the time of the attack, and had turned his back on their Order, when it was alluded that a Kao member had been involved. His self-righteous indignation had seemed genuine by all reports.

However, Mother Mizpah had always told her to look beyond appearances and open her senses to 'see'. With the information sent to her by her informant, she had laid out all information concerning all known attacks from the Naming Ceremony onward, and had timelined it with what was known of the Protector's movements. Gradually a pattern had emerged. She was now positive that the Protector was the elusive Phantom. She had planned to send the information to the Viceroy discreetly, but with the arrival of the twins and the Book of Ahn as well as the Overlord, she had not had the opportunity.

Now, with the prophecy and her knowledge of the Phantom's identity, the spell that the Overlord had mentioned sent warning bells through her head. As she fired off rapid questions to the Overlord concerning the ceremony, everyone grew silent. Talia was the first to realize the significance of Sunni's questioning, and she paled slightly as the time frame registered with her. The Overlord couldn't understand the sudden tense silence that permeated the group. R.L could see that his father was starting to recede into the Overlord demeanour at Sunni's questions, so he just blurted out the prophecy that the Book of Ahn had revealed.

One thing that R.L could credit his father with; was his ability to think fast. He willingly provided them with all the pertinent details for the ceremony thereafter. Sunni thanked him for the information, and then released the wards off of the holding area. He was being released to Tabitha's and Talia's custody while she made arrangements for his immediate departure. She was sending him back to try to stop the Protector from performing the spell. She left him with Talia and Tabitha because everyone at the settlement respected them and Sunni was counting on the goodwill that the refugees had for them, to prevent them from trying to attack the Overlord while under their care. She then motioned for the twins to follow her as she briskly left the holding area.

The twins had to jog slightly to keep up with Sunni's pace. She moved swiftly towards an area which had a gazebo-like structure in the center. At this place, there was a circle of mages who acknowledged her presence. Sunni re-told the narrative that the Overlord had inadvertently let slip. Some within the circle of mages paled at the mention of the name of 'Nok'. Finally, one of them elected to speak with her. R.L didn't know these mages, but from the respect that Sunni and Novo accorded them, they were probably important.

So when one of them deigned to speak in a light whispery voice, he made the effort to listen. She told them that the name she had mentioned was one that had been banned by the superiors of their original circle years before. That mage had belonged to the Circle and had been extraordinarily gifted and much-admired within their group before he had gone rogue. His secret activities had been discovered accidentally by her sister, Alyssa, and she had subsequently reported it to the head of the order at that time. The investigations by their superiors had been slowed down considerably when Alyssa had left the group soon after. The investigation may have been stopped if not for the tenacity of one of her friends.

So the superiors had made further investigations into the matter. They finally discovered that the rogue Circle member had been delving into an area which called into question all that the Kao had held as truth. He had even gone so far as to initiate experimenting. He had been called upon to defend himself. No one at this circle knew what occurred between the superiors and the rogue mage that night, but the next morning a decree had been passed that no one was to have any dealings with him again.

So if what Sunni stated was true, then the Protector must have somehow completed the work that the fallen Circle member had started. If that was the case, then the entire world as they knew it would be affected by whatever it was that the rogue member had created. It had been grave enough to be considered a threat by their superior's years before, while in its incomplete state, much less for now in its finished state. So since the threat had been identified somewhat, it could be said with certainty that the place which the prophecy spoke of must be the Holy Citadel of Rhys. Everyone at the Circle had nodded their heads in agreement at this.

Novo had asked why before he could stop himself. The member who had been speaking merely smiled. For a while both Novo and R.L thought that she wouldn't answer their question, since technically it was Sunni who was addressing them, but she surprised him. She told them that right after the rogue mage was banned, a direct order was issued from the Kao echelons that under no circumstances the rogue mage was to be allowed access to the Holy Citadel, in fact no Circle member was.

Before they had all thought that it was due to the fact that the Kao didn't know who else the rogue mage may have been working with and wanted to prevent the fusion of such powers with the ancient magic that the Citadel was still steeped in. Now they realized that the Kao had somehow suspected that whatever ancient power located at the Citadel which kept it as it had always been through generations must also contain a power source that could repel whatever the rogue mage had sought to unleash.

With that Sunni had bowed to those within the Circle, and left with the twins in tow. As she walked she talked to them. She wanted to make sure that they had the amulet and ring from their mother on them. When they told her yes, she was considerably more relieved. She deposited them at Tabitha's, and told them to pack what they thought might be needed on a short trip, and instructed Novo to make sure that both he and R.L were ready and at the lookout in fifteen minutes. Before she left, she ensured that they were wearing their inheritance. She told them that the only way to the Citadel right now would be those heirlooms. She asked them if they could remember the Citadel. Both twins nodded. They remembered the garden with the bough and the rainbow they had created. Thus assured, she told them to focus solely on that location, then departed to find Galine and Ravi.

* * *

CHAPTER EIGHTEEN

' THE DEMIGODS '

'And as it began, so shall it end!'

<u>Thirty Minutes Later</u>
<u>At the Citadel</u>

Galine's body still felt out of sorts from the journey to the Citadel. The twins' amulet and ring made the journey incredibly easy, as they merely thought of their childhood abode and then found themselves in a garden of sorts with two old trees which had a rainbow and fluffy clouds over them. In the blink of an eye, they had gone from being in the refugee settlement to being in what was formerly known as the Holy Citadel of Rhys. R.L had held onto her arm, while Novo did likewise with Ravi: they then counted to ten before closing their eyes and wishing they were back at the place of their birth. Sunni had thought it wise that the twins take Galine and Ravi to assist them in locating the last of the Demigods.

Talia had been more than a bit disappointed that she couldn't accompany them but Sunni hadn't been sure if the amulet and ring could transport more than four at any one time. Aside from that, she had also voiced her sentiment that she wanted Talia to accompany the Overlord on his return to the palace. Although he was amenable to cooperating with them to try to stop the Protector from unleashing the darkness of the prophecy, she was of the opinion that he would need assistance.

It was true that the Overlord was a powerful mage; however, he was still one against the many followers of the Priory. So Sunni had asked Talia to put together a small tactical team to accompany the Overlord to the palace to stop the Protector. Sunni had insisted that at least one member of this team belong to the Circle, since this might give them an edge. Talia had reluctantly complied, because she saw the value in attacking the problem from different angles. However, she was still not contented with just giving them a detailed map of the Citadel from memory. Sunni had also given them the deactivation spells that had been put in place by the last mages to leave the Citadel.

She had given them the deactivation codes more as an afterthought, just in case something went wrong. She honestly didn't think that they would be necessary as the twins were going to transport themselves directly within the confines of the Citadel. The spells had been put in place for those seeking to enter through more conventional means. Plus, it was still undisputed fact that as the only mages to be born within the Citadel (within her knowledge), the Citadel was likely to sense their return and eliminate any possible threats to them.

So, with this in mind, Sunni, Talia, and a selected member of the Circle had gathered on the outskirts of the settlement, away from the rest of the refugees, to see them off. Given the highly secret nature of their mission, Sunni thought it best to keep the twins' part hush-hush. Personally, Galine thought that Sunni was probably hoping that the Overlord, Talia and her tactical team would succeed and there would be no need to restore the Demigods. Nevertheless, the last sight that the twins, Galine and Ravi had of the refugee settlement was of that solemn small gathering blessing their venture as they disappeared from sight.

The next sight that greeted Galine was that of a garden. As she opened her eyes fully, she saw the trees and a glimpse of colour coming from above. The rainbow came as a surprise. There was no way to tell how much time had passed in their journey. It had felt like an instant, and according to the dial that Ravi carried with him, less than a minute had passed since they were at the refugee camp. So a journey which by conventional methods should have taken at least a week by her estimate was achieved in an instant. Yet, her body felt as if she had been traveling for a week instead of an instant. For some reason, she felt extraordinarily exhausted, so much so that it was a struggle to keep her eyes from closing. She valiantly resisted the temptation to curl up and nap since they were racing against a deadline.

Within twelve hours the Protector would unwittingly release the darkness which the prophecy spoke of. They had to find the Demigods, discover a way to transform the Demigods to their natural state, and then get them to cooperate to save the mage world. Unfortunately, her need to sleep overwhelmed her; and after a while, even Ravi noticed and thought it best to order her to take a short nap. She made him promise to awaken her in an hour or before, if it should become necessary.

She didn't want to disturb the twins from their exploration, so she quietly fell back and returned to the rose garden which she had spied upon her arrival. The multi-coloured rainbow, complete with fluffy clouds, which had caught her eyes upon arrival, appeared comically out of place, situated as it was over two old trees. Nevertheless, upon closer inspection she discovered that below the two old trees there was a bench which was more in the nature of a lounge chaise made of boughs and flowers. As she sat down, she was surprised at how comfortable and spacious it was. It was just right for a leisurely siesta.

Within a few minutes of curling up, she was fast asleep and dreaming. In her dream, she saw a great and terrible battle in the distance. Immense dark clouds towered over an area of darkness, which was lit up intermittently with flashes of lightning and rumbles of ominous thunder. The entire world seemed dark and dismal and covered in a thin film of grey. It seemed as if she was observing through the eyes of another, and even from this vantage point she still felt afraid.

She was distracted from the battle in the distance when she caught sight of six creatures just like her but on a larger scale stealthily make their way over the threshold of the Citadel. They entered the domain of the Citadel and surrounded her with such speed that all she had time to do was instinctively bow in obsequiousness to them. Somehow she knew that these were

Demigods. By the manner in which they entered the Citadel, a place reserved only for special occasions and considered neutral territory by all Demigods, she knew something was wrong. It seemed as if they were fleeing from something or someone. For a Demigod to flee meant that whatever was in the distance at that battleground surrounded by thunderclouds was to be feared.

The Demigods bade her rise and be at ease. At this request she had been surprised. No Demigod who had ever entered the Citadel before had bothered with the comfort of the mage keepers of the Citadel. One of the Demigods, seeing her bewilderment, felt a stir of pity and motioned for her to join them. At this point she was more confused than she had been before. They were acting not like Demigods, but almost like mages. She was sorely tempted to find out if this was a trick by some mages to get into the Citadel by disguising themselves as Demigods. However, she held her tongue and listened instead. What she discovered saddened her immensely by the end of its telling.

The Demigods had challenged their Creator, and these few believed that it was only a matter of time before they were all destroyed. It was the first time they spoke of Mother Gaia. The Demigods had always viewed Mother Gaia as a distant parental figure who left them to their own devices. However, as the tale unfolded and she learned of the horror that the other Demigods had inflicted on her species in a conflict and Mother Gaia's subsequent response, even she felt that their Maker had been justified.

Nevertheless, as she heard the sorrow in their voices, compassion moved her to propose something a bit outlandish. For the first time she didn't stop to think, she only felt moved to help these creatures who had been considered all powerful by her until this moment.

As one, all the Demigods turned to her and waited for her to give her view. What seemed like a crazy idea grew and by the time she finished speaking, the Demigods looked thoughtful as they pondered her idea. If they transformed their forms into innocuous items then it would be unlikely that Mother Gaia would find them. Everyone knew that the Demigods were arrogant creatures who looked down upon the mages. So what better place to hide them than in plain view as harmless looking items? They would be aware of everything but in a form which could only be unlocked by mages' hands, and with an enormous source of power. Of course, Mother Gaia could just as easily destroy them if it found them in those forms. However, she vowed to them at that moment that if she could transform them, she and her descendents would safeguarded them until elements aligned to release them.

The Demigods had remained silent at this point as they mulled over this possibility. It was so different that it might actually work. Mother Gaia would definitely not be looking for any of its children amongst the mage population after what they had tried to do to them. As they looked at each other, one by one they consented to her idea. The Demigods agreed to trust her, a mere mage, with their lives.

As she prepared this complex spell that would transform the Demigods into items, she decided to hide the spell to their reconfiguration in two parts. One would be in the Citadel itself, and the other in one of her own memories which she would pass down through her descendents. The passing down of memories to chosen descendents was a tricky one. She had to ensure that only one descendent from each generation had the memory encoded into their being. What's more, this memory could only be activated in the presence of the Citadel, which held the other part of the spell. For this she sought the Demigods' assistance since, as makers of her species, they would be able to encode what was needed and ensure transmission to a descendent with a particular composition.

The other part of the spell was to be hidden in the transformed essence of one of the Demigods, who would become part of the Citadel's structure. The spell would be revealed to the chosen descendent of hers once they slept within the precinct of the Citadel. The memory would be triggered in that descendant's dream state and that part of the spell would be revealed. If the Demigod hidden within the Citadel felt that it was the right time to be transformed, then it would reveal the second part of the spell to her descendent upon waking.

When this intricate spell had been entirely formulated, she bade them to form a circle around her. To power the spell, she asked each to give a particular portion of their power. However, before she could start, the Demigods surprised her. Though they had no need to, each one asked her permission to bless her. She was dumbfounded, to say the least. Never in the history of their creation had any Demigod been known to perform such an act to a mere mage. A blessing was the highest honor that a Demigod could bestow onto another of its kind. Her look of astonishment at their request made them feel sheepish for having treated the mage kind so shabbily before.

So without further ado they spoke words of blessing over her and her future descendents, who would be the chosen memory carriers. The main blessings consisted of: protection against all forms of harmful magic, the gift of healing, the ability to recognize another of their kind and be able to disguise themselves from that Demigod if they so wished, and the gift of a highly developed sense of intuition. The last two blessings were not revealed to her, and performed by two of them touching her forehead. As the last Demigod bestowed their blessing upon her, she felt a sense of serenity and peace. At that moment, they showed themselves to be true Demigods, worthy of being called the creators of her kind.

As she spoke the words of the spell and combined their magic, she felt a tremendous amount of energy flowing through her being. She belatedly realized that one of the unknown blessings enabled her to serve both as a facilitator and conduit for the flow of power that passed through her very essence. Nonetheless, by the time the spell was finished, she was exhausted. A quick perusal made her realize that the spell had worked. On the ground lay two unusual bracelets with intricate workings, a matching amulet and ring, and an extraordinarily pretty trinket. As she glanced at the walls of the room of the Citadel, intricate designs spontaneously began to decorate the walls, letting her know that the last one had indeed been transformed into the Citadel's essence.

After securing the items safely on her person, she lay down outside the circle in which the spell had been cast and slept. She was still asleep when the battle that raged between Mother Gaia and the rest of the Demigods finished a few hours later. In fact, at this point, Galine seemed to separate herself in this dream state from the sleeping woman, and once more became an observer. She heard the deafening silence a few hours later which was to signal the end of the battle between Mother Gaia and the other Demigods. She saw the soft golden glow of light bathe the Citadel then move on. She heard the mournful keening sound that went through the world a short while after the golden glow had passed over the Citadel.

She saw the arrival of a small group of refugee mages to the Citadel, one of whom awakened the sleeping woman. This particular mage who woke the sleeping woman was the one to bring with him what Galine now recognized as the Book of Ahn. She saw the subsequent marriage of that woman and the mage who had awakened her, and a long line of the faces of mages descended from her who carried the memory. The last face she saw as she drifted from that dream state into consciousness was her as a child listening to her maternal grandmother telling her the legends of the

Demigods.

As her consciousness aligned itself to the present reality, Galine realized now why she knew certain things instinctively. It was as if a missing piece of a puzzle long dormant had finally been solved. The Demigods had been as good as their word, and their blessings had indeed been transmitted throughout the spellcaster's line of descendents. As she opened her eyes and looked at the fluffy clouds above her, she saw symbols indented in the clouds. With her ancestor's memory now activated, she was able to complete the indented symbols to formulate the retransformation. It seemed that the Demigod within the Citadel had deemed that now was the time to reclaim their true forms.

She jumped up quickly and went in search of Ravi and the twins. She realized now why her senses had always been heightened around Ravi. He was the lost Demigod that the prophecy had spoken of. She found them in the same room she had seen in her dreams. They were puzzling over something when Galine interrupted them. She had recognized the unusual bracelets with intricate workings from her dreams as the ones worn by the twins. She knew for a fact that the matching amulet and ring were also worn by the twins around their necks as heirlooms passed on to them by their mother and aunt. The Viceroy had given her the extraordinarily pretty trinket for her birthday the year before, and she always kept it on her person for luck.

She gleefully filled them in on her dream and told them of the revelation of the way to re-transform the Demigods. Ravi had been extraordinarily resistant to the idea that the Demigods had transformed themselves into such inanimate objects until the Demigod hidden within the essence of the Citadel chose to assert itself. All the objects that hid the Demigods were taken from them and floated into the same symbol which had been on the Book of Ahn. Ravi paled as it was finally brought home that not only were a handful of his brethren left, but that they had endured an existence far worse than his. Even Galine could see that Ravi was shaken by this. No mage could ever be privy to the thoughts of a Demigod, but when her power level started to spike, she realized that his emotions were allowing his true form to manifest itself.

She reacted instinctively by grabbing hold of both his arms and ordering the twins to call their power from within through the physical routines that she had seen each perform. She did not require their powers to be called by magic. Rather the spell required the true essence of them, which flowed out as they performed their routines. The twins stood at opposite ends then touched the opposite hand of the other in a way which allowed the other's energy to flow to them at this point. Thus, a circle of sorts was formed, with Galine and Ravi in a double clasp, while the twins' hands went slightly over that double clasp, touching the other at the wrists. The objects which had been floating over their heads formed themselves into a circle which surrounded them. Once the objects were in place, the twins began to move in a slow, swaying movement. Galine could feel their energy beginning to flow; once she judged that it had reached an appropriate level to start the re-transformation process, she began her part.

She called the true forms of the Demigods into being by naming each. She identified each and every one of them. Ravi's mage form was unraveling as his energy just poured out unto her, and she merely directed that energy to each of the circling objects. The objects began to spin faster and faster, as the energy from Ravi and the twins' essence combined to form an amazing amount of power. When she felt that the twins had reached their limit of endurance, she raised the double clasp to join with the wrist points of their hands until Ravi's essence joined with theirs.

It was at that singular moment when time seemed to freeze that she was able to focus that power onto the spinning objects. She saw the power swirl around each of the objects, and saw forms begin to take shape. She saw six different forms emerge from the spinning objects. She held Ravi's arms and the twins by extension, until each one of the forms was fully emerged, only then did she allow herself to sink into oblivion.

*

At the Palace

Sunni had worked a minor miracle, and had somehow managed to get Talia's group and the Overlord from the refugee settlement to the palace approximately an hour before the Protector's ceremony was scheduled to begin. On their journey to the palace, they had worked out a reasonable explanation for the Overlord's sudden appearance in the Varga dome. Talia continued to watch him closely for any indication that his cooperation wasn't merely a ruse on his part to get them to let him go.

He had surprised her by asking her questions concerning Delia and his son. It seemed as if he genuinely wanted to know more about the mages he called family. Talia had obliged, and spoke to him of her childhood with Delia. She told him of how Delia was the one who had always managed to remain unruffled at her various escapades when they were younger. She had been Talia's cohort, best friend and confidante. She spoke of how when they were little girls Delia had dreamed of having a family and settling down. Talia had wanted to see the world, but Delia had told her that the world that she would create with the family she made would be enough for her.

Talia remembered how she had scoffed at Delia for having such simple dreams. Looking back now, Talia admitted that Delia had always been the wiser one. In a way, she thanked the Overlord for making Delia's childhood dreams come through. It had often been a point of consolation for Talia that her sister had achieved her wishes before passing on.

She had spoken to him of his other son and how he had been raised. Novo had been blessed to have so many parents at the settlement. She had been clueless as to how to raise a child. Then

Mother Gaia had sent her Tabitha and her clan, and their Aunt Sunni, and then Thom and Ravi. Novo had never lacked for love, and he had loved them all in return. He had been such a remarkable child when he was young, and he had grown into a remarkable mage as he grew older. He was the quintessential child she never had, and she thanked Mother Gaia each day for blessing her.

The Overlord looked at her continued references to Mother Gaia. He couldn't understand how she could believe in a deity they had never seen. Over the years, he had noticed that all of the Kao they had captured had adamantly refused to renounce Mother Gaia. They had sought refuge in Mother Gaia's teachings when captured, and in some instances tortured, by the Priory. It was as if Mother Gaia was much more than a mere deity, but something infinitely more personal to its believers. He didn't understand it. If Mother Gaia was such an all-powerful deity, why couldn't it just stop the Protector from unleashing this great threat?

Talia was challenged to find the words to explain Mother Gaia to an unbeliever. So she gave him her own personal testimony of Mother Gaia. She explained how Mother Gaia wasn't a faceless, nameless deity. In fact, Mother Gaia, though called by that feminine name, was both female and male. Mother Gaia was their ultimate Creator, and had preserved the lives of mages from the Demigods' carelessness. Talia spoke of the history of the mage race as passed down through generations of Kao.

Few persons outside of the Kao were made to learn mage history in such an intensive manner; and as a result, for many Mother Gaia had remained merely a distant deity. Mother Gaia was within each and every one of the mages. She was that spark of life within each mage that extinguished at their passing. Mother Gaia was in every living being within the world, from the mages to the shrubbery that grew. She was in the warmth of the sunlight that they felt on their skins during the day. Mother Gaia was the source of all life.

Talia told him of how her mother had taught her children to thank Mother Gaia each day for the many bountiful mercies and blessings that she had bestowed and was to bestow upon them. She spoke of the time that Mother Gaia had directly manifested itself in her presence when Thom had been injured after the tournament so many years before. Before, she had merely acknowledged Mother Gaia because of the teachings instilled into her by her mother.

That had been her turning point, whereby she went from acknowledging to really and truly believing in Mother Gaia as much more than a mere impersonal deity. Talia had gone on to outline instances when Mother Gaia had worked through mages to achieve a particular outcome. There was historical evidence in the archives of the Kao which spoke of instances when disasters of immense proportions had been averted by mages who had inexplicably felt called to do something. Mother Gaia was known to never interfere directly unless there was a good reason. Her ways were not the ways of the mages.

However, didn't the Overlord find it strange that the prophecy had revealed itself at just the right time to the right mages? Or that the Overlord himself was now going to assist them in stopping a threat to a deity he had never given much thought to? Talia was going to try to stop this threat because if the prophecy was correct, then all mages could be wiped out as well. They were dependant on Mother Gaia's existence for their survival. If one eradicated Mother Gaia, then the spark of life within each one of them would be destroyed as well.

The Overlord lapsed into thoughtful silence after Talia's discourse, and she could see that he was struggling to comprehend what she had told him. She silently asked Mother Gaia to open his mind so that he could truly understand. Her mother had taught her that faith was something personal, which one had to come to on one's own terms. No one could force-feed faith to another, nor was there a magic spell which could bring about the birth and maintenance of one's faith. It was something that had to come from the individual mage, and it was something which would always be tested. So after saying that silent prayer, she left it all in Mother Gaia's hands.

When they arrived at the palace unannounced they were greeted by the Viceroy almost immediately. As efficient as ever, Sunni had somehow managed to get word of their pending arrival to him prior to their actual arrival. He recognized Talia as soon as he saw her, and looked considerably more relieved that she was there once more. He quickly filled them in on all he had managed to find out about the ceremony. The Protector had been keeping a very close lid on the spell. He had tried to stop the proceedings, but the Protector in an unprecedented move had foiled him by using some obscure protocol which had been in place for many centuries.

The Protector had also reinforced his security detail, and was now heavily guarded. In fact, the Protector was now more guarded than the acting Overlord. In addition to this, there was now a substantial body of Priory members now within the confines of the dome. The Viceroy had taken all this into consideration before wisely opting not to order the Protector's detainment, since that would surely have triggered the Protector into moving up the scheduled time.

The Viceroy's spies had not been able to discover much in terms of the spell they were planning to use or anything directly concerning the proceedings. He woefully conceded that they had to stop the Protector at the ceremony itself. The Viceroy had alerted his most trusted personnel, and they were to accompany them to this ceremony and were prepared to assist them against the members of the Priory. They had to strike decisively and quickly to contain the Protector before anyone from the normal contingent of Priory members could react. The main threat would come from the Protector and his entourage.

There was little time to lose, so they all made their respective way to areas where they could change into suitable clothing before proceeding to the Great Hall. The Great Hall was already packed to capacity, as many of the followers of the Priory had gotten there early in order to view the ceremony. The general mood was one of eager anticipation. The Overlord and the Viceroy made their way to the raised dais where they had designated seats as accorded their respective ranks. The Viceroy's personnel and some of Talia's group flanked them, then dispersed as they thought fit in order to find suitable positions in the general crowd. Talia and the Circle member situated themselves obliquely behind the Overlord and Viceroy, posing as members of the Overlord's security detail.

The Protector swept into the Great Hall with his entourage a few minutes later. He looked condescendingly to those already seated at the raised dais. The Overlord inclined his head slightly to acknowledge his presence. The Protector called the audience to silence, and then proceeded in an eloquent tone to discuss the ceremony. He eventually moved on to give special thanks to a mage with extraordinary vision who had created the special spell they were to witness at the proceedings that night.

Talia could feel the Circle member tense beside her at the Protector's praise for the mage who had gone rogue. However, that tension changed somewhat as the Protector moved on to the part they were all there for. As soon as the Protector called for silence then introduced the mage known as 'Nok' who had created the spell, the Overlord and Viceroy moved as one to stop him. The Protector had been taken by surprise at this unexpected attack, but he recovered quickly. He called his entourage as a shield between him and the Overlord and Viceroy while he continued. At this point,

Talia and the Circle member launched their attack, and were able to stun him. Unfortunately, some of the members of the Priory from the audience, seeing the Protector under attack, rushed to his aid. The Circle member was able to create a barrier between them as Talia dealt with the Protector. The Overlord, Viceroy and the others who had been selected were busy trying to break through the shield that the entourage had put in place in order to assist Talia and the Circle member.

Amidst the chaos, no one noticed that Nok had quietly started the spell. Mages first began to realize that something was dreadfully wrong when the temperature in the Great Hall dropped drastically until it was extremely cold. Tendrils of darkness started to emerge from under the feet of Nok. In horror, all watched as Nok's expression of jubilation turned to fear then to stark terror. Then, in an instant he vanished within the thickly gathering darkness. This darkness was beyond anything Talia had ever known. It was not of this world, and it was fearsome.

Unfortunately, this was not a dream, and the darkness kept building. It sucked the life-energy from everyone within its reach. The Protector and his minions had been amongst the first to be engulfed. Talia, the Viceroy, the Overlord and the others had focused all their powers onto this creeping darkness, but to no avail. It merely sucked their blasts into its vortex of darkness. Talia belatedly realized that this thing had no feelings or emotions or life. It was just a vast emptiness, and there was absolutely nothing they could do to stop it.

Talia could feel herself becoming numb; and as she watched, she saw that the others of her group were similarly affected. The last thought that moved through her mind was a plea to Mother Gaia to help them.

Mother Gaia probably decided to listen to her plea, because at that moment she saw huge beings, much like the mages, bathed in a soft glow of light, appear. These beings surrounded the darkness in a circle, and bit by bit they forced the darkness back. In what seemed like slow motion, they were able to banish this dark emptiness back from whence it came. Gradually, everything returned to normal as these creatures suffused their power into the Great Hall. Through their dispersed power, Talia quickly felt more like herself. As she quickly perused the area she discovered that though Nok and the Protector otherwise known as the Phantom, and his cohorts had perished none of their group had fallen.

Talia caught sight of her nephews and Galine in the midst of these great creatures. With one accord, everyone in the Great Hall bowed as they realized that these creatures had saved them from certain doom. As the twins introduced the mages to the last of the remaining Demigods, a soft light began to fill the Great Hall. It was like the warmth of the sunlight mixed with all the essence of goodness. It was a comforting presence that calmed every pore of one's being. All the terror and fear that had been experienced previously was simply replaced with a sense of peace and happiness.

Mother Gaia had found her children, and she was happy. They had been forgiven, and even the mages felt her joy. The Demigods bowed as the light got brighter and brighter, as if they felt unworthy to be forgiven for their sins. The mages, on the other hand, prostrated themselves in obeisance, as they beheld the gift of Mother Gaia's presence. Then, as suddenly as the light had appeared it disappeared along with the Demigods. There were certain things that were beyond the abilities of the mages to be a party to, and this was one of them.

As the mages got up one by one, there was a consensus amongst each and every one of them. They had been blessed, and Mother Gaia had restored them from their folly through her children. Never again would they depart from her ways. This event was to be recorded as part of mage history. As Galine, the twins, Talia, the Overlord and the Viceroy made their way to one another in the midst of this Great Hall, they could not contain their joy about having experienced such a blessing. Though Ravi was no longer with them, they remembered and gave thanks for the time which they had been privileged to spend with him. Now each one, was faced with the task of helping to transform their world into a better one. One in which Mother Gaia would be restored to her original place of honour. It was going to be a struggle but at that moment, they all felt a deep-seated belief that all would be well.

* * *

KERI AMANDA KITSON

Keri is a novice part-time writer with a penchant for popping in and out of places at the oddest moments. She is an avid lover of the sea and a regular attendee of Macueripe Beach, where she has been known to sweet talk others into venturing out to the furthest point of the bay.

When she's not pursuing her career in law, she spends time reading (especially different variations of 'Pride and Prejudice'), watching Korean dramas and eating roti. She currently resides in Trinidad and Tobago.

For news and upcoming releases please visit her Amazon Author page or her website at www.kerikitson.co or email her at kitkeri@yahoo.com.